Fistful of Fog

A Novel

- - - - - - - - -

Rinkesh Ghosh

Chardowar Books

San Francisco

Fistful of Fog is a work of fiction. Names, characters, places and incidents are either the product of the author's imagination or are used fictitiously. Any resemblance to actual persons, living or dead, events or locales is entirely coincidental.

Copyright © 2018, 2019 Rinko Ghosh
All Rights Reserved.

This book was self-published by Rinko Ghosh under Chardowar Books. No part of this book may be reproduced in any form by any means without the expression permission of Rinko Ghosh. This includes reprints, excerpts, photocopying, recording, or any future means of reproducing text. If you would like to do any of the above, please seek permission first by contacting Rinko Ghosh (email: **rinkoghosh@live.com**).

Published in the United States by:
Chardowar Books, San Francisco

ISBN: 978-0-9600153-1-3
Subjects: Coming of Age | Romance | Adventure | Intercultural | Himalayas | California | Strong Female Lead

Printed by KDP
Cover Art by Lynn Sondag (www.lynnsondag.com)
2 4 6 8 9 7 5 3 1
First Edition

For:

Kathy Anne Zuercher

(1966-1992)

CONTENTS

Translator's Note	1
Part One: Break-up Day	5
Chapter 1: Don't Forget Me	7
Part Two: A Year To Remember	13
Chapter 2: Dream-Chasing	15
Chapter 3: Losing My Religion	17
Chapter 4: Fifty-Fifty	49
Chapter 5: A Fragile Union	61
Chapter 6: Death Or Glory	107
Part Three: Six Miserable Months	133
Chapter 7: Alienation	135
Chapter 8: Homecoming	153
Part Four: Another Memorable Year	169
Chapter 9: A Second Chance	171
Chapter 10: The Jungle Blues	211
Chapter 11: A Brief, Mostly Happy Reunion	237
Part Five: A Day I'd Like To Forget	245
Chapter 12: Don't Forget Me (Revisited)	247

Translator's Note

This memoir would not have been written if I hadn't dragged Jay back to campus. The first brush of spring had stroked the manicured Dominican campus with a flourishing green. But a sprightly sapling, planted to replace an old magnolia tree felled by last winter's storm, appeared to send a jarring reminder that there is nothing sadder than going back to your old haunts and finding the grand remnants of your memories erased, as if your time in college was an illusion.

He got down on his knees and rummaged through the pile of wood-chips discarded along the roadside. And when he found a wood-chip that had their initials (which Zoe had carved many years earlier), he picked it up and used his shirt-sleeve to wipe it clean.

Getting back up on his feet, he turned to me and said, in Bengali: "First love is fragile, like a daydream. You enjoy it's embrace for a moment and then it disappears. The best dreams have short lives but first love never dies."

Using the pretext of a celebratory luncheon (I'd recently been approved for a faculty position), I'd dragged him back to a place he had tried to forget. I was keen to learn more about his romantic adventures with his college love, Zoe, who his mother had once forbidden him from dating.

The previous month, after I'd announced my engagement to a wonderful woman from Colorado, my father had stopped speaking to me. Like many Sherpas of his generation, he was opposed to me being in an interracial relationship. But Sister Julia Fernandes (who used to be Zoe's roommate and now ran the campus ministry at Dominican) said if I could get Jay to talk about his intercultural relationship with Zoe then it would restore my faith in love's ability to overcome barriers.

Jay had not set foot inside the picturesque grounds of Dominican University for a very long time. But I was his godson. He couldn't say no.

Earlier that day, he had visited the Conlan Center. I'd warned him the athletics honor board only had room to display sport-stars from the 21st century. More than 25 years had passed since Zoe had been named student athlete of the year at Dominican But he was dejected, after discovering her name was no longer listed on the board.

Jay kept staring at the vacant space which used to hold the felled magnolia tree, under whose branches he used to sit with Zoe. I could visualize him picking up the splintered pieces from his past.

"Why don't you write about her? That way Zoe and Jay can stay together not just as words on a page but also in the minds of future generations," I said.

"But I'm a painter not a writer," he said. "Besides, when it comes to writing about personal matters, I prefer Bengali to English."

"Then tell me everything that happened?" I said, clicking on a voice-recording app on my cellphone. "I will translate your story into English and make sure she is not forgotten here, in her homeland."

His dark eyes lit up with a glow I hadn't seen before and he said: "Thank you, that would be the best gift anyone could give me. But make sure you keep it real because Zoe didn't like it when I hero-worshipped her or got too sentimental. So, don't skip over the messy bits or sugar-coat any shortcomings. And, whatever you do, please don't bring God into it or blame fate."

"I will make an honest effort to avoid those writerly pitfalls but I can only hope she would not have been displeased with my portrayal of her in this memoir," I said.

We parked ourselves on a bench near the felled tree. It was a gorgeous day with the luxurious green sprawl of spring extending across the Dominican campus, all the way down to a rolling wildflower meadow. And where the meadow left-off the blue-green hills began. There were hills behind those hills and they ran their slopes down to the endless Pacific.

Translator's Note

He began telling his story in a comforting, sing-song voice, as if he were chanting. I closed my eyes and allowed myself to be transported to my birthplace: a rocky amphitheater of bright icy mountains where heaven seems so close that if you reach up you can almost rub the giant star-belly of the universe. As I listened to him speak, the cracks in my broken spirit began to heal.

We never made it to lunch that day. But, by the time he finished, I realized Sister Julia was right: this story will restore your faith in love.

For allowing me to retell his inspiring story my indebtedness to Jay remains everlasting, like snow on Kanchenjunga. Therefore, it is only fitting I close with his words. When I asked him why he had risked everything to help Zoe in her attempt to become the first woman to stand on the summit of the third highest mountain in the world, he said he had learnt the hard way that the worst thing you can do when you love someone is play it safe.

Dawa Sherpa, Ph.D.
Associate Professor, English and Cultural Studies
Dominican University of California

Part One:

Break-up Day

(October 1, 1990)

Chapter 1: Don't Forget Me

Norbu's sky burial was held on a rocky plateau, near Green Lake. I used a flashlight to part the darkness, which concealed a group of people crowding around his cloth-shrouded body. There was some banter, some weeping, some laughter.

The gloomy dawn lined the plateau with an ambiguous, confusing light that hinted at darkness as much as it hinted at sunshine. After my eyes adjusted to the light, I looked closely at Norbu's face, the only part of his body exposed to the heavens. A large, red gash ran across his temple. He seemed to have a slight smile on his face but the laugh-line running from the side of his nose to the corner of his mouth appeared weathered, like the mountains that surrounded us. Death seemed to have aged him.

Lama Pasang, his lips reddened with betel-juice, walked over to where we were standing and bathed us in incense. Soon, the place began to smell of juniper and sage.

We kept a respectful distance from the two body-breakers who were moving the corpse to a frost-free patch of plateau. After sharpening an assortment of knives on a rock, they tied plastic aprons around their waists and began to strip first cloth and then flesh. The vinegary odor of death brushed aside the incense-laden air and forced us to take a step back.

One of the body-breakers, bespectacled and equipped with a machete, sliced open Norbu's stomach in one clean, sweeping motion. After extracting a bone saw out from a blood-stained backpack, he started to cut off the limbs.

Squatting next to him, his bearded companion used a cleaver to separate flesh from bone. A few minutes later, having traded his cleaver for a hammer, he placed a yellowy femur on a flat stone and smashed it to pieces.

The bespectacled man began to separate the mound of meat from the pile of bones. Then, with a flick of his wrists, he sent a large piece of sliced flesh flying toward the birds.

Fistful of Fog

Vultures (also called sky-dancing angels by the lama) descended in a mass of beating wings and tearing beaks. They began to devour chunks of flesh, fighting each other for choice bits. The feeding frenzy had begun.

Zoe's normally serene face appeared haggard. Her eyes, bloodshot by a mixture of altitude and insomnia, resembled those of the corpse. And having run out of her favorite brand of chewing gum, she had started to munch on a slice of *chhurpi* (a rock-hard, Himalayan cheese made from yak milk) which a Sherpa porter had given her.

The lama chanted in Tibetan (which I translated into English, for Zoe's benefit): "Life on these mountains is tenuous. And today the time has come for Norbu to summit the Last Mountain: the mountain you climb when you are done conquering mountains."

Her gaze moved towards Kanchenjunga, coming into view as the lethargic sun broke free from the clutch of monsoon clouds. First the eastern summit, and then the two summits adjacent, started to glow as the rays fell on the mountain. After that it was the central summit, which began to shine silver. Finally, the sun shone on the western summit. Soon, all five summits of the Kanchenjunga massif glittered like icy beacons.

The mountain looked majestic in her early morning splendor but I couldn't bear to look at it. I used to love that magnificent mountain but now I feared that giant icy slab of killer rock like one fears a malignant tumor.

I closed my eyes and prayed, first for my father and then for Norbu.

Two years earlier Kanchenjunga had ended my father's life. And, the previous day, it had taken the life of my climbing friend, Norbu, whose body, now broken into pieces, rested inside the stomachs of the scavengers surrounding us.

The birds grew noisier.

Don't Forget Me

Someone in the crowd must have started beating on a large drum because soon I heard slow rhythmic taps reverberating across the mountains.

I wondered if the drum-beats were meant to drown out the awful sound of the birds gorging on flesh.

A chilling vision of birds feasting not on Norbu's corpse but on Zoe's body forced me to open my eyes. I was relieved to see her still intact and standing, next to me. She was staring, transfixed, at Kanchenjunga.

Of all the giant rocks in the world she could have picked, why did she want to climb the killer mountain whose shadow darkened my home in Darjeeling? And what was with this extreme American confidence that I routinely encountered in Zoe and some of my other college classmates.

In the Himalayas, even the most decorated climbing Sherpa, someone who may have climbed Everest multiple times, will tell you that climbing any 8000-meter peak is extremely hazardous. Most of them participate in these expeditions only to earn a living and (if given a choice) they would rather be doing something less risky. But in America you had young amateurs like Zoe aspiring to climb the world's most challenging mountains based on only a handful of climbing experiences and an assumed birthright of incurable optimism.

Junko Tabei had claimed Everest in 1975 and K2 had been bagged by Wanda Rutkiewicz in 1986 but Kanchenjunga was yet to be summited by a woman. It was the only one left (out of the "big three" Himalayan summits) where a woman could cover herself in glory, after making a first ascent. And Zoe, who had graduated from college earlier that year, wanted to be that woman.

I didn't know whether to call her attitude arrogant or naive but when it came to Himalayan mountaineering, the expression – "let's give it the good old college try" (which Zoe and her climbing friends routinely employed) – seemed hopelessly inadequate and potentially deadly.

Fistful of Fog

There was no escaping Kanchenjunga. I could visualize its icy tentacles, having choked the life out of my father and Norbu, now metastasizing to Zoe's brain.

The lama continued with his chanting: "Let us remember Norbu and prepare ourselves to deal with the loss of our dear friend. We must never forget those who die, especially those who die young. As body-breakers sever his flesh, let us feel the harmful cord of attachment, which had tied him to his past, disappear into thin air. Let us extract his fear of failure, which had prevented him from pursuing his dreams, and let us smash those fears along with his bones. Let us pay attention to how his spirit leaves his body and enters the stomach of these giant birds. And, as these great birds fly up high, let us watch his spirit dance on the celestial skies."

The drumming intensified but Zoe's gaze remained cemented (as if she were in a trance) on the mountain.

One of the body-breakers blew on an old, Tibetan trumpet. The deep drone of the trumpet ricocheted off the mountain face and floated into the valley below.

As the sun began to rise, the shadow of Kanchenjunga crept in between us.

Taking her hand, I looked pleadingly into her eyes and said: "Please don't climb this killer mountain. If you do then I'm not sure I can continue with our relationship."

After withdrawing her hand from mine, she removed the turquoise ring from her finger. The stone embedded in the center of the ring matched the color of her pupils and my mood.

She gave me a long, sad look. Then, handing me the ring, she said: "I'd honor your request if I could but you know I can't."

The feeling of dread that had been gnawing at my insides all morning worsened after Zoe walked away.

Don't Forget Me

Our relationship had been broken, like Norbu's body. And I'd been served another painful reminder that love, like life, can be short-lived.

Although we had been together just a few months, her liberating touch had ended my conflicted youth. Cocooned inside the blissful daze birthed by her unforgettable love, I had never imagined our relationship ending. But how long can one hang on to a rainbow before it fades?

Prior to meeting her in California my life's trajectory had been constrained by my family's religious traditions and by my isolated Himalayan upbringing. But she had rescued my soul from its puritanical cage and had flown it up to intoxicating heights, from where I'd seen a new world opening up.

As clouds shrouded the sun once more, and darkness descended upon the Himalayas, the body-breakers began to depart. Standing on the icy plateau, now deserted except for vultures picking at the last morsels of flesh, it became clear that a future without her would make me utterly miserable.

I had to win Zoe back.

Part Two:

A Year To Remember

(September 1989 -September 1990)

Chapter 2: Dream-Chasing

That year, the precursor to the technology boom in San Francisco fueled the whirlwind known as dream-chasing. This phenomenon swept through the city streets and tossed everyone into the midst of a soul-searching escapade. One couldn't step into any café, bar, or office in the city without hearing someone talk about how they were going to give it all up and follow their life's dream.

The laid-back town that everyone had associated with the Summer of Love was undergoing a radical transformation, as it started its meteoric technology rise. It was fashioning itself to become a booming metropolis, soon to be filled with start-up companies and choking with rush-hour traffic. Memories of the counter-culture movement were fading and one could sense a manic, capitalistic spirit permeating the city. This newfound energy rebuilt neighborhoods and pushed real-estate prices up. Artists and tie-dye shops made way for tech-worker housing and clothing emporiums. Even the homeless guy on Van Ness Street changed his cardboard begging sign from "I need a beer fix" to "I need to fix my BMW".

It wasn't just San Francisco that was going through change that year. Walls were about to come down and national boundaries were about to be redrawn. The cold war was coming to an end and everyone across the globe seemed to be embracing the American way of life.

For a lonely college student living in the isolated Himalayas, there seemed no better place than California to learn about America, my father's adopted homeland. Throughout my high school years I used to daydream about escaping Darjeeling (where I lived with my mother) and traveling to America (where my father lived, after their acrimonious divorce). But my mother hated the idea of me visiting him and my family had no savings. So, I never expected my travel dreams to materialize.

Fistful of Fog

Everything changed during my junior year in college, when I received a call from an American attorney. My father had left me money in his will. I was still mourning my father's death but sensing my miserable mental state the attorney said attending an American college as an international exchange student could help me get my groove back.

After I began my journey to California, I glanced outside the airplane window. Kanchenjunga – queen of the Eastern Himalayas, pride of Darjeeling – came into view, shortly after take-off. The Himalayas seduce many with their promise of immortality, bestowed only to a few lucky climbers. But for less fortunate climbers, like my father, these tall, majestic mountains often turn out to be unforgiving, icy killers. After whispering a prayer in memory of my father, I rolled down the window-shade and shut my eyes.

When the airplane landed at San Francisco airport, everything seemed shiny and new. The novelty of the western world had not yet eroded and I was thrilled to ride an escalator for the first time. My fascination for the west, full of shiny mysterious things that made me want to press buttons when no one was looking, began with that escalator ride.

Chapter 3: Losing My Religion

Despite my vow of celibacy, I was mesmerized when I saw her for the first time. Her hair spun gold in bushy waves around her bare shoulders. Her eyes were not the blue of electricity but a shade darker, like the color of music from the Mississippi delta.

Moist, thrashing bodies were slam-dancing around her, creating a fleshy ring with her as the centerpiece. She looked like a Celtic goddess overseeing an ancient mating ritual.

I'd never slam-danced before. I tried to copy the moves of the guy in front of me but I fell down.

Just as I was beginning to get the hang of it, the band started to play 'Straight to Hell' by The Clash and several pairs of hands lifted me up in the air. I got passed around. It seemed fun until I was unceremoniously dropped onto the grass.

Not wanting to die under a stampede of boots, I was relieved to see a hand reaching down to pull me up from the grass. A second later, I was thrilled to discover the hand belonged to her.

"Jeez, you've fallen down more times than Charlie Brown kicking the football. Are you ok?" she said, as she pulled me back up on my feet, which stood unsteadily on the lush lawns of the on-campus amphitheater.

Her smoky voice carried just a hint of seduction. Her skin, the color of rolled oats and free of make-up, radiated outdoorsy wholesomeness. She was a few pounds too substantial to be considered anything other than an average American beauty but she was blessed with a great sun-fed cheeriness, which made her stand-out even at a college like Dominican, where beauties thrived, like ivy on campus.

I didn't understand the Charlie Brown analogy. My head was spinning. And my back hurt. But I said: "I'm fine."

"Great," she said. "By the way, I'm Zoe."

"Hi, I'm Jayanta," I said.

"J-what?" she said.
"J-A-Y-A-N-T-A," I said.
"Nice to meet you," she said.

It was clear from the look on her face that she found my name impossible to pronounce.

The delicate crescent brush of the moon slipped-in through the trees and marbled the outline of her T-shirt, pale against the blackness of night. I tried not to look at the faint outlines of her nipples, standing up straight in the cold air. They seemed to be staring at me like two tiny puckered doorknobs, twin gateways to forbidden pleasures.

I was mortified to find my repressed sexuality reawakening at such an inappropriate time and redirected my gaze towards the stage. Hayden, the lead singer of the band, had just announced he would be taking a break. He had recently graduated from Dominican but his boyish face and blonde dreadlocks made him look like a cross between a young reggae-star and a new-age *sadhu*. Before leaving the stage, he implored everyone to donate generously to the Sierra Club volunteers, who were making their way through the crowd gathered around the stage.

A few months earlier, Exxon Valdez had spilt oil in Alaska and many students at Dominican had gotten inflamed. The Sierra Club had organized a fundraising concert to benefit victims of Exxon Valdez.

A few days later, I would discover Zoe was passionate about all matters relating to the environment and she was an active student member of the Sierra Club.

Forest Meadows, the on-campus amphitheater where the concert was being held that evening was packed with students.

"Here, let me wipe the mud off you," said Zoe, rubbing her fingers over the polyester shirt on my back, as a lanky sophomore wearing a fringed leather skirt stepped onto the stage as Hayden's replacement.

Losing My Religion

The feel of Zoe's fingers on my spine spawned an unruly wave of lust inside me.

I tried to calm my hormones by saying a silent prayer in memory of the Exxon victims but that didn't work. Soon, slivers of guilt began to ride on top of the lust-waves gushing through my brain.

"I don't remember seeing you at any prior Sierra Club event," said Zoe, pausing my stream of inappropriate thoughts. "Are you an environmental major?"

"No, I'm majoring in religion, with a minor in painting," I said, stuttering in an attempt to hide my excitement. "I'm an exchange student from Darjeeling. Recently arrived."

"That is an unusual combination," she said. "Are you planning to become a painter-priest, like Fra Angelico?"

"I'm not sure but I'm in awe of his painting of St. Dominic," I said. "Are you catholic?"

"I don't believe in God," she said. "In fact, I wish folks here wouldn't waste so much time talking about religion. My faith in life is sustained by the kick-ass beauty of nature and by music that doesn't suck."

Her statement fascinated and repelled me. How could she not feel the need to believe in a higher power? And how did she deal with guilt after doing naughty stuff?

The band reconvened on stage but without Hayden this time. The leather-skirted sophomore, trying her best to sound like Kim Gordon from Sonic Youth, started singing 'Kissability'.

Zoe started dancing again. Her bouncing hips, which occasionally touched mine as she twirled around, reminded me of the celestial nymph Madhura, who had tempted Lord Shiva into having coitus when His consort was not around. I hushed the waves of guilt surfing inside me by forcing myself to stop thinking about God. Instead, I tried to treat the song like a hymn and repeated each line, slowly.

19

Fistful of Fog

For a few seconds I felt my blood cool down but when I heard the lyrics – "you're driving me crazy, give us a kiss," – I couldn't contain myself any longer.

I moved towards Zoe. But Hayden came between us and pulled her towards him. They kissed and I had to pause my lust.

Over the coming months, this initial feeling of uncontrollable lust would grow into a novel and unforgettable emotion that can only be described as first love. I would resist this exciting (but forbidden) new state of affairs and try to return to my old, celibate ways. But the intoxicating glow from Zoe's love, starting with that first meeting, would erase the shadows surrounding my puritanical youth. And when that light would get extinguished, I would sink into a restless adulthood marked by failed romances and an incurable need to hold on to the past, an exercise as futile as trying to prevent a fistful of fog from vanishing.

As I rode my bike back to the dorm, I spotted a fat lizard basking under the glow of a roadside electric lamp. I felt the venom (which Hayden had produced in me) flow through my legs and endow them with a new, manic energy.

Pumping the pedals hard, I steered the bike towards my target. The lizard was just about to get off the asphalt and escape into the bushes growing on the side of the road when the front tire of my bike arrived at its target destination. The tire, inflated to the perfect point where its width matched the length of the lizard's body, squashed the reptile. I rolled the wheel back and forth a few times to make sure that not much more than a bloody watermark remained on the cold asphalt.

That act of reptilicide slaked my anger. But a few moments later I was overcome by disgust. How could I have killed an innocent creature?

I said a quick prayer of repentance but that night I couldn't stop thinking about Zoe. I tried to conquer my desire for her by meditating but when I woke up, I was ashamed to discover a wet dream had messed-up my bedsheet.

Shame dragged me over to the campus chapel. I knelt in front of the altar and said: "I try to keep my mind pure, like an unpolluted Himalayan stream. But my loins drag me into muddy ponds, from the depths of which blossom blemished lotuses, girls like Zoe, girls who don't believe in God. I try to get my soul out of the mud but the fragrance makes me dive back in. Dear God, please purge this terrible lust out of my system."

Most relationships begin with a kiss but Zoe began ours with a slap.

It was my first day in Professor Harker's Environmental Lab. (I'd signed up as a laboratory assistant to make some extra cash). I was thrilled to find Zoe in the lab but we got into an argument when she caught me tossing a six-pack holder into a garbage can.

"How can you assist in an environmental lab if you don't even know to cut apart plastic webbing on six-pack holders so ducks don't get their necks stuck in them?" she said in a passionate voice.

As I got to know her better, I would find it ironic that Zoe, who didn't seem to worry too much about sticking her neck out in some of the most dangerous places in the world, could be so passionate about protecting the necks of others. Maybe it had something to do with the fact she had been born in Berkeley, the protest-capital of America. But no cause, be it protecting birds or native-American lands, seemed too small for her to ignore. And the weaker the defender of the cause, the more empathy they garnered from her.

But I wasn't aware of this trait during my first month at Dominican, so I wrongly interpreted Zoe's passion about six-pack holders to be an accusation directed towards me, which made me angry.

Part of my anger stemmed from being treated ... like an ignorant foreigner (especially one who wasn't from a desirable European country but from the third-world) ... by some of my privileged classmates (many of whom drove up to class in BMWs handed to them by their parents).

Zoe's WASPish looks had led me to assume she (like many of my classmates) hailed from a wealthy family. Later, I'd discover her family had limited resources and she was attending Dominican on an athletic scholarship.

"How am I supposed to know all the rules when I haven't even been in this country a month?" I said, angrily. "We don't have these sort of six-pack holders in my country."

"Come with me after this lab is over," she said. "I'll loan you my copy of the Environmental Handbook. That will give you an idea of basic environmental dos and don'ts."

As we walked together after Harker's lab, I felt a strange sense of elation. It was a typical summer afternoon in the Bay Area, with freezing fog in San Francisco requiring jackets and sweatshirts, while (a few miles inland) students on Dominican campus fought 90-degree heat with tank-tops and flip-flops.

Zoe had adjusted her wardrobe to the weather. Her freckled arms, normally covered, were exposed in a short, sleeveless dress. Her scalp, often bare, lay submerged under a large-rimmed and loose-fitting sunhat.

The scent of magnolia blossoms flirted with the warm air, making me pause my walk to inhale the exuberance of a summer day, before the fog forced its way inland and transported me back to my normal, restrained self. I asked her if she wanted to sit under the shady branches of an old magnolia tree. But she kept walking, saying she was late for volleyball practice.

A few minutes later, we entered a shadowy alley behind the campus chapel. The alley was slippery with water (from sprinklers providing moisture to adjacent flower beds). I found the cool, damp darkness comforting. In a mad moment of summery abandon, I decided to kiss her.

Hastily, I put my arm around her waist and drew her close. And then, just as I lowered my head to plant my lips on hers, a sudden gust of wind removed the hat from her head.

Prying herself loose from my embrace, she stood up on her tippy toes and turned a quick quarter-circle. Raising her free arm, she reached behind her to snatch her hat back from the wind.

All off this happened very quickly. It was too late for me to pull my puckered lips back. And I was caught off-balance.

I ended up tasting: first, the humidity of a scorching summer day under her arms ... and then, a second later, a slap on my cheek.

"What in the world was that?" she said, sounding less than amused. "Was that an attempt to kiss me? I sure hope not, because you are not my type."

As she walked away, the shameful sound of that slap reverberated inside my head.

Trudging back to the chapel, I begged God to restore my dignity.

During those first few weeks in America, my life often felt like an old car skidding on new ice.

Everything my upbringing held sacred was challenged by the new country. I debated whether to glide in the direction of the skid or apply the brakes of my puritanical compass and resist with all my will power. Currents and counter-currents swirled inside me, leaving me confused. On most days, I missed my simple, old life in Darjeeling.

Fistful of Fog

I turned to my roommate, Ron, for advice. He had been born into a middle-class Parsee family from Bombay and his birth name was Roshan. He was a business major at Dominican. He had lived in the U.S for only three years but he spoke with a flawless American accent. I admired how he effortlessly slipped in and out of accents: American when classmates were around and then, when he was alone with me, his accent would revert to the rapid, lyrical English one hears in Parsee colonies across India; words spoken as if one is singing while running to catch a commuter train. That semester I'd signed up for ESL classes and hearing Ron express himself like a native English speaker made me jealous. How easy would life at Dominican be if I could speak English as fluently as he? And would Zoe have rejected me if my vocabulary hadn't been so limited and if my accent hadn't sounded so alien?

"Of course, you are not the type of guy Zoe would go for," he said. "Have you seen yourself in the mirror recently? You look like a Satyajit Ray movie character from the 1950s. Shave off that mustache, trade your glasses for contacts and put on a pair of jeans instead of those dreadful polyester threads you call pants. And while you are at it, shorten your name to Jay. Do you think anyone in California can pronounce Jayanta?"

"But that is the name I was given by my parents," I said.

"So, what?" he said. "With a name like Jayanta you are guaranteed to remain a virgin, here in America. But a name like Jay can get you laid."

That night he drove me to listen to an Indie rock band playing in San Francisco. I'd grown up on a steadfast diet of classical Bengali songs, sprinkled with the occasional Bollywood tune. American music did not feel rhythmic to my ears.

When I confessed to Ron that I missed music from the old country, he said: "Stop acting like a *desi*. You need to learn this music fast. The best way to impress a girl like Zoe is with your knowledge of rock-n-roll."

Whenever Ron got frustrated with me that semester, he would call me a *desi* – a person of rustic Indian origin – a term he knew I hated.

That weekend, he took me to a vintage shop on Haight Street and made me buy a second-hand leather jacket and a new, blister-inducing pair of steel-toed boots. Then, for the next several nights, he drove me to various bars in the city and had me listen to different types of bands: alternative, indie, punk, heavy-metal, jazz, bluegrass, and country. In an attempt to fit-in, I ignored my sonic discomfort and tried to learn how to dance to this new beat. But when we returned back to campus at the end of each night, I felt dazed and exhausted.

One night, when Ron saw me praying before going to bed, he said: "Stop wasting your time. The only God you should worship in this country is money."

On most nights, I would tune into cricket commentary on BBC radio. Sometimes, I felt closer to the voice of the BBC commentators than to Ron, or anyone else on campus. I tried to share cricket scores with Ron, but he said he had absolutely no interest in any sport, "unless they involve hot rods or hot women".

He was into cars like I was into cricket. The only thing he ever watched on TV was Indy 500 races. He worked weekends at a second-hand car dealership and would bring a car home on some nights. He never went to a bar without his "wheels" or without slipping on a fake "engagement" ring on his finger. He said a girl trusted a guy more if he flashed a ring and if he had a car to drive her home (or make-out in if he couldn't wait).

"You must learn to drive," said Ron, one morning. "Otherwise you will never get anywhere with a hottie like Zoe."

Although I had procured an international driver's license, I had never driven a car on the right-hand side of the road before. So, he gave me driving lessons at a grocery store parking lot.

Fistful of Fog

After a few practice rounds, I took the car out on the main road. But I got my turns confused and hit a parked delivery truck.

No serious damage was done but my pride was dented.

Just before the tow truck arrived, Ron said: "Have you heard that old Japanese proverb about the unruly nail getting hammered into submission? Well, you certainly look like one miserable foreign nail that has been sprinkled with an extra layer of culture shock. What you need is a friendly hammer like me to beat your *desi* upbringing into a shape that will be more familiar to American eyes."

I knew Ron was upset, but I wished he would stop calling me a *desi*.

———

Since I was getting nowhere with Zoe, Ron suggested I get to know her roommate, Julia.

She was majoring in nursing at Dominican, but she was always hanging around the chapel on campus. I decided to friend her in Bible Study class.

The class went excruciatingly slowly, as the campus minister droned on about Dominican ideals. And, as soon it ended, I followed Julia outside.

"You seem to know all the hymns by heart," I said, shielding my eyes from the sunrays bouncing of off the crucifix necklace around her neck. "Where did you learn to sing like that?"

"Goa," she said.

"No way," I said. "You don't look very Indian. I thought you were Italian or something."

"I get that all the time," she said, in Hindi. Then, switching back to English, she said: "My parents were Portuguese but Sister Carmen at St. Anne's convent in Mapusa grew me up. Believe me, I am as Indian as you. I love Bollywood movies."

"I'm from Darjeeling," I said, thrilled we had a country in common.

She said: "Since you are from Darjeeling, I have to ask: have you climbed Kanchenjunga?"

An image of my father's body, lying inside a wooden coffin at Kanchenjunga base camp, flashed through my brain. Even though a year had passed since his death, the mention of climbing Kanchenjunga made me feel nauseous.

I had never gone further than Kanchenjunga Base Camp but after losing my father I'd replaced my climbing boots with a sketch-book. I'd sketched my father's portrait from old black and white photos which my mother had buried deep inside the drawers of her almirah.

For a while, I'd left those sketches alone. Then, I'd colored them in with paint. Capturing, with the soothing strokes of a paintbrush, the different angles of his face displayed in various shades of brightness had helped me survive the dark months following his death. Painting had proven more effective than prayer in dealing with the shockwaves that had engulfed me during that difficult time.

"No, why do you ask," I said, surprised at her question. "Do you know it is the third highest mountain in the world and difficult to—"

"I know all about Kanch," she said. "I climbed Denali this summer with Zoe. We are members of the American Alpine Club. The club is screening a documentary on Aconcagua this weekend. You should come. They always have free food."

"I'm not much of a climber," I said.

"But having grown up in the Himalayas you must have done some climbing," said Julia, bringing me back to the present.

"I took a few classes at the Himalayan Mountaineering Institute during my sophomore year in college but I'm not into climbing anymore. However, I do like to paint the unique light that shines on the Himalayas at dusk and dawn. My house in Darjeeling has water-colors of several peaks," I said.

"I didn't realize you were a painter," she said. "I love going to museums, but Zoe is so preoccupied with Hayden right now that she doesn't seem to have time for anyone else. Do you want to go to the Legion this weekend? They are having a special lecture on Italian religious painters from the 15th century."

Upon hearing Hayden's name, a jealous, little monster sprouted inside me.

"I thought Hayden and Zoe were just friends. Are they serious?" I said.

"Interested in Zoe, are you?" said Julia, with a chuckle. "Well, take a number. There are quite a few men lined up before you."

"No, I'm not interested in Zoe, or any other girl for that matter," I said. "I'm in a relationship with God."

"Then why did you blush when I mentioned Zoe's name?" she said, laughing.

I didn't have a good answer for her.

After Julia mentioned Professor Harker's Environmental Ethics seminar was one of Zoe's favorite classes, I enrolled in the course. And when Zoe showed up to class, I rushed to grab a seat near her.

The late afternoon sun tossed the shadow of her seductive profile onto the blistered classroom wall. The voluptuous contours of her breasts displayed against the wall turned me into a guilt-filled, lustful mess.

I prayed for her to drop a pencil, so I could rescue it and "accidentally" touch some part of her body, as I returned it back to her. But nothing of that sort happened. And I was reduced to watching the shadow of her breast rise and fall against the wall, as her breath fanned the cauldron of unrequited desire flaming inside me.

Losing My Religion

Hoping to ask her out on a date I followed her outside, after class.

But before I could engage her in conversation a jock with tennis-ball calves came by, looked at me with obvious disdain, and then whisked her off to an on-campus soccer game. And I was left nursing my shame.

Shame may feel like a foreign country for some, but for anyone with a puritanical upbringing like mine it is well-worn territory. My upbringing had conditioned me to recognize all desire as evil. And hypocrisy, the ever-present alter-ego of shame, ensured I remained in an endless cycle of masturbation and confessional prayer.

There were plenty of god-loving students at Dominican, especially in my religion class. I decided to friend them and stay away from atheists like Zoe.

Why waste my time talking to someone who didn't believe in heaven or karma, or any of these other life and death questions I had been wrestling with my entire life?

But the next time I saw her on campus, an unbearable excitement flushed and confused me.

Having grown up in a country obsessed with fair skin, I was fascinated by the lightness of her features, perfect except for a slight redness on the tip of her nose. Other than that little blemish, her skin appeared flawless but fragile. It had a diaphanous, dream-like quality, so ephemeral that a few minutes without sunscreen could make any exposed part of her flesh match the redness on her nose. Over the coming months, despite Zoe's best efforts with cream to tame it, the redness on her nose would grow, and my fondness for her would grow along with it.

And her golden hair, which had only intrigued me at first, now began to fascinate me.

Fistful of Fog

    I was seven years old when I first laid eyes on a blonde. That year my mother had invited an English school-teacher, Ms. Rowbotham, to our house in Darjeeling for afternoon tea.
    Her appearance fascinated and frightened me. Also, she reminded me of one of the extra-terrestrial villains in a movie about outer space I'd seen the previous night.
    "Ma, why is her hair made of jute and her feet webbed like a duck's?" I whispered, when Ms. Rowbotham excused herself to go to the washroom. "Do you think she is an alien from another planet?"
    Ma explained that Ms. Rowbotham was wearing transparent, flesh-colored stockings (which made her toes appear as if they were joined together).
    I had never seen stockings before. But Ma was in no mood to hear my reasoning and warned me not to make any more rude comments about Ms. Rowbotham's appearance.
    My unfamiliar, tropical eyes did not rest on another blonde until I met Zoe at Dominican. Whenever she got bored in class, she would curl a few strands of her hair around her finger and rub it on her nose.
    I wondered if blonde hair smelt different to mine. One morning during Harker's class, I leaned forward to sniff Zoe's scalp. Instead of getting a heavenly whiff, which was what I was expecting, I smelt chlorine.
    Later, I would learn Zoe often came to class directly from swim practice and she used shampoo infrequently because she believed suds in wastewater were suffocating fish in San Rafael Creek.
    Many delicate moons have waned since Zoe left Dominican but I still can't walk past a swimming pool without thinking of her.

Losing My Religion

The next time I saw Zoe, she was chained to an old magnolia tree.

This tree, which everyone at Dominican called Maggie, sprawled over that part of campus which used to be known as magnolia valley. Her branches were crinkled with age, her roots tempered by seismic fault-lines. She stood on a sloping hillside, defying gravity and the Pacific fog, which sometimes stretched its way over to her corner.

Lightning had trimmed her aspirations, leaving the upper corners of her branches brittle and leafless. On good days, she appeared as a tall, green beacon of hope for the survival of local forests. On bad days, she resembled a shipwrecked mast with fishnet sails.

Real estate development had reduced the number of magnolia trees on campus. Now, the valley was down to just Maggie and two of her arboreal sisters, who survived in adjacent plots. Tree-removers had been summoned earlier that day. The business school was expanding and Maggie had been earmarked for removal. But before the tree-removers could unleash their chain-saws, Zoe had student volunteers from the Sierra Club tie her to Maggie's trunk.

As dusk deepened, a group of students surrounded Maggie. Some students traded their protest banners for candles and they started a vigil. From a distance, the candles resembled a ring of fireflies, encircling Maggie.

Professor Harker gave a passionate speech about the need to preserve the environment for future generations. His speech was followed by a violin recital performed by the chapel choir group, led by Julia.

After the violin recital was over, I helped her untie Zoe from the tree.

"Thanks, Jay," said Zoe. "Didn't expect to see you here."

"I asked him to come," said Julia. "His friend from Darjeeling is planning an expedition to Kanchenjunga. I thought you may be interested in talking to him."

"There is nothing I'd like more than becoming the first woman to plan her foot on top of Kanch," said Zoe, with a dreamy look on her face. "Can your friend find me a place on his expedition team?"

"But Kanchenjunga has one of the highest death rates. Aren't you afraid?" I said, stunned to hear she wanted to climb the same mountain that killed my father.

"Of course, I am afraid of dying, just like anybody else," she said. "But how can I pursue my dream if I'm not willing to take any risks? And you? What's your dream?"

"I'm not sure," I said, surprised.

Her question had caught me off guard.

"The only thing more depressing than not following your dream is not knowing your dream," she said, with a look of slight disdain.

―――

I walked into Professor Harker's cluttered office in Guzman Hall on the Monday following 'Black Friday' (Wall Street had coined this term because the stock market had suffered a sudden collapse on that day).

He paused his reading of 'Scientific American' and asked me to take a seat.

After we had exchanged pleasantries, I said: "I've been trying to figure out what to do after graduation but I'm not sure I want to major in religion anymore."

"Why the sudden change of heart?" he said.

I said, hesitantly: "Well, I met this girl so now I am thinking—"

"There is always a girl involved in these sort of things," he said, chuckling and stretching the laugh-lines around his eyes into leathery check-marks. "You bring back memories of my college days."

"I come from a long line of Brahmin priests and my mother believes it is my destiny to also become a temple priest. But after attending your class I'm finding myself drawn more to logic and less towards blind faith. I think I'm developing a special interest for environmental causes. What shall I do, Professor?" I said.

"In the east, they say destiny is pre-ordained. Here in the west we believe we make our own destiny. Duality can be your strength. Why don't you switch your major to environmental studies? You may have to take a few extra classes to make up for lost time but I'm sure you'll manage. After you return home, you can integrate the technological advantages you see here with the nature-based traditions of your homeland. That way you can have the best of both worlds," he said.

"I know environmental jobs pay decently but do they offer security or are they subject to the whims of Wall Street?" I said.

"There is no better time to be working in the environmental field," he said, his voice filling-up with conviction and pride. He paused to clear his throat, before continuing: "First Love Canal, then Bhopal, then Chernobyl. Disasters will happen as long as corporate greed and nuclear saber-rattling exist. And as long as man-made disasters continue to happen, you will never have trouble finding a job in this field."

After assuring me he would get my new major approved by the dean, he told me a bit about himself.

Like a lot of men from his generation, he was self-made. He had been raised on a farm in Illinois. After active duty in the Korean War he had attended college, on the GI bill. Several years spent in the African savannah and two graduate degrees later he was now regarded as one of the world's leading experts on environmental conservation.

He had never married but if he had had a son, he said, he probably would have been around my age.

Fistful of Fog

I was about to ask him if he had visited the Himalayas when he looked at his watch. I thanked him and left his office but that night I kept tossing and turning in bed.

Would God find a way to punish me for turning my back on Him? And how would my mother react, when she found out I'd reneged on the vocation that had sustained my Brahmin family for generations?

Unable to sleep, I got out of bed and opened my dorm-room window wide. It was cool and windy outside but I was moist with sweat. After standing by the window and savoring the gusty breeze that came pouring into the bedroom, I climbed back into bed. A few minutes later, I reached out in the darkness and tried to touch the clay statue of Lord Shiva, which rested on my bedside table. I wanted to touch Shiva's feet and ask for forgiveness. But my fingers touched emptiness. I got out of bed and turned on the light. The statue was lying on the floor, head severed clean from the body.

The head of God stared at me with blank eyes, as if reflecting the stiffness of death.

I was filled with dread, which worsened the following morning when the fault-lines in Northern California rumbled and life changed for many at Dominican. Ron had his car, which he had parked outside a strip club, crushed by a collapsing brick facade near Market Street. Professor Harker had his apartment building on Beach Street collapse, while he was lecturing at Dominican. My dorm was spared any damage, but my spirit was rattled.

A few days later, my mood darkened further when Tenzing, my best friend from Darjeeling, called and said Jerzy Kukuczka (the second mountaineer to climb all 8000-meter peaks) had plunged several thousand feet to his death, while attempting to summit the unclimbed South Face of Lhotse. My thoughts immediately turned to my father, who had also fallen to his death, while trying to climb Kanchenjunga.

That night I prayed for my father and for Jerzy.

Isn't it strange how the mind associates one untimely death with another, unrelated, one? And how a loved one's death, which you are trying hard to forget, springs back to life because you are reminded of the haunting youth of a different, unrelated, victim?

A candlelight vigil was held in memory of the Loma Prieta earthquake victims. But campus remained gloomy. Everyone seemed to be on edge, as if waiting for aftershocks.

―――

After our mid-term presentations, Professor Harker invited our class to dinner at an off-campus barbecue restaurant. He arranged for a van to drive us and, when we arrived at the restaurant, I managed to procure a sit next to Zoe.

"Nice presentation today on those moon jellies," I said.

"Thanks," she said. "Loved your watercolors of Mount Tam. Didn't know you were interested in conservation challenges facing the Tamalpais watershed. You are such a good painter."

Hearing the encouragement in her voice inspired me to say: "Hey, would you like me to paint your portrait sometime?"

"I'd love that," she said.

"Gr-gr-great," I said, stuttering, as a sudden wave of anxiety descended on me. "How about tomorrow afternoon?"

"Ok, let's plan for six-ish, after volleyball practice," she said.

A warm sensation flushed my face. I was about to turn my head away but mercifully her attention was diverted by the arrival of our waitress.

There wasn't a single vegetarian item on the menu, which put me in a bind. Having grown up in a vegetarian household, I'd never eaten meat. My mother had impressed upon me that killing an animal for meat was sinful. But Ron had said not eating meat was "un-American". And I didn't want Zoe to think of me as un-American.

"I'll have the beef ribs," said Zoe.

"The same," I said, after mumbling a silent apology to God.

A few minutes later, our waitress reappeared and deposited a gigantic plate of steaming beef ribs in front of us. I tried to drown my ribs in barbecue sauce. I hoped the sauce would cover-up both the awful leathery taste and my guilt.

"Sheesh, you must really like that sauce," she said.

"How come you don't have any on yours?" I said.

"The 'cue is smoked on mesquite wood. Why ruin good meat with sauce?" she said. "I don't put sauce on my barbeque. And I don't put make-up on my face. What you see is what you get. Why cover up the way nature intended things to be?"

I looked at her gorgeous, rosy face and thought: yes, why cover up a good thing?

A few minutes later, my stomach began to ache. The fatty beef ribs had combined with hot sauce to turn my abdomen into a gastric volcano. I tried to douse the fire with diet coke, but the carbonation made my belly growl louder. I attempted to hide chewed bits of gristly beef-rib inside my napkin. But this restaurant was a real dive. The napkins were paper-thin and couldn't hide a sneeze.

Before I could force the next beef-rib into my groaning belly, I had to run to the restroom. I sat on the toilet and tried to rid my bowels of chunks of dead cow kicking inside me. It felt like my intestines wanted to have an out-of-body experience.

Having grown up in small-town India, I preferred using water, rather than paper, to clean my bottom. But there was no mug in the bathroom. I panicked when I realized I'd have to use toilet paper for the first time in my life. Not knowing how much swiping would be enough, I used-up an entire roll. Unfortunately, the plumbing jammed and toilet water, speckled with the semi-solid remains of my ill-digested meal, overflowed and started to exit the restroom.

Losing My Religion

"Did a skunk die in here or something? Yuck, it smells awful," said Zoe, walking into the restroom.

Then, turning towards me she said, with a freckled smile: "Didn't they teach you in religion class that cleanliness is next to godliness?"

I realized she was pulling my leg but I was mortified.

The San Marco Art Studios – an assorted mess of scattered paper, brushes, books, tubes of paints, wooden frames and rags – always had a soothing effect on me. Whenever I had troubles that year, I'd escape into the studio and paint. Sometimes, in between classes, I would stretch out on the baggy sofa that occupied a dusty corner of the studio and read one of the books lying around or take a nap.

It was the most relaxing place on campus for me but that afternoon, as I waited for Zoe to show up, I began to feel anxious.

Would she like my work? Or would she dump my portrait onto the unkempt heap of books and stuff piled-up inside her dorm room?

My angst did not subside when she showed up, late, and said: "Sorry, volleyball practice ran over. I hope this doesn't take much time because it is Grampa's birthday and I'm taking him out to dinner. Maybe we should reschedule."

"Don't worry, this won't take any time. I will use watercolor instead of oil so we can be fast," I said, desperately hoping that she not cancel the appointment. "I'll do as much as I can now and finish up later."

"Ok," she said, settling into a chair.

I sat down on a skinny stool which was facing her. Reaching into my backpack, I extracted a drawing-pad, a #2 pencil, a water-color paint set and a sable paintbrush.

Fistful of Fog

My fingers shook slightly as I began to sketch the outlines of her face, resplendent in the late afternoon light. Then, after mixing paint with water from my bottle, I started to brush paper with paint. Each brush-stroke felt more assured than the one before and brought a greater feeling of calm. Soon, I felt completely relaxed. But I must have lost track of time because I was startled to look up and find her standing over me.

"Looks great," she said. "When will it be ready?"

"The paint's almost dry," I said. "I don't have a suitable frame to hang this on but as soon as I find one I will bring the framed painting over to you."

"That's terrific," she said, before making her way towards the door.

Then, just as she was exiting the studio, she turned around and said: "Hey, the Cramps are playing at the Halloween Ball next Tuesday at The Fillmore. I have two tickets. Want to come?"

"Sure," I said.

I'd never heard of the Cramps but I was thrilled to get an invitation from her.

"Let's dress up. There will be prizes for the best costume," she said.

I'd never been to a Halloween party. As I planned for my date with Zoe I worried endlessly about details.

Would we go to her dorm room after the event or would she come to mine?

Would we take public transportation, or would we drive?

"You need some hot wheels," said Ron. "Otherwise you will never get laid by a hottie like Zoe."

He took me to the dealership where he worked part-time and "borrowed" a Mustang convertible.

When the big day arrived, I ran to the store and bought new bed-sheets. (I hadn't yet figured out how to use the washing machine in my dorm). Then, I chilled a bottle of Champagne but it was only when she rang the doorbell, that I remembered I didn't have any wine glasses. I rescued an empty plastic water bottle from the recycle bin and quickly cut a cup out of it.

"Nice costume," she said, after I opened the door.

She had dressed up as the Hollywood hooker, Vivian (from the movie: 'Pretty Woman'). And I had dressed up as the Dalai Lama. I sported a maroon outer robe, a golden upper robe, and a silk scarf tied around my waist.

It was a Tibetan scarf, symbolizing compassion and colored white to show the pure heart of the giver.

A few months earlier, Lama Pasang (the head-lama at a Himalayan monastery located near Kanchenjunga base camp) had gifted that scarf to me, after saying: "When you get to America, you must show love for all people in your new homeland. This scarf will help tear down boundaries and bring you closer to everyone there".

The scarf wasn't a part of the Dalai Lama's normal wardrobe, but I wore it that Halloween night, hoping it would improve my luck with Zoe.

When we got to The Fillmore, we joined the long line of people waiting to get inside. Many faces were painted for the occasion, but the dim light made it difficult to distinguish between the costumed ghouls, rock-stars and superheroes prancing around that evening.

We hung out near the bar area and chased shots of tequila with pints of beer. But when The Cramps took center stage we pushed our way towards the front and started to dance.

As Lux Interior sang – 'Can Your Pussy Do the Dog' – I turned toward Zoe.

Removing the silk scarf from my waist, I draped it loosely around her athletic shoulders.

Fistful of Fog

Slowly, I turned her toward me and kissed her on lipstick-free lips that smelt of beer and bubblegum.

For a few seconds, she reciprocated.

Then, she abruptly withdrew her tongue from inside my mouth and said: "Jay, I like you, I really do, but I have a boyfriend."

Her words killed my buzz.

Our stars had aligned briefly that evening but their paths would remain crossed a little while longer.

After returning to my dorm room, I scissored the portrait of Zoe I'd painted (but not yet framed).

Depositing the shiny pieces of shredded paper into the stained toilet in the bathroom, I turned the flush. Rust-colored water emerged and swept away the pieces.

A lone blank piece of paper clung onto the side of the toilet-bowl: one lost little white ray of hope battling against the rising tide of dark water.

I flushed again. This forced the errant ray to flee into the dark noisy maze of the apartment's plumbing, where the rest of its shredded companions lay buried.

The act of portrait-destruction made me feel a little better but I couldn't get Zoe out of my mind.

After bible study class the next morning, I asked Julia: "Is Zoe still seeing Hayden?"

"No," she said, pulling down a campus chapel window to prevent the fog from getting inside. "The new guy's name is Juan. You must have seen him play basketball for the Penguins. He is from Buenos Aires. You should check out his photos from our Denali expedition this summer. They are hanging in the library. He has taken some crazy shots of Zoe, I tell you. She is planning to spend Christmas with him in Argentina."

Losing My Religion

Of course, I had seen Juan. His physicality had made him a pillar of the Dominican basketball team. His long arms endowed him with a wingspan that made him look like he could fly to the top of any mountain by simply flapping his arms. The thought of her spending the holidays with him in the Southern Hemisphere birthed a jealous, angry monster inside my head. I didn't see Zoe again that semester, except in my nocturnal fantasies.

―――

Two weeks after Thanksgiving, Zoe left for Argentina. It was the business end of the semester, with finals looming.

As Christmas neared, red-n-blue ribbons brightened the store fronts but blue-n-black chains of homesickness dampened my spirit. I scoured San Rafael and the surrounding suburbia searching for something, anything, to remind me of home. But with malls and condos dotting the landscape, and no snow-capped mountains to be seen anywhere, the edges of my life felt flattened.

Whenever I felt blue, I would climb a hill behind Dominican and paint Mount Tam. Whether it was foggy or sunny, lit by moon or sun, the act of turning a bleak canvas into a symphony of color lifted my spirits up a bit. But there was no hiding the fact I missed Zoe.

"Time for you to forget Zoe," Ron said, on the last day of finals week. "Semester is over but you remain a virgin. Let me help you end your V-curse, despo."

I wished I hadn't revealed my secret to Ron. I was 22 years old but still a virgin.

My family followed strict Brahmanical rules and our home in Darjeeling had always been puritanical. But Ma's religiosity took a turn for the worse after my father left us and moved to America with his yoga student, Angela.

Fistful of Fog

My teenage years were filled with Ma's impromptu, shame-inducing lectures on why one must abstain from sex before marriage. And, after she divorced my father, she expanded her definition of abstinence to include meat, alcohol and Bollywood movies.

Most men in my family were priests but I wasn't sure I wanted to follow in their footsteps. When I shared my feelings with Ma, she said she wouldn't let me go abroad unless I reassured her, in front of God, that I would remain a virgin in America, the land where my father had lost his religion.

A few days before I left for Dominican, Ma had taken me to the Kanchenjunga temple in Darjeeling, where my uncle served as headpriest. With my chest bare and my head bowed, I sat cross-legged on the marbled floor in the inner sanctum of the temple. After my uncle marched me through an elaborate ceremony, filled with much hymn-chanting and water-sprinkling, Ma made me take a vow of celibacy, in front of Lord Shiva's statue. Earlier, while training as a priest's apprentice, I had taken other vows, like not eating meat.

After landing in California, I'd been surprised to find students talking about virginity as if it was a disease. But, as long as Zoe had been on campus, I hadn't given much thought to spending time with other girls.

Now that Zoe was far away, and in the arms of another man, I started to wonder what I would do, if an opportunity presented itself.

But if I slept with a girl, wouldn't God get mad at me for breaking my chastity vow?

This dilemma made me seek Ron's counsel, which turned out to be a terrible mistake.

When I look back at my eventful first semester at Dominican, there is nothing I regret more than what followed shortly after I revealed my V-secret to Ron.

Losing My Religion

As soon as our finals ended, Ron drove me to The Foxxxy Kitty, a strip club located on the neon-lit side of North Beach.

After we entered the club, he murmured a few words to the hostess at the entrance, who surprised me by greeting him by his name.

A few minutes later, a blonde (whose face bore a slight resemblance to Zoe) came into our private booth which smelt like day-old sushi sprayed with Pine-Sol.

As she began to dance, I feigned a bored look and lit up one of Ron's cigarettes. Her gyrations escalated with the music and before long she had shed all her clothing.

I tried to look elsewhere but my eyes, channeling the hunger of a thousand lonely nights, zeroed in between her legs.

After a few minutes of acrobatics, she turned her back toward me and shoved her plump butt-cheeks inches from my face. And I began to fantasize that it was Zoe's body (and not the stripper's) I was viewing.

Bringing her crotch so close to my nose that I stopped breathing, she bent over and spread her buttocks open with her hands. She held that pose for a long minute.

My penis, which had been throbbing violently, couldn't stand the strain. I sneaked my fingers under the table and touched myself. Soon, I ejaculated.

I was mortified and quickly crossed my legs to hide the stain but Ron laughed, saying: "Consider this your new temple of learning. No better place for you to learn how to deal with girls. I'm going to leave now so you can have her to yourself. I've already paid her to take care of your V-curse, so make sure you get much more than a lap dance from her."

After he left the booth, I told her I didn't want a lap dance and asked if we could talk instead.

She was worried about not getting paid but after I reassured her I wouldn't tell anyone, she put her clothes on and started chatting.

Fistful of Fog

She had left her hometown, Mostar, shortly before the breakup of Yugoslavia.

She hadn't met anyone from India before but felt she knew the country because of Bollywood movies. I told her I'd never met a blonde Muslim before.

For a while she talked about Bosnia. Then, after saying it was more tiring to talk in English than dance, she started shaking her hips again, Bollywood style this time.

Later, as we walked towards our hotel, Ron continued with his inane banter, saying: "Always carry a spare condom ... remember, girls that talk a lot don't fuck ... the quiet ones trying to blend into a wallpaper are your best bet ... go where there is no competition, like Fisherman's Wharf, which is teeming with single tourists and tell them you come from the land of the Kama Sutra ... stay away from graduate students, those geeks never get laid ... and remember, even if all else fails never sleep with a *desi* girl because she will find a way to chain your balls to a wedding ring."

After we checked into our Russian Hill hotel room, I lay on the rickety bed and tried to erase the unsavory evening from my mind. But later that night, the stripper from the Foxxxy Kitty appeared in my dream. She was dressed in the same sort of clothes (torn jeans, a sweatshirt displaying the Dominican University logo, and an Oakland *A*'s baseball cap) that Zoe often wore on campus.

After removing all of her clothes, the stripper asked me to come to her side. Then, when I hesitated, she began to laugh demonically.

When I looked up, I saw the stripper's face had transformed into that of the goddess *Kali*, the consort of Lord Shiva. A few drops of blood trickled down *Kali*'s lips and hung on her outstretched tongue.

As my eyes moved slowly down to *Kali*'s torso, I saw her chest sporting a necklace of severed heads and a large Black Widow spider crawling between her legs.

She began to dance, slowly at first and then she twirled swiftly. I tried to avoid looking at her but the spidery vortex between her legs sucked me in. And when she turned her back towards me, I saw the dime-sized whitehead, right above her rectal opening.

The whitehead looked ripe, and ready to detonate. It kept growing, at first the size of a marble but soon a melon, until it exploded and drowned me in an ocean of puss.

I woke up screaming.

A few months later, I would hear R.E.M.'s song – 'Losing My Religion' – and I would think back to the influence Ron had on me during my impressionable first semester at Dominican. Even though Zoe (who enjoyed deciphering the meaning of songs) would say I'd misinterpreted the lyrics, that tune would trigger memories of the crass, questionable methods Ron had employed to help me cut the puritanical cord which had tied me to my past and the unsavory aftertaste his shenanigans had left behind.

It was a typical San Francisco morning, deserving of warm layers that would soon be peeled-off as the day grew. Hyde Street was empty, except for a few early-bird tourists taking pictures of Crooked Street. Two grey-suited men raced to catch the cable-car, heading towards the financial district. You could tell the locals from the tourists; the former carried an extra layer of clothing.

A few more turns brought me up a hill slope and onto the row of glitzy shops and moneyed houses, beyond which lay the eternal Pacific. The city took the air out of my lungs and breathed life back into my hungover body.

Fistful of Fog

I sat down on the grassy mound near the top of the Vallejo Steps and watched the city wake up. Russian Hill glowed in her morning splendor but Chinatown was covered in a congee of fog. The cable car lines sang in empty silence in the street below, a few minutes of rest for the wooden ships before ferrying people up and down again in this vast amusement park of a city, where possibilities were endless, where new love and newer wealth seemed just around the corner.

I felt a strange sense of familiarity as Edwardian mansions in sunny Russian Hill neighborhoods gave way to cramped, subsidized apartments glued together in the mist that had just started to creep into the Tenderloin. The dual forces of sun and fog seemed to have split the city's rich and poor districts better than the Board of Supervisors.

A tranny with tall legs and the previous night's clothes hustled toward me from a street-corner and said: "Come here my little cupcake, let me start your day by tossing your salad."

After ignoring the tranny's proposal, I picked up my pace and walked away.

Civic Center was its usual blend of lethargy and activity when I got there. Food peddlers and farmer-vendors were setting up their stalls on the edge of Market Street. And an assorted bunch of hobos moved aimlessly amongst corporate types, hurrying to work with lattes in hand.

The thickening arterial traffic started to clog the streets leading down to the freeway.

I got off the busy intersection and walked down smaller alleyways, zigzagging my way around the Tenderloin – an urban surfer sliding up and down on the sleazy shimmering underbelly of the city.

The walk up to the top of Twin Peaks was sweaty but once I got up there the breeze cooled me down. The vast cityscape lay sprawled below me, the commuter maze extending into the groin of the city, thick and slow-moving.

Losing My Religion

The fog reappeared to play peekaboo with the TV towers but the western horizon of the city, clear of mist, stared invitingly back at me. I decided to walk downhill.

Golden Gate Park was quiet when I got there. I ignored the dread-locked dude who rode up on a bicycle and showed me his bag of pot. The dude must have thought I was Mexican because he spoke to me in Spanish.

When I arrived at Ocean Beach, it was sunny on the water's edge where the surfers played and foggy where the hobos huddled over a bonfire. I bought a six-pack of beer from a nearby store and parked myself atop a sand dune.

As I was finishing my first beer of the morning, I heard the fading moan of a fog-horn in the distance. It sounded haunting, like a Tibetan trumpet calling from the top of a Himalayan peak.

I decided to go home for the holidays.

Chapter 4: Fifty-Fifty

I had gone to some length to reinvent myself in America. But I didn't anticipate this causing any issues when I returned home. During orientation week the international student office at Dominican had warned incoming foreign students about reverse culture shock setting in upon returning home. Thinking it was a nonsensical concept, I'd laughed back then. But after a few days in Darjeeling, a feeling of alienation started to grow inside me, making me feel homeless (even though I had a house to live in).

My disorientation started shortly after my plane landed at Calcutta airport and I rode the crowded train towards Darjeeling.

I looked outside the train window as the hinterland flashed by.

For a brief moment, I was entranced by the timeless beauty of the countryside: ducks feeding endlessly on green algae ponds; rice paddies bursting with grain; coconut groves whistling softly in the wind. But a few minutes later, I was repelled by the appearance of the filth and chaos of the shantytowns: a blur of concrete amidst a churning medley of humans, animals and debris.

A cloak of humanity descended upon us as soon as the train pulled into its final stop.

I let the chaos that greeted the arrival of the train subside before getting down to the platform and jostling my way through the human maze that packed the station.

Hawkers competed with each other to get my attention as they yelled: "... tea-coffee? ... hello, rickshaw? ... salted peanuts! ... hotel, sir?"

Just as I was resigning myself to hiring a taxi, I heard the familiar voice of my uncle, Kaku, yell from behind: "Jayanta, so sorry I am late. Jeep had a tire puncture."

Fistful of Fog

Sweat beads, made shiny by melting sandalwood paste, lined his forehead like a silvery screen. As an ardent follower of Lord Shiva, he never appeared in public without the sign of the holy *tilak* marking his forehead. His *tilak* comprised of three horizontal lines. It was made from a mixture of sandalwood paste and ash procured from the sacred fire burning inside the Kanchenjunga temple, where he had served as head-priest since the year my father, Baba, had unexpectedly vacated that post and emigrated to America.

As we drove out of the train station, I squinted through the dust haze filtering through the jeep. The open drains lining the road presented a familiar sight; its syrupy sediment attracted dogs, insects, squatting beggars and urinating street urchins. Adjacent to the drains, rows of shops displayed a collection of stringy vegetables and fly-crusted sweets. Cross-legged men, squatting inside these kennel-sized shops, sold tea, cigarettes and the ubiquitous betel-leaf. Betel stains pock-marked the asphalt like a crimson skin-rash.

This was not the welcome from my home state I wanted to experience immediately upon arrival but it is impossible to travel by train and not see the unpleasant underbelly that surrounds most railway stations in India.

The jeep's driver shifted into 4-wheel drive as the vehicle wound its way up the hillside. The dust settled behind us like a chalky bedspread. The vehicle swerved through a maze of potholes, pedestrians and livestock.

A bus, overflowing with humans (some of whom were sitting on the roof) forced our jeep into letting it pass. The driver swore colorfully, as the bus-driver honked him into submission.

Serenity reigned once more as we drove uphill and the countryside reappeared: tea-bushes clinging on to steeply terraced hillsides; monkeys feasting on trees heavy with fruit; ribbons of heather swaying silken in the breeze.

Fifty-Fifty

The first wave of Himalayan fog rolled in, as we left the frenetic plains and climbed up into a steep road that led to the mountains. The jeep meandered uphill through forests of pine and oak. Then, just after we passed a sign that read – "Welcome to Darjeeling" – the struggling sun freed itself from the silent clouds and began to shine on my old nemesis: Kanchenjunga.

I readjusted my seating position by turning my back to the mountain. Then, I closed my eyes.

Although more than a year had passed since I'd last set foot on that mountain, the memory of Baba's last steps on its icy slopes still haunted my nightmares.

In his younger days, he used to be a recreational mountaineer. He and Kaku had taken classes at the Himalayan Mountaineering Institute (HMI). Together, they had climbed a 6000-meter peak near Lavose, a Himalayan village nestled in the lap of Kanchenjunga. Baba liked to say he was following in the footsteps of sages, who for centuries had traded the pollution of the plains for fresh Himalayan air, known to clear the mind of existential difficulties. According to him, the Himalayas were the best place to search for answers to life's most difficult questions: like whether God existed.

After Baba eloped to America with Angela, we didn't see him for a decade. Then, he showed up unexpectedly at my grandfather's funeral. It took me a while to recognize him. His tanned skin had turned yellow. It was bruised from constant scratching and it was falling off in places.

Angela, he informed us, had left him for a younger man. He had tried to win her back, even converting to Christianity (to impress her Italian-American family). But when he didn't succeed in reviving their relationship, he started to drink heavily. Other than a frayed copy of the Bible, a bottle of whisky had been his only companion that year.

Ma refused to let Baba inside our house, so Kaku took him to Lavose, a place he had dearly missed during his time in America. They got a room at the monastery. With help from Lama Pasang (who used to be Kaku's classmate) he nursed Baba back to health.

Fistful of Fog

    Baba wanted to return to America and make one final attempt to reconcile with Angela but when he heard Pemba (his ex-instructor from HMI) was leading an expedition on Kanchenjunga, he decided to join. Kaku tried to stop him from climbing the mountain. But a successful summit bid, said Baba, would impress Angela and allow him to win her back.
    The next time I saw Baba, he was lying inside a coffin. Ma had sent me to Kanchenjunga Base Camp with instructions to bring his body back to Darjeeling and cremate him according to Hindu rites. But Pemba handed me a note from Baba. It stated if Baba were to die during the expedition, then his corpse should be shipped to a cemetery in New Jersey, where deceased members of Angela's family were buried. When Ma saw the note, she flung Baba's Bible into the kitchen fire.
    Kaku never forgave himself for not being by Baba's side during that fatal expedition, but he was in no shape to climb any mountain. After years of sedentary activity, accompanied by a great fondness for snacking on temple sweets, Kaku had turned obese. Having lost part of his leg to complications arising from diabetes, Kaku now walked around Darjeeling, assisted by a crutch and boosted by mountaineering tales from his expired youth. He frequently complained about his long days at the temple, spent helping devotees negotiate celestial contracts with various deities. But it was his longer nights, spent drinking bhang (a cannabis-infused alcoholic preparation, which he claimed was Lord Shiva's chosen drink) with patrons of the temple that had made the fleshy sacks under his eyes droop.
    It is traditional for Bengali uncles to overlook the flaws of their nephews and allow them a fair degree of license. But with me, Kaku rewrote the rulebook on that tradition. He had taken my side at all times, even when he knew I could be making a mistake. If it hadn't been for him, I wouldn't have survived the bitterness that germinated in Ma, after Baba left us and went to live in America.

Fifty-Fifty

I arrived home with feeling emotionally drained. But my suitcase was full.

(I hadn't told my mother about my decision to not become a priest. Instead, I'd tried to replace the guilt I felt for abandoning my family's chosen vocation with gifts from various San Francisco malls).

But before I could open my suitcase and impress her with the new microwave oven I'd bought for her, she hurried over towards me and said: "*Chi-chi*, what in the Lord's name has America done to you? You've changed so much I barely recognize you."

After attending the Halloween concert with Zoe, I'd stopped cutting my hair. Now, I'd become attached to my curly, lengthy hairdo. But when Ma said she wanted the temple-barber to shave my head, I didn't protest because I was mad at Zoe for having disappeared from my life.

That afternoon, Ma had Kaku drive us to the Kanchenjunga temple. After a brief prayer ceremony, she escorted me into the temple courtyard, where a barber was waiting. When the barber had removed the last vestiges of my hirsute vanity, Ma massaged my bare scalp with water from the Ganges, considered by her to be the most sacred river in the entire world.

"Shaving your head symbolizes the removal of all undesirable foreign influences picked up during your time abroad," said Ma. "This is the traditional way by which a native son is accepted back into our homeland, after his sojourn in heathen lands. Now, you can resume your training as a priest's apprentice."

As soon as we left the temple, my scalp began to itch. When I visited a doctor, he informed me that I had developed an allergic reaction to the bacteria living in the Gangetic water. But my mother blamed the dysfunction on my newly-Americanized body's inability to absorb the holy water.

53

Fistful of Fog

Dysfunctional families, like unskilled mountaineers, carry more baggage. And mine became dysfunctional in 1977. I remember that year well because first Coca Cola left India and then my father, Baba, left my mother and moved to the U.S. with Angela. Now, a dozen years later, a familiar sense of dysfunction resurfaced when I told Ma I'd decided not to become a priest.

"Why do you feel the need to abandon this great calling your ancestors have made their vocation for a thousand years?" she said. "Didn't your grandfather risk everything to join the temple? And what did your Baba do? He gave up everything: his religion, his family, and his country. If you want to follow in his shameful footsteps, then go back to America."

A tear rolled down her cheek. She was like a withering banyan tree; the hardness on the outside caused by her divorce still visible but her insides were slowly turning mushy as seeds of hope began to decay, unable to withstand the double onslaught of aging and my father's death.

When I saw Ma crying, I remembered all the sacrifices she had made while growing me up. Walking over, I cradled her in my arms and said: "Don't worry, everything will be all right."

I felt a discernible shudder pass through her body and enter mine. I wondered if the entire weight of my family's history – hundreds of generations of my Brahmin ancestors – had now transferred over to me.

―――

I went outside and hit a cricket ball deep into our backyard. Cleopatra, our aging Labrador Retriever, ambled after the ball but gave up when she couldn't find it amidst the jungle growing in our backyard. It used to be a neat backyard with Kanchenjunga visible in between the pine trees fencing the lawn. But now the lawn was hopelessly overgrown and root fungus was killing many of the pine trees.

Fifty-Fifty

My thoughts flashed back to the day when Baba had tried to teach a much younger Cleo, how to fetch a ball. That day, Cleo (she was just a puppy then) had fetched a leathery object, which turned out be an egg. She had started to chew on it, like she did with every ball, and before anyone could do anything, one little cobra had climbed out of the egg shell and crawled inside her mouth. Watching Baba get the snakeling out of Cleo's mouth had been the most frightening experience of my childhood years. But the dog had stood there, unfazed.

Cleo, much older now, had lost her care-free sense of play. The fear of unknown creatures, living more in her imagination than in our backyard, had dampened her spirit and made her look worn out. I wished for a younger Cleo to reappear and take me back to a time when the yard was well kempt and Baba was alive.

The old, colonial-style house stood on top of a hill on a defunct tea estate. It had been built by the British and had seen better days. In 1949, after securing the post of the head-priest at the Kanchenjunga temple, my grandfather had relocated his family from Calcutta to Darjeeling. And my family had lived in that house ever since.

Like Cleo, our house looked washed out that afternoon. I decided not to spend any more time digging-up old memories buried in the yard. I was about to head back inside when I heard the crunch of a walking stick on the gravel path that led from the house to the backyard. I turned around. It was Kaku, slowly making his way into the backyard.

After Baba left my mother and moved to America, Kaku had taken me under his wing. It was under his tutelage that I had trained as a priest's apprentice.

"I have good news," he said, as he limped his way forward on the path. "I was able to convince your mother that there are many ways to serve God. Just because you've decided not to become a priest doesn't mean you will stop serving Him."

I went over and gave him a hug. "Thanks, Kaku," I said.

"There is one catch," he said, pausing to slip a piece of candied betel-nut into his mouth before saying: "Since you no longer are required to remain celibate, your mother wants you to get married. She is arranging for you to meet a few local girls this week."

"But I don't want to marry any of her chosen girls," I said, angrily. "Can't you see what she is doing? She is agreeing to let me off the vocational hook in exchange for my freedom. I won't stand for it."

"One step at a time, Jayanta," he said. "First finish your studies at Dominican. Then we will worry about what marital arrangement makes most sense for you."

"But can't you understand I'm not ready to get married," I said. "I want to see the world first; travel to a few different countries, try a few different jobs, do the usual things people my age do."

"Look, I know this has not been an easy homecoming for you but give your Ma some time, ok?" he said. "She is terrified you may meet someone in America and abandon her, like your Baba did. That is why she wants you to marry a Bengali girl."

After meeting Zoe, I'd begun to question the wisdom of arranged marriages. But since Zoe had chosen another man, what was the point in protesting my family's time-honored customs? I decided to not voice my objections (regarding an arranged marriage) to Kaku that day.

Now that I was no longer planning to sign-up for the priesthood, my mother quickly developed a new obsession: arranging my marriage with an appropriate Brahmin girl.

"Wake up; Rama has arranged for you to visit her friend's niece this afternoon," said Ma, shaking me awake, before handing me a cup of tea.

"Her name is Rita. Here, look at her photo. Doesn't she look divine, just like the goddess Durga?" said Ma. "She is a proper *Kulin* Brahmin. Now, that is the kind of girl I want you to marry. Her father just got elected to the position of treasurer at the Shiva temple. He will be a good mentor to you."

She looked admiringly at the photo she held in her hand.

"Can this wait a few days?" I said, struggling to cope with my jetlag. "I have a few other things to take care of first."

"Jayanta, you will be graduating in a few months," she said, sighing, as she sat down on the bed next to me. "No good Brahmin should remain a bachelor after completing their studies."

"But I may want to get a job in America, after I graduate from Dominican?" I said, wincing as sunrays hit my half-open eyes. "Marriage will have to wait."

"Aren't you coming back to Darjeeling after graduation?" she said, in an agitated voice.

"Obtaining American work experience will help me get a well-paying job here," I said.

"*Chi-chi*, when did you become so money-minded?" she said. "They may have more money in America, but we have richer traditions. Don't give up on your culture like your father did. Marry a good Brahmin girl and continue our tradition."

I hated that whenever Ma was upset with me, she often compared me to my father. As the eldest child in the family, Baba had had weighty expectations placed on his narrow, Brahmanical shoulders. And when he had rebelled by eloping with Angela, it had created a big scandal within the Darjeeling Brahmin society my family fraternized with.

"Here, give me that," I said, snatching the photo out of Ma's hand and tearing it into pieces.

"That temper of yours will land you in trouble someday," she said, sighing. "How will I find a decent girl who is willing to marry you, unless you learn to control your temper?"

"Sorry, I didn't mean to upset you," I said.

"Ok, that's settled then," she said. "I will call Rama and let her know you are ready to meet Rita."

"No, that's not what I meant," I said, raising my voice again. "Can't you understand I'm not ready to get married? I want to live a little first. See the world, that sort of thing."

"Don't speak to me in that tone, Jayanta," she said, angrily. "I've raised you to be a proper Brahmin. Don't forget that. You are the last male of reproducible age left in our family. If you don't marry soon and something happens to you in that faraway land our ancient *Kulin* lineage will be extinguished. You must settle down soon, with an appropriate girl."

"Please don't talk about settling down," I said. "That word reminds me of dead winter leaves falling from old trees and laying down on the dank grounds of a graveyard."

"Then go back to America and die alone," she said in a voice laced with disappointment. "And when they plant you next to your father's grave don't expect me to come visit."

After a few rainy days in Darjeeling, I became drenched in nostalgic thought.

I missed Zoe. And I missed California.

Friends and family continued to make snide comments about me having changed in appearance, habits, and behavior because of my tenure abroad. But I found not much had changed in Darjeeling and the same old stuff I had tried to leave behind now staring back at me.

I felt fragmented into two: a western half that craved rock bands and burgers and an eastern half that hankered for the songs of Tagore and aromatic Bengali curries.

The two factions seemed to be in constant conflict. But after studying abroad, now I could only see Darjeeling through a lens clouded by my experience in America.

For the remainder of my homestay I decided to go into hibernation mode and seek out only those things (like cricket) which I had missed during my time abroad. The sound of live test commentary from The Ashes series made me feel more at home than all the "homecoming" parties my mother had arranged (so I could meet girls of her choice).

I wouldn't have bothered showing up at the New Year's Eve party but I decided to go when I heard Tenzing was going to be the deejay. During my time at Dominican, I'd missed him more than anyone else from Darjeeling. But, as soon as he saw the mineral water bottle in my hand, we got into an argument.

"Why are you drinking mineral water like a foreigner?" said Tenzing. "Just because you live in the U.S. now doesn't mean this water isn't good enough for you, does it?"

The sound technician came by at that moment to discuss an issue with the speakers and we had to pause our argument. Then, a few minutes later, I got into another argument with Tenzing. This time it was about his choice of music.

"Don't teach your father how to fuck," said Tenzing. "Other than what you learnt from me you knew nothing about rock music before you went to America."

"I've been listening to live bands in America while you've been jerking off to the same old albums," I said. "You know I love Bob Marley too. But how about playing some Sonic Youth or something else from this decade? You need to change and keep up with the times."

"I don't even know who you are any more," said Tenzing. "You've been gone only a few months but already you are acting so confused. You used to listen to only Indian music, remember? Now you are acting like such a pseudo, talking about change and shit like that."

"Don't judge me," I said. "You have no idea what changes I had to make just to be accepted in America. It isn't as easy as you think."

Fistful of Fog

"Then stop with the fake accent," he said. "And stop trying to show-off with your knowledge of the latest bands and that kind of stuff. We may not have the dollars, but we have pride. At least I chose to stay here. You sold out and left."

I couldn't stand his taunting any longer.

"You bastard," I said, locking my arm around Tenzing, drawing him into a bear hug, and wrestling him down to the ground.

Small, but wiry and strong, was Tenzing. He stayed down for a couple of seconds but soon wriggled out of my grip and, grabbing my face, pinned me down into the floor. I started to suffocate on a pile of old cigarette butts and was about to pass out when his girlfriend, Naz, rushed over.

"Cut it out, you two!" she yelled. "It's almost time to wish everyone Happy New Year!"

Tenzing released his grip on my neck. We got up and dusted ourselves.

Naz forced us to shake hands.

After getting back on our bar stools we resumed drinking but stayed silent. The coldness between us remained for the rest of the holidays.

When the time came for me to return to California, neither Tenzing, nor Ma, came to see me off at the airport. There were no lively scenes at the airport, like the first time I'd left for the U.S. Not many seemed to care about my departure this time.

After I landed in San Francisco, the immigration official said: "You haven't completed this form. What's your home address?"

"I'm not sure," I said.

That was the truth because I was having doubts about which place to call home.

Chapter 5: A Fragile Union

1990 escorted-in big changes across the globe. Walls came down, old regimes collapsed and new countries emerged.

Most college students feel their generation will change the world. My Dominican classmates were no exception. Many embraced buzz-words like globalization, to reflect the new world order. But I didn't pay much attention to the myriad changes happening around the world. For, in my tiny corner of the universe, a big change happened as my final semester got underway: Zoe did not return to campus. According to the campus rumor-mill, she was still in Argentina, where she was said to be recuperating from either a climbing accident or an abortion or both (depending on who I spoke to).

During that first week of the spring semester, I oscillated between the two floors of the Dominican Library. Armed with a Spanish-to-English dictionary, I leafed through every Spanish-language newspaper and magazine. I looked for any headline(s) that would clue me in on Zoe's whereabouts. On a few occasions, I had to get the Mexican cleaning lady to translate some words for me.

I couldn't find any mention of Zoe's name in any of the articles I read but one caught my attention. It was from Reuters and read: "Rescue on South Face of Aconcagua: Anne Kirchner was rescued by a team of Argentinian climbers in a canyon above Piedras Blancas. She had almost made it to the top along a new route on the south face but had to retreat when she got hit by a snow-storm. When the climbers found her, she appeared lost and was showing signs of acute hypothermia. They radioed the park ranger at Nido de Condores for help. Anne, now resting at Camp Colera, told Reuters she was lucky they found her when they did because it is unlikely she would have survived a night alone in that icy canyon. Later this week, she plans to make another summit bid, by the normal route this time."

Kirchner was Zoe's surname, which is why the article had caught my gaze.

I conducted additional research but that surname appeared to be a common one in Argentina (several politicians seemed to bear that name, often hyphenated). I found two Anne Kirchners but both were local politicians and neither seemed to match Zoe's profile.

After spending a few days digging around in the muck generated by Argentinian politics, I gave up hope of finding out more about Zoe's whereabouts.

Nine weeks after the start of the spring semester, Zoe finally returned to campus.

It took me a few moments to recognize her. She had shed a few pounds and her hair was shorn short. The rest of her face was concealed in layers of make-up, a commodity she had avoided in the past. But it wasn't just her appearance that threw me off; it was also her new aura – one that made her look older but also more vulnerable.

I had spent months trying to reinvent myself and become the sort of guy Zoe would go for. And I had anxiously awaited her return. Now that the moment had arrived, I ran up to her and asked if everything was all right.

"Jeez, of course everything is all right," she said, testily. "Take a few weeks off and everyone acts like the sky is falling on their heads. Will you people just leave me the heck alone?"

Her words made me angry. After all the time I'd spent fretting about her well-being this was the reception I got from her?

I decided to avoid her for the rest of the semester.

A Fragile Union

That spring sea-lion pups washed up on the beaches of California. Global warming, said Professor Harker, was causing mothers to abandon their pups and go into deeper waters in search of food. It was as if the ocean had caught the flu and marine creatures were suffering, he said.

Volunteers from the Sierra Club had feverishly patrolled Bay Area beaches all week. Then, on Friday afternoon, one of them called Harker and said they needed help with a pup stranded on Ocean Beach. He asked me to drive his pickup over to Ocean Beach.

When I arrived at the beach, I found Zoe trying to herd the pup into a dog-carrier.

As I would get to know Zoe better, I'd be amazed by her willingness to help creatures (human and non-human) in distress, no matter what condition she was in. In the coming months, my Sherpa friends would find her willing to risk limb and life to save any of their colleagues on the slopes, even when she was in a precarious position. And whenever I'd complement her on her selflessness, she would shrug her shoulders in an aw-shucks manner and say: "If I needed help, I'm sure they would do the same for me."

After a brief chase with a herding board, we maneuvered the sea-lion pup into the safety of a carrier.

I lifted the carrier and placed it on the bed of the pickup. The pup waddled forward a few inches before surrendering to exhaustion.

The pup lay down with its face aimed upwards at the sunrays, filtering in through the carrier's opening. Its furry white whiskers stood out against its peanut-brown skin, making it look like an old man, catching an afternoon snooze.

Zoe fastened the carrier with a sturdy piece of nylon rope onto metal hooks on either the side of the truck.

The pup opened its eyes briefly to look at us before shutting them again.

Climbing down from the bed of the pickup, she said: "Uncle Whitey here looks like a survivor. But we need to get him over to the Marine Mammal Center quick. Otherwise, he might not make it."

"Isn't it heart-breaking to see these beautiful young animals so close to death?" I said.

"Death sucks," said Zoe. "You go about your merry way and then one day, boom, the person you care about the most dies and the world becomes a meaningless, terrifying place. It's been four years since mom left me but I miss her so much."

"I know what you mean," I said. "I hadn't seen my father in years but it still hurt a lot when he died. Art saved me."

"A similar thing happened to me," she said. "Not with art but with nature, especially the unspoiled kind of wilderness you encounter on the high mountains. Nature helped me heal."

"So sorry for your loss," I said.

"Me too. I'm sorry to hear about your dad," she said.

A strange calmness came over me as I realized we shared a sad commonality – both of us had lost a parent.

As we left the tranquil sands of Ocean Beach, and drove along the Great Highway, Zoe said: "Appreciate you rushing over to help, Jay." Then, turning her head and looking back towards the bed of the pick-up, she said. "I thank you. And Uncle Whitey back there, thanks you."

The cold grey Pacific fog began to seep inside the truck as we crossed the Golden Gate Bridge. Fiddling with the knobs on the radio until the warm voice of a baseball commentator filled the truck's cabin, she said: "Hey, the A's are playing tomorrow. Want to go?"

The fleetingness of varsity relationships is well known. Friends become lovers and lovers turn into frenemies. But even when it appears as if there is no hope left for a romantic lift-off, nothing can change course quicker than the fate of a college romance.

A Fragile Union

For nine frustrating months, I'd oscillated between Zoe's indifference and my denial. During this time, she had noticed me amongst the sea of potential suitors as much as one notices a candle in a room blazing with lightbulbs. And I had kept assuring myself I wasn't going to fall for atheistic beauty like Zoe, one who made me question my belief in God. Now, as my final days at Dominican got underway, and I prepared to head home to Darjeeling, I had given up hope of forming any sort of relationship with Zoe. But my luck changed with that most American of all sports: baseball. I used to think of baseball as cricket's dumbed-down, new world cousin but that afternoon I accepted Zoe's offer and secured myself a date. My date with Zoe would extend into an unforgettable night and leave me hooked on the ephemeral magic of first love.

The previous year the Oakland Athletics had won the World Series. Zoe was an ardent A's fan. To get her fired up, I bought a Yankees shirt and put it on before entering the Coliseum.

"Who invited the enemy in here," she said, smiling.

"My father used to live in New York; I am a huge Yankees fan," I said, thrilled to discover that she hadn't invited anyone else from Dominican to attend the game with her.

Zoe looked a bit shabby and a lot desirable that evening. On her scalp rested a baggy A's cap, its faded gold logo glittering in the fading light. The color of the logo matched the mustard-stain on the sleeve of her T-shirt, stretched snugly across her curvy chest. Her left hand touched a well-worn baseball mitt, resting on her lap.

Before the game started she made a big deal about how the Yankees would have no answer to Moore's curveball. I got her to agree to a bet: the loser would buy the winner drinks.

Fistful of Fog

I didn't really care about which team won. All I wanted was to hang out with her after the game.

"Bring it on," she said, "we are going to whup your sorry Yankee asses today."

It was a warm afternoon at the Coliseum – perfect for beer and baseball.

After the game started, I threw in a few buzz-words (which I'd picked up from a baseball-for-beginners book). I had to check myself a couple of times and make sure I didn't use any cricket references.

I cheered for New York. And I loved it when she (and the crowd) booed me. It didn't matter because Canseco and Henderson ensued an easy win for Oakland.

She rejoiced. And I did also, silently. But outwardly I feigned disappointment, as we drove towards San Francisco after the game.

———

The Misty Maiden Tavern was located on a stretch of Polk Street that was gradually getting transformed from seedy to gentrified.

A deejay stood crouched over a turn-table at the far end of the long, crowded tavern. A few people danced haphazardly around the deejay, but most patrons hung around the bar area.

Wanting to impress Zoe, I was about to order champagne from the bar-tender, but she said she preferred beer and tequila.

After our drinks arrived, she began to talk about her plans after graduating from Dominican but just then the deejay put on a song by Sonic Youth, which made her jump up from the bar-stool and say: "Let's dance."

Like most couples who know each other but are not intimate we danced awkwardly.

She said her favorite bands at that moment were Sonic Youth, The Stone Roses and Nirvana. Despite never having heard of either The Stone Roses or Nirvana, I said those three were my favorite bands as well.

As we danced into the night, I could feel my life, which until then had comprised primarily of discordant moments, slipping into groove.

I thought back to the vow of celibacy I'd taken before leaving Darjeeling and I felt a twinge of guilt. But the longer we danced together, the desire to sleep with Zoe overpowered every other emotion. And I decided to put God out of my mind for the rest of that evening.

We left the tavern only after it closed. I was too drunk to drive. Zoe took the car keys. While opening the car door she lost her balance and fell, onto the sidewalk.

Laughing, she said: "I guess I'm not as sober as I'd thought. Let's take a cab back to campus."

I couldn't think of anything clever to say to keep her with me a little bit longer. So, I changed the lyrics to the song 'Too Drunk to Fuck' by the Dead Kennedys (that the DJ had played earlier that evening) and I sang: "I went to a party ... I drank 16 beers ... now I'm jaded ... but sober enough to fuck."

I shouldn't have twisted the lyrics to a great song. But it made her laugh. Which gave me the courage to kiss her.

She kissed me back. It lasted only a few seconds. But it made my soul sing.

"Look, Jay, I like you, I really do!" she said, after extracting her tongue from inside my mouth. "But graduation is around the corner, so what is the point of starting something now."

"But graduation is a five days away. We have until then," I said, desperate for any excuse to spend the night with her. "Wait a minute, are you still seeing Juan?"

"No, we broke up last year but I'm not looking for a relationship right now," she said.

In a desperate, last-ditch attempt I said: "If we sleep together once then we will get it out of our system. Then, we can go our own separate ways."

"That is the worst pick-up line I've ever heard," she said, her voice gurgling with throaty, drunken laughter. "I'm sure I'll regret it tomorrow but ok, let's try this. Just once, never to be repeated, understand? And don't share this news with Julia, or anybody else on campus?"

"Don't worry, it will be our little secret," I said, thrilled but incredulous that this was finally happening.

The more time I spent with Zoe, the less my chance of returning unscathed from the seductive grip of forbidden love. That realization wobbled the bounce in my step, as we walked into the lobby of an old Russian Hill hotel, its shabby edges veiled under bright lighting.

My Sherpa friends say when they get close to a great Himalayan peak, they immediately started thinking about coming down. Not because the view up top isn't spectacular but because lingering on the peak can prove fatal.

While we waited for the night clerk to check us in, I placed three fingers inside my trouser pocket and sought reassurance by rubbing the ribbed plastic outline of the condom. But as soon as the clerk handed me the key to our room, waves of angst began to pound against my chest.

It had been a long warm day. It was muggy inside our hotel room.

I followed Zoe onto the skinny balcony outside and watched her light up a fat joint. We sat down on adjacent deck chairs. After a few deep puffs, she handed the joint to me.

A Fragile Union

In my eagerness to hide the fact that I'd never smoked pot, I inhaled a large mouthful of smoke. I coughed until my lungs got so irritated that a sliver of stringy phlegm shot out through my lips.

I was embarrassed but she laughed.

"You remind me of my boyfriend from high school. Never smoked before, have you? Not a big deal. Tonight's as good a night as any to begin. Here, let me show you how," she said.

After a few tries I finally got the hang of how to inhale. I began to relax a little.

I put my arm around her shoulder. She rested her head on my chest and said: "This feels nice."

I wanted to kiss her again, but my tongue felt like leaded sandpaper. I was having trouble standing straight. I told her that I wanted to get back inside.

She followed me back into the room but when I saw the double bed, I began to panic. She was more experienced than me. What if she found out I was a virgin? Would she still go through with it? And how would she react when she saw my penis? Would she freak-out because I wasn't circumcised?

After a locker-room shower during my first semester, I'd noticed a guy checking me out. When I'd asked Ron if he knew the reason, he had said: "It's because you got a worm-dick. You better trim that bad boy before it scares the bajesus out of some poor girl."

I remembered the time when Tenzing had cajoled Salim, the only Muslim boy in our Darjeeling high school, to show his penis to us. There are not a lot of circumcised boys running around in the Himalayas. I had found Salim's penis revolting and fascinating at the same time. We had made fun of Salim that day, calling him "cut-cock" and all sorts of other nasty names. But at Dominican most men were circumcised and the joke was on me.

Stop worrying about your foreskin and try to focus on the job at hand, I said silently, as I watched Zoe peeling off her clothes.

Fistful of Fog

I felt sweat trickle down from under my arms; my deodorant was failing me when I needed it the most. My sense of smell had been heightened by pot, so I sniffed around. But I couldn't tell if the faint odor of mustiness was coming from me or from the dusty old furniture that outfitted the room.

She had taken off all her clothes, except her panties. I followed her lead and took off my clothes but getting the plastic wrapper off the condom proved challenging. My shaking hands refused to cooperate with the packaging. I tried to hide my frustrations by biting into the packaging but that didn't work either.

"First time isn't it?" she said.

"No," I said, after deciding this was not the time for truth.

"It's ok," she said. "Nothing to be ashamed off, silly. Here, let me help you with that thing."

After refusing her offer for help, I joined her inside the covers and sniffed her golden hair tangle, which smelt faintly of ball-park mustard. I kissed the tip of her nose and then her lips. Slowly, I moved my head down towards her lovely pink breasts. With her every breath they swooped elegantly upward, before rolling gently back down. I sent a free hand down to cup one. The fleshy globe heaved uncertainly before resting pale and pink in the cushion of my brown fingers. I lightly kissed one nipple and then the other. Sliding my body further down, I tugged at her panties, gently. She wriggled out of them, revealing her labia, which appeared like petals plucked out of a Georgia O'Keeffe painting. Spreading apart her plump lips and gently inserting my index finger inside, I rejoiced at the gooey velvety touch. But then I made the mistake of bringing my nose next to it and inhaling the vinegary smell of her. The yeasty smell of her genitalia played on my pot-addled brain and instantly took me back to Norbu's sky burial. His corpse had reeked of that same pungent smell. And (despite the lama's attempts at covering the pungent smell of death with incense) the odor of Norbu's corpse had remained with me for weeks.

A Fragile Union

My English teacher had talked about the 'madeleine effect' described in Proust's famous novel: 'Remembrance of Things Past'. As a result, I understood that memories could sometimes be conjured up by images from our past.

But why was my mind thinking of death when I was about to make love to someone as sensual as Zoe?

And why did sex and death always seem to go together?

Was it because they were the only two things that mattered in life?

Or was it because one led to the beginning of life and the other to the end?

Stop thinking about death, I told my stoned brain, and focus on the delicious prospect of having sex with Zoe.

I recalled a cousin saying that whenever he went to a funeral he couldn't wait to return home and have sex with his wife. I wondered if the reverse was also true. Did he always think of death after he had sex with his wife?

"Is everything ok down there?" said Zoe, bringing me back to the present.

Everything was not ok. I was having an almighty struggle putting the condom on my limp penis.

"Here, let me help you," she said, sitting upright on the bed.

"No, no, I'll manage," I said, as I clumsily forced the condom onto my penis.

A few seconds later, when she saw me struggling again, she helped me get inside her.

I began to move with hesitant, awkward strokes.

After a few more interminable moments, she began to stir in a slow, surrealistic way, as if she was living inside a Fellini movie.

After a few more strokes, I became uncontrollably animated and before I knew it I'd finished with a thunderous sigh, which captured the suffering of a lifetime of wasted ejaculations.

"Sorry," I said, sheepishly. "I wanted it to last longer."

"No worries," she said. "We can try again, later."

Fistful of Fog

Afterwards, she fell into a softly-snoring sleep.

The fading moon slipped in through the hotel room window and caressed her face, radiant with afterglow. The soothing moon-rays kicked away the guilt storm, threatening to restart inside me.

She lay there like a great sleeping beauty, my very own All-American dream, but just for one night.

Upon returning to campus, I found my mother waiting in my dorm room.

"What are you doing here?" I said, alarmed that she had landed, unannounced, on my college doorstep.

"How could I not come to my only child's graduation?" said Ma, as she opened her handbag, bursting with photographs of prospective Brahmin brides.

She scooped out a fistful of photos from inside her bag and laid them out on my desk.

There were photos of: tall and tawny girls; curvy and creamy girls; sitar-players and dancers. It was as if all the eligible Brahmin girls of Darjeeling were now living in her handbag.

"We must start planning now so we can have the wedding as soon as you return to Darjeeling," she said, excitedly.

"But I'm not ready to get married," I said, angrily.

"I'm not getting any younger you know," she said, her voice turning soulful. "I need a grandson soon. You only have a few days left at Dominican. If we don't start planning now we will never be ready on time. Don't you remember how long it takes to get anything done in Darjeeling?"

It depressed me that Ma was counting the days to my graduation, desperately waiting for me to return home.

The brief wondrous afterglow of my night with Zoe departed. And, as I watched her place Lord Juggernaut's chariot on my bookshelf, the guilt storm came rushing back in.

"Doesn't it look grand?" she said, looking at the chariot with obvious pride.

It was a wooden replica of the chariot of the Hindu god, Jagannath (whose anglicized name, Juggernaut, was familiar to some of my American classmates). Ma had acquired the chariot after making a pilgrimage to the holy Hindu city of Puri. It was her graduation gift to me.

"Like this chariot, you will become unstoppable and march forward to fulfill all your life-goals after Dominican," she said, her voice filling-up with purpose and her tone seeking instantaneous approval.

"Ma, there is something I need to tell you," I said.

"What?" she said. "Do you have an upset tummy from eating too many of those chili *pakoras* I brought for you?"

"No, not that," I said. "It's just that I'm not majoring in religion any longer. You will find out during commencement so you might as well know now."

"How could you do this to me?" said Ma, sitting down on an armchair with a sigh. "It's one thing for you to say you are not ready to sign-up for priesthood. But to give up on religion altogether? What's next for you? Eating beef?"

"After studying at Dominican I've become more interested in science and logic. Now, I have less tolerance for blind faith and superstitions, the kind they preach at the Jagannath temple in Puri," I said.

"*Chi-chi*, let me cover the Lord's ears," said Ma, getting up from the armchair and placing a tablecloth over the chariot. "I don't want Him to hear this sacrilegious nonsense coming out of your mouth. It never ceases to amaze me how quickly people change after coming to America. Look at what happened to your father?"

Ma's insistence on comparing me to my father (every time she and I disagreed on something) made me very angry.

"Stop telling me what I can or can't do," I yelled. "And I don't want that rickety old chariot on my brand-new bookshelf anymore."

"How can you speak to me in that tone?" she said. "Have you forgotten you are a Brahmin?"

"I have my own dreams to pursue, you know?" I said, in a passionate voice. "On some days, I wish I had been born anything other than a goddamn Brahmin."

"Watch your language, Jayanta," she said. "Don't speak like a low-class person. And don't forget we are the chosen caste. You must behave appropriately."

I'd had enough.

"Forget it, Ma?" I said, unable to stop myself from yelling. "I have no desire to be a Brahmin anymore. All I wish is for you to leave me alone. Here – take your chariot back."

Raising my hand like an axe, I delivered a karate chop. The wooden chariot splintered into multiple pieces.

That destructive act released my pent-up stress and made me feel better. But then I saw Ma crying and I was flooded with regret.

"I don't know how to handle that temper of yours," she said, sobbing. "Someday you are going to hurt someone."

"I'm sorry, Ma," I said. "Don't worry, I will glue the pieces back."

I walked towards her and tried to hug her but she moved away.

"I will pray to Lord Shiva tonight and ask Him to drill some sense into that confused head of yours," she said. "Forget this western nonsense about following your dreams. Priests in Darjeeling may not make a lot of money but their jobs are secure. You are a Brahmin. You must fulfill your destiny. Trust me, nothing good can come from trying to alter your destiny."

The misty spring campus at Dominican soon turned into a heated battle-ground. My mother pursued me relentlessly, never losing an opportunity to get me to phone-chat with one of her chosen girls. And I used every excuse to keep her away from campus, so she wouldn't run into Zoe.

Everything was working according to my plan, until Ron ushered Zoe and Julia into our dorm room one morning, just as I was waking up.

"Happy birthday, sleepyhead," said Zoe, holding a chocolate cupcake in her hand.

Rubbing sleep out of my eyes, I looked up towards them.

Zoe sported a torn T-shirt and cut-off jean shorts; her shapely bare legs were tucked into a pair of raggedy sneakers.

On the other side of the bed, Julia stood upright on denim-covered legs which extended all the way down to the top of her shiny new sandals. The reflection from the silver crucifix, sparkling between her demure breasts, stung my eye.

They were like two mismatched peas in a pod; like the Dominican Choir and Sonic Youth playing at the same venue; opposites who balanced each other perfectly; like the twin symbols of Yin and Yang at a Himalayan monastery.

My mind said a girl like Julia would make a more appropriate life-partner for me but even in my half-awake state I desired Zoe with my entire body and all of my soul.

"Girls why don't you get into bed and give the birthday boy a kiss," said Ron, holding a camera in his hand. "I'll take a photo of the three of you in bed. Pretend like you are making out, so the birthday boy has something to brag about later."

Just as Ron was about to click on the camera, my mother walked in. When Ma saw us in bed the box of temple sweets she was carrying slipped out of her hand and fell down. Soon, sticky, white syrup began to dribble across the linoleum floor.

"Jayanta, you must stop fooling around like this," she said, later, when we were alone.

"But Zoe is my friend, Ma," I said.

Fistful of Fog

"To come here and find that blonde temptress in your bed with her tongue hanging on your cheek like that? *Chi-chi*," she said. "It hasn't even been a year since you left Darjeeling but America has turned you into such a loose character that I can't even recognize you sometimes. Nothing good can come from marrying someone who prays to a different God. Don't you remember how the temple priests couldn't find a single auspicious date when Rama's cousin wanted to marry that Muslim doctor? I will pray to the Lord and ask Him to keep you away from these tempting campus girls, with their skimpy clothes and skimpier morals."

"Zoe is not Muslim," I said. "And who said anything about marriage? We are just friends; it's not serious or anything."

My mother had her hierarchy of "proper" girls that I could marry. A Muslim girl was the lowest on her list; even lower than the lowest-caste untouchable. Better to die alone than marry a Muslim, Ma had said to me once.

I hated Ma's bigoted views. But I loved her.

"If you must pick one of these girls for friendship, then my vote goes to Julia. At least she is Indian," said Ma.

That afternoon, Ma took me to a temple in Livermore.

A corpulent priest performed a *puja* in my name, in front of a statue of Lord Shiva. Towards the end of the ceremony, he tied a piece of sacred thread tightly around my waist. With a vigorous nod of his head, he assured Ma it would act like a chastity belt on my conscience. Then, he moved around the shiny bronze amulet, which was attached to the sacred thread, until it settled into the hollow of my navel.

I bent down to touch Ma's feet and get her blessing. The amulet reflected off the temple's pond and stared at me like a metallic third eye, embedded inside my navel. I wondered if this was Ma's way of saying that (from now on) she was keeping a permanent watch over me.

A Fragile Union

That week Julia was hosting a group of Dominican nuns, visiting from France. They were from Fanjeaux: home of Saint Dominic and the epicenter of the Dominican Order.

Hoping to find out more about Fanjeaux, I joined their cafeteria table for lunch. But all seats adjacent to the nuns had been taken. And I found myself placed next to Julia's fiancée, Mark.

Julia had met Mark at a bible retreat in the smoky mountains during summer break. Their relationship had blossomed quickly and she had recently traded her purity ring for an engagement band. The sight of Julia walking around campus holding hands with a pompous fuddy-duddy like Mark made me want to grab him by his clerical collar and shake sense into his shiny bowling ball of a head.

"She could have done so much better," I said to myself. "What was she thinking?"

Mark had enrolled in the graduate Divinity program at Vanderbilt University but he seemed to spend most of his time at Dominican. That afternoon, he sat outfitted in a heavily-starched clerical collar, fastened so tight that his neck had turned an angry red and his Adam's apple looked ready to pop. And when we shook hands, it felt like his large chunky fingers were trying to strangle mine.

What I disliked about Mark was that he wore his knowledge of Christianity like a medal, always name-dropping passages from the Bible to make his point.

He loved discussing religion and he went around campus asking everyone questions. When he asked me questions on Hinduism and Buddhism, I was hesitant. I suspected his desire for discourse on other religions was motivated by the need to prove that his religion was superior to others. But he assured me, in his slow southern drawl, that his interest in world religions was genuine, which I didn't believe for a microsecond.

"I may be from the place they call the buckle of the bible-belt, but my true interest lies in understanding how all religions are connected," said Mark, as we sat in the cafeteria and debated, with the Fanjeaux nuns, the merits and disadvantages of various global religions.

"The true religion of this country is capitalism" said an international exchange student from England, sitting near us. "If you want to spread American faith across the globe then ditch that Divinity degree of yours and get an MBA."

A few minutes later, Mark asked me the question I dreaded most: "So, Jay, do you think you will stay here or return to India after graduation?"

I hated both the question and Mark's condescending tone (which implied that no one in their right mind, if given an option, would chose my impoverished country of birth over his rich homeland).

It was a question I had been wrestling with for days.

Did I want to stay longer in this exciting new country and savor the prospect of spending more time with Zoe.

Or did I have to go back to my birthplace and don the shackles of familial responsibility?

I wasn't sure which path I wanted to pursue but I didn't want to give Mark the pleasure of feeling superior about his country of birth.

"I'm not sure," I said to Mark.

And then I left the cafeteria.

As I began my final days at Dominican, I felt a sense of impending gloom. With commencement around the corner, college life would soon be over, and a new reality would beckon. A reality which required me to move 12 time-zones away from Zoe.

A Fragile Union

Tenzing liked to say that once you've summited a Himalayan peak, climbing any other mountain feels like an anticlimax. Even if my desire to extend my relationship with Zoe were to remain unrequited, she had shown me the highs only true passion can generate.

I wanted to find a way to extend my stay in San Francisco and spend more time with her. And there was only one person on campus who could help me resolve this issue: Professor Harker.

When I entered his paper-sprinkled office, I found him speaking into a telephone.

"I am not sure I can change your grade. The best I can do is give you is an incomplete. You can repeat the course next semester," he said, in a resigned tone.

The effort of dealing with yet another unmotivated undergraduate had made the large blue vein on the professor's forehead crawl up into the higher reaches of his scalp.

After he hung up the phone, I handed him my resume and said: "I know it may be a bit late to put my application in now, but I would like to apply for an internship at GreenEarth. I've been trying to figure out what to do now that college is over. My mother wants me to go back to Darjeeling. But I want to stay in San Francisco for a little while longer."

(Harker was Chairman of GreenEarth Conservation International, where Zoe was planning to intern that summer).

"Do you have the necessary paperwork required to work in the U.S.?" he said, placing my resume on top of his brief-case, balanced precariously on the paper jungle on his desk.

"My student visa is expiring soon, and it has been extremely challenging getting the INS to grant me an extension," I said. "On some days, I feel like giving up."

"Never give up, because one day even the shrinking forest will be able to reclaim land back from the encroaching city," he said. "Maybe, we can get GreenEarth to sponsor you for a H-1B visa."

"Thank you, that would be great," I said.

After assuring me he would get me an internship in his firm, he paused to answer the phone, which was ringing again.

Sounding belligerent, he said: "Yes, Dean, I know Aaron is Mr. Goldman's nephew, but an incomplete is the best grade I can give him."

I left Harker to his professorial troubles and went looking for Zoe.

A few minutes later, I found a champagne-sipping Ron sprawled on the lawns of the Forest Meadow. He was surrounded by several of his B-school classmates. They were celebrating his new investment banking job.

"Did you hear how much Ron will be making in his first year?" said a girl who had her hair strung into a limp ponytail, which hung between her toothy shoulder blades like the mangy tail of a chewed-up animal.

"I wish some of his luck would rub off on me," said another student, outfitted in a three-piece suit. "After all the rejections I've received, I could sure use some luck."

"Let's drink to life after Dominican," said Ron, handing me a crystal glass filled with cheap champagne. "Here is to all of us misfits prospering in life and making a ton of money."

Despite all his peacocking on campus in second hand Armani jackets and recycled Bruno Magli shoes (custom-heeled to overcome his severe lack of inches), there was a smell of insecurity about Ron that no amount of Brylcreem (applied together with a base-ball cap strategically angled to cover a premature bald spot) could hide.

"Here, have another drink," said Ron, uncorking another bottle.

The popping of the cork seemed to delight him and he looked around with an air of naked expectancy, as if expecting applause. After declining his offer, I said goodbye.

Just as I was about to give up searching for Zoe, I found her sitting on one of Maggie's low branches. She had each leg hanging from either side of the branch, which was as broad as a horse's back.

"Come up here and join me," she shouted. "I'm reading from 'Baron in the Trees'. Reading out aloud is the only way I'll remember anything for my comp lit exam tomorrow."

Normally my fear of heights would have kicked in. But my excitement at seeing her temporarily overwhelmed my worries. Leveraging a low-hanging branch, I propelled myself up and sat next to her.

As she began to read from Italo Calvino's novel, I began to feel a deep sense of wellbeing. The fog-free sun shone softly on the old magnolia tree. And the gentle drone of hummingbirds, pollinating the nearby flowerbeds, imparted a soporific calmness to the afternoon.

When Zoe (role-playing Cosimo) declared she had decided to spend the rest of her life living up in that tree, I heard a voice yell (in Bengali) from below: "Jayanta, I've been looking everywhere for you. Come down. I need to talk to you."

It was Ma. She looked flustered. Normally, I would have panicked at the thought of her catching me with Zoe but that day I didn't care. I didn't want to climb down from that tree.

"Wait in Meadowlands, Ma," I said, in Bengali. "I'll join you there, in a few minutes."

"If you stay with that girl one second longer, then I'll leave you here and return home," said Ma, in Bengali.

"Jay, is everything ok?" said Zoe, as she watched Ma walk away.

"Yeah, everything will be fine," I said, "but I wish we could stretch out time. I'm not ready for all of this to end."

"Why don't we carve our initials into Maggie before we leave?" she said. "You can take half the wood shavings with you and I'll take the other half. That way, a bit of us will remain here and a bit of college will remain with us."

Fistful of Fog

There were so many things I wanted to say to her. But when I looked at her in the late afternoon light I felt the universe expand. It was a perfect spring day which balanced perfect content with perfect longing. Soon, I would have to leave this sheltered world behind and head over to a non-collegial world, where an alternate reality and possibly a gloomier life beckoned. But on that day, I didn't care too much about the future. I just wanted to share a few moments with Zoe before the world grew up. And we with it.

Our summer of love began with that great American office sport – softball. I used to view softball as cricket's pudgy, new-world cousin but, as soon as Zoe was chosen co-captain of GreenEarth's softball team, I signed up to play.

Those co-ed office league games were played at Golden Gate Park. Zoe turned up for the first game wearing an angled Oakland A's cap, a well-oiled catcher's mitt, and a forearm bruise, still red but parts of it turning purple.

Never having played softball, I tried to catch the ball without gloves, cricket-style. She had never seen anyone do that. When I managed to get a batter out by catching the ball barehanded, she came over and said: "Way to go, Jay!"

That catch wasn't enough. We lost the game. But my mood brightened up when Zoe invited me to a Nine Inch Nails performance that evening.

The I-Beam was packed that night with NIN fans. We drank and shoved our way up to the floor by the stage.

When Trent Reznor sang – 'Head Like a Hole' – Zoe started to slam-dance with a group of bare-chested guys, who were circling the mosh pit. I tried to join her but I gave up after ending-up on the floor and getting kicked in the small of my back. Despite the pain I felt great when she asked me, after the concert, if I wanted to go to her place.

A Fragile Union

A cab dropped us off outside her Alamo Square apartment. As she searched her purse for keys, I looked at the old building, hazy in the late-night light.

The forgiving fog had rubbed-out the wrinkles on the building, lending it an air of immortality. The building was an old Edwardian, which stood close to the row of houses that locals called the 'Painted Ladies'. Tour buses seldom stopped in front of her building but the Edwardian showcased a decaying beauty that was a throwback to grand old San Francisco.

Six months later, the building (like my relationship with Zoe) would cease to exist. One morning on my way to work I would stand and stare nostalgically at the empty lot where the building used to be. The memory of my unforgettable nights with Zoe in that old Edwardian would appear imagined, any trace of reality absent, like the building, removed, as the city remade itself by extinguishing a tiny bit of San Francisco history.

But that night after the NIN concert, my body filled with beer and lust, I wasn't thinking about the history of San Francisco. As Zoe hunted for keys to the front-door, I attempted to kiss her. I thought she would push me away but she surprised me by taking my hand in hers and guiding me towards the bedroom.

A month had passed since our unforgettable first night but everything felt familiar. The sex was sloppy but terrific. And it felt better when we did it again the next morning, with both of us still hung-over. Not wanting to wash the smell of our lovemaking off of me, I went to work without showering.

"Look, what the cat dragged in," said my boss, as I walked past her in the hallway.

I ignored her smirking and walked slowly to my cube, leaving an air of unwashed joy in my wake.

Fistful of Fog

When Zoe met Tenzing, who was visiting from Darjeeling, she immediately proposed a climbing trip to Mount Shasta. I was thrilled the American Alpine Association had decided to honor him in San Francisco with an award (the previous year Tenzing had rescued two American climbers stranded on Kanchenjunga). But my mood soured when he accepted Zoe's Shasta proposal, despite my request not to do so.

Zoe had picked the challenging Hotlum Glacier route. Because of its ice falls and seracs it would serve as useful training ground for any future Himalayan expedition, she said. I tried to talk her out of undertaking such a dangerous climb but she refused to listen. And the following day my mood worsened when I found us stuck in a traffic jam, soon after leaving San Francisco.

"The traffic situation in the Bay Area is getting out of control," said Zoe, as she poked her head out of the front passenger window of the Jeep Wagoneer. "Doesn't look like we are going anywhere anytime soon."

"Looks like everyone is heading somewhere this weekend," said Julia, seated in the back of the jeep, next to Tenzing.

"But they can't all be heading north," I said, from behind the steering wheel of the jeep. "I'm sure this traffic will thin out soon. Just give it a minute."

"We don't have this problem on Kanchenjunga," said Tenzing. "Plenty of open spaces in the Himalayas."

"There is nothing I'd like more than climbing Kanch," said Zoe, letting out an audible sigh. "I bet the world would look very different from up there."

I turned towards him and mouthed a silent "no" but he ignored me.

"I'm leading a Kanchenjunga expedition this fall," he said. "Want to join?"

"I'd love to. Can you get me on your team?" said Zoe.

"Sure, no problem," he said, his voice filling with Himalayan pride.

A Fragile Union

I couldn't believe my ears. I turned around and glared at him.

21 months earlier, he had been on the same expedition which had killed my father. Like many Sherpas, his livelihood depended on expeditions so I couldn't fault him for ignoring my request to stop climbing. But he knew how much I hated (after my father's death) the thought of anyone climbing Kanchenjunga. For him to invite Zoe to climb that deadly mountain, even after everything I'd told him, made me furious.

"Thanks, Tenzing. You will not regret having me on your team," said Zoe.

The thought of Zoe climbing that killer mountain made me nauseous. "This traffic is terrible. Why don't we get some coffee while we wait for the traffic to thin out?" I said, trying to change the topic of conversation.

"The only traffic we have to worry about in the high Himalayas is yaks," he said, breaking into a crooked smile.

"Yaks on Kanchenjunga must move faster than this," said Zoe. "Whatever happened to the Great American Dream? Of living in open spaces surrounded by nature and not debt? Being slaves not to technology but to one's whim? Flying on horses and not stuck inside metal coffins, breathing traffic toxins? Living off the land and not off plastic packages?"

"It lives elsewhere," he said. "I know Sherpas who will give up their life before their freedom. Many tourists visit our village near Kanchenjunga. They come to my cousin's shop, wanting to buy this and that. Hats, horses, whores. If they could, they would even buy blue sky. But they don't know there are many things money can't buy."

"That's what Kerouac said," said Zoe. "He was my hero. It is a shame most people get so caught up in the great American trap – mortgages, car payments and all that nonsense. I wouldn't have survived teenagerhood without Kerouac."

"But that would be like living in the dark ages," said Julia. "No jobs, no future. Would you like such a life?"

Fistful of Fog

"Well, let's be honest here. A bit of security is ok. Food on the table and a roof over my head I can't do without. But the rest of this stuff? All these trappings of modern living: pills and Porsches, saunas and sitcoms, colas and condos. Do we really need them? And at what price? Take the microwave. Wasn't it supposed to free up time? To do what? So, we can slave away at jobs we hate to pay for things we don't need, like the microwave?"

"Sister Catherine from Fanjeaux said most Americans are free with their money but stingy with their time because they are always slaving away, trying to make as much money as quickly as they can, without realizing that no amount of dollars can buy back lost time," said Julia.

"My cousin says brave Sherpas should worry more about freedom than money or death," said Tenzing. "Before our Kanchenjunga expedition last year I tried to buy him life insurance. But he refused, saying that betting against our lives was stupid. He will be joining us again next spring. You will meet him at Base Camp."

"It'll be so much fun meeting everyone. Boy, I can't wait to climb Kanch," said Zoe, as I shifted gears to speed up and get ahead of the traffic, which had begun to move again.

She lit up the jeep with her smile but the specter of the mountain darkened my heart.

Zoe was crazy about live music.

She would often get goose bumps when a favorite song came on. I tried to get goose bumps to the songs she liked but my arms didn't always cooperate. Sometimes, I'd rub cocktail-ice on my arms and then show her my goose bumps.

We chased bands across the great state of California. My feet were exhausted but my spirit was invigorated.

A Fragile Union

The golden state and the golden girl kept spinning their music. I twirled fast and furious, trying to keep pace. And I stopped listening to tunes from the old country.

"Dude, how come you never hang with me anymore?" said Ron, one evening over cocktails at the Misty Maiden Tavern.

"Work has been busy," I said.

He said: "Sure, banging office chicks can be hard work. Trust me, I know all about that kind of work."

"Zoe is not that kind of girl," I said, angrily. I must have raised my voice because a few heads turned towards us.

"Dude, don't tell me you're in L-O-V-E?" he said.

"No," I said. "I just like hanging out with her, that's all."

"Is that why I don't see you much anymore?" he said. "You are so glued to her smelly bits that I wouldn't be surprised if she gets you to put a ring on her finger soon. It's a typical Indian love story. Sex-starved boy falls in love with the first girl who lets him sniff her smelly bits."

"Nothing like that," I said, angrily. "We just like doing things together, that's all."

"Just be careful," he said. "Don't get too serious too soon."

"How many times do I have to tell you: this isn't serious," I said.

He smiled and said: "That's what the hunter said before he shot his first deer. But once he acquired a taste for blood there was no turning back."

After pausing to take a sip of his martini, he continued: "Wait a second, are you planning to marry her and become legit, like Depardieu did with MacDowell in that Green Card movie. Now that would make a lot of sense."

"No, of course not," I said, annoyed that he would think of something crass like that.

"Find a way to get the damn green card," he said. "Then apply for citizenship. Give yourself options. Last week, I applied for my Australian passport. Someday, I'm going to become the rainmaker at the Sydney office of my bank."

Ron acquired passports like a shopaholic collected credit cards. They were not only an escape ticket from a life past but also a calling-card for future adventures.

With him it wasn't just wanderlust; it was a genuine case of never being satisfied with where he was.

"I'll look into it," I said, trying to muster enthusiasm but apprehensive that a green card would drive a deeper wedge between my mother and me.

"Now that we have reconnected, I hope you will be able to ignore your booty call once in a while and hang out with me more often," he said.

But Zoe had become much more than a booty-call for me.

That evening, as I lay in her warm arms, intoxicated after another round of racy sex, I said: "I think I'm developing feelings for you."

"Well don't fall in love or anything serious like that," she said. "This is just a summer thing, remember? We'll be separated in a few weeks. Until then let us just have fun – hang out, play ball, and listen to a few bands, ok?"

With Zoe on my arm, I forgot my old rhythm. I started dancing to a whole new beat. San Francisco began to feel like home and I dreaded the thought of returning to Darjeeling.

———

My life fell out of groove when Hayden, Zoe's ex-boyfriend, showed up at The Stone. We were standing on the outer-edges of a frenzied, sweating sea of people dancing next to the stage.

Social Distortion was into the tail end of their setlist, when he pushed his way up to Zoe and said: "Hi."

Zoe, whose flaming hair bounced around madly as she lip-synched to lyrics from the song – 'Ball and Chain' – screamed when she saw him.

"Oh my God, Hayden, what are you doing here? So great to see you," she said.

"I've missed you," he said, running his fingers through his dirty blonde dreadlocks.

"I've missed you more," she said.

They started jump-dancing together.

I tried to keep up their frenzied pace but stopped after getting hit on the nose by a flailing arm.

When the song ended, he said to her: "I'm here with a guy who went to high school with Mike. He is taking me backstage to meet the band. Want to come?"

"Love to," she said. Then, turning to me, she said: "Want to join us?"

"Have to work early tomorrow so I'm going to call it a night," I said, as I massaged my ears to stop them from ringing.

"Ok, see you later," she said as Hayden took her by the hand and guided her toward the back of the stage, which was filling up with people trying to make their way towards the band.

Seeing her disappear behind a door at the back of the stage crushed me. I shouldn't have let her go with him.

Zoe did not come to my apartment that night.

Or that weekend.

The music in my life began to slow down.

I went joylessly through the motions of my life with the sole intent of killing time until the day she came back to me.

Then, when she said Hayden (who was visiting from Portland) had decided to stay an extra week, the music came to a screeching halt.

As I rode my bike toward the Zen Center at Green Gulch Farm, I decided to take the scenic route and climb up into the Marin Headlands. After parking my bike on the side of the road, I walked up to a vista point high up on the headlands, above the Golden Gate Bridge.

Fistful of Fog

There she was: San Francisco, home of the perpetual gold rush, city of never-ending dreams.

A freezing fog came out of nowhere and started to blot out the bridge. It reminded me of what Zoe had once said: "If you can see the bridge, the fog is about to come in. If you can't see the bridge, the sun is getting ready to shine again."

A few cars, headlights darting briefly like fireflies before disappearing into the belly of the fog, zipped across the bridge. In the distance, the sun shimmered on the fuzzy cityscape, which mirrored the dreams of a new generation of wealth-seekers, this group obsessed more with silicon than gold.

I fortified myself with chewing gum and mounted my bike again.

My arrival at Green Gulch Farms went unnoticed by the group of devotees planting seeds with macrobiotic passion. I stopped to smell the herbs in the nursery before making my way down to the meditation hall.

Inside the hall, an old Japanese monk was speaking with a slow drawl to a group of young devotees. My entrance must have disrupted his concentration for he opened his eyes and looked directly at me. I tried to slink into an empty seat at the back of the congregation, but the monk motioned me to come up and take an empty place in front, not far from him.

The monk's voice, more at ease with chanting words than speaking them, said: "...the struggle within is the struggle without ... life without attachment ... love without lust ... desire without fulfillment ... to live, to love, to dream, to desire, is human ... to do so without attachment, hatred, or jealousy is the way to enlightenment ... *Om mani padme hum.*"

Normally listening to the monk's chants made me feel calm but that afternoon his mantras didn't help much. I'd tried not to fall for Zoe but the angst triggered by Hayden's arrival signaled it was useless to deny I was deeply in love with her. And, judging from the considerable amount of time she was spending with him, my love felt doomed to remain unrequited.

A Fragile Union

When the meditation session was over, I walked behind Green Gulch Farms and made my way up to a trailhead. A cold foggy front had been going through Marin County that week. The freezing air cut through the bundles of woolens I had layered on me and made me shiver. Only after I got to the top of the hill did the sun start to take a hold of me.

When the first droplet of sweat appeared on my forehead, I began to feel warm again. I sat down on a stony ledge and retrieved a sketch-book and a pencil from my backpack. A few minutes later, I began sketching the outlines of Mount Tam. The meditative scraping sound of a #2 pencil on paper settled a wave of calmness over me.

The evening after Hayden left, I asked Zoe to meet me at The Misty Maiden Tavern. She arrived with tired, sleep-deprived eyes. Her normally shiny hair was uncombed and its ragged edges seemed to be revolting against a worn ponytail-holder. As we waited for our drinks to arrive, I said: "So, are you with him or with me?"

"What's the big deal?" she said. "I didn't think we were exclusive. Are we? Didn't you tell me your mother was trying to arrange your marriage with some girl back in Darjeeling?"

"That's different," I said. "What did you tell him about us?"

"Nothing, just that we are friends. Same as he and I," she said, after taking a sip from her beer mug.

"So, you are not sleeping with him?" I said. "No friends with benefits arrangement?"

"That is none of your business," she said.

"This may sound crazy but it bothers me that you've slept with so many men," I said.

"My sexual history hasn't prevented you from sleeping with me any chance you get, has it?" she said, sarcastically. "Anyway, I'm telling you he is just a friend, that's all."

"So, if he is just a friend, then you can stop seeing him anytime, right?" I said.

"I think so," she said.

"Have you read that French novel where this boy falls madly in love with a girl just after one sighting?" I said. "I think it's called 'The Lost Domain' or 'The End Of Youth' or something like that. Anyway, he is not able to forget her, ever."

"On the other hand, isn't it scary how often people say they are in love but a few weeks later they break up?" she said.

"Is that how you feel that way about me? That I'm just a crush and this phase will go away soon?" I said.

"I don't know," she said, twisting a few strands of her hair around her finger and rubbing her lips with it. Then, after asking for a refill, she said: "Hey, instead of worrying about the future, can we enjoy the time we have together?"

A wooden bench, carved out of a salvaged tree trunk, stood inside a grove of redwoods in the Presidio of San Francisco.

Attached to one corner of the bench was a metal plaque which read: "Anne Marie Kirchner (1947-1986): She danced on top of the mountain and drank from the fountain of dreams".

One afternoon, as I sat on this bench with Zoe's head resting on my lap and her eyes staring at the fragmented sunlight filtering in through the lofty branches of the redwoods, she started talking about her mother, Anne Marie Kirchner.

Anne had wanted to become the first woman to summit Mount K2 but cancer put an end to her dream.

Zoe's grandfather, who had summited three Himalayan peaks in the sixties, had wanted Anne to join him on his expeditions. But it was only after meeting Arlene Blum (who led an all-women ascent of Annapurna in 1978) that Anne became interested in mountaineering.

Anne feared American women were falling behind other nationalities when it came to Alpine-style climbing, so she tried to shine the spotlight on U.S. women mountaineers by summiting two unclimbed peaks in the Pamirs.

Zoe was cruising along in high school when Anne got diagnosed with squamous cell carcinoma. After Anne died, Zoe's world crumbled. She felt suicidal for weeks and none of the antidepressants her doctor prescribed seemed to help. Then, her grandfather took her rock-climbing in Yosemite and she felt like a new person. The more challenging the slope, the more exhausting the climb, the better she slept at night.

That year Wanda Rutkiewicz became the first woman to summit K2. A few days later, Zoe decided she would make the first female ascent of an 8,000-meter peak and dedicate her climb to Anne. But first, she set herself a goal of climbing all 13 peaks in California over 14,000 feet. Her middle name was Anne, which was the same as her mom's first name. She started using Anne as her climbing name but getting money to support her climbing lifestyle was challenging (being single had been hard on Anne and she didn't have any savings).

Zoe took on odd jobs to support herself. She waited tables, gardened rich people's homes, and, for a brief while, she even worked at a funeral home. She didn't care what she did as long as she made enough money to climb in her spare time. Within a span of 12 months, she managed to get all 13 California peaks under her climbing boots. Then, after Dominican University's volleyball coach promised to get her an athletic scholarship, she decided to become the first in her family to attend college.

"I can't imagine what you had to go through, after losing her so suddenly," I said, when she had finished.

My upbringing had trained me to be judgmental of people who appeared different to me. But after hearing Zoe's backstory I realized much of my assessment of her character had been based on superficial observations and incorrect assumptions. And it became clear to me that the life she had led had been very different to the life I'd imagined for her.

Fistful of Fog

From that day forward, I began to see Zoe through a new lens: that of a grieving girl prepared to do whatever it took to memorialize her mother in a meaningful, unforgettable way.

"I miss mom so much," she said, her voice cracking up a bit. "The hardest part was that after her funeral no one, other than Grampa and me, seemed to mention her name ever again. It was as if she had never even existed. Death sucks."

"I know what you mean," I said. "Every time I see the tomb of the unknown soldier, I get depressed. How tragic for someone to give their life to a cause they may not even believe in, yet no one is even able to identify their remains, let alone remember them?"

"Exactly," she said. "Archibald MacLeish captures it well in his poem, 'The Young Dead Soldiers Do Not Speak'. Have you read it?"

Meshing my fingers with hers, I said: "No, but I'm sorry you had to go through all this."

"Don't be sorry," said Zoe, as she got up from my lap and sat upright. "It will be worth it when I stand on top of Kanch and plant a banner with mom's name on it. The world will remember her once more."

Pockets of wildflower on the hillside, matched the colorful patches on her tied-dyed T-shirt. The backwaters of the Pacific, iridescent in the afternoon light, circled the Bay like a briny necklace of pearls and emeralds. The world, from my vantage point on top of Mount Tam, looked like one giant happy oyster.

"Do you know what you are going to do after your internship is over?" said Zoe, biting into a crunchy apple.

I drank in the beauty of the vista surrounding me and pondered how best to answer her question.

A Fragile Union

Until that summer, I hadn't spent much time dwelling on my calling in life, other than coming to the realization I didn't want to become a priest. But now that I was earning a paycheck at GreenEarth, I'd begun thinking more on this topic.

Unlike Zoe, I wasn't passionate about my environmental job. A few times I'd thought about quitting and following my real passion (studio art). But the fear of being separated from her had kept me from acting on my impulses (because losing my work visa would mean having to leave her homeland).

"Not sure," I said, after a brief pause. "I would probably want to pursue painting full time, maybe get an MFA or something, but I don't want to be a starving artist. So, I'm thinking of applying for the position of a forest ranger at a tiger sanctuary near Darjeeling. It comes with a secure paycheck. I could protect tigers from poachers and paint scenes from the jungle in my spare time."

"Protecting tigers is such a noble thing to do," she said, wistfully. "You know, sometimes, you remind me of Mowgli from Jungle Book. He was my favorite Disney character growing up."

"And you remind me of Princess Rapunzel," I said, caressing her hair.

"She didn't become a princess until she met her Prince Charming," said Zoe.

"You will always be my golden princess," I said. "From now on I'm going to call you Rani, which means queen in Bengali. Are you ok with that?"

"Yes, but only if you let me call you Mowgli," she said, smiling.

I put my arm around her shoulders. Drawing her towards me, I kissed her.

"I don't love you, Mowgli, not even one tiny bit," she said, smiling, after we surfaced for air.

"Neither do I, Zoe-rani, not even a smidgen," I said.

We kissed again.

Fistful of Fog

"Sometimes, I dream about us having a future but then I worry it won't last," I said.

"Life is short so our dreams need to last," she said. "That's what my mom used to say. The past is dead so why bother with it. And the future doesn't matter for it is not within our control. All that matters is right now. And right now I'm living my dream, being here with you, amidst these precious trees."

I sat soaking in the sunlight and reflecting on her words. A warm glow began to envelop me.

The label – "undocumented alien" – has the power to cause more shame and fear than almost any other set of words in the American lexicon. Yet those words (always directed at people who find themselves in the sort of arbitrarily-defined situations I found myself in that year) lose their meaning after getting thrown around so much it makes the recipient literally feel sick. Being unwanted in a foreign country is a depressingly common plight for many new immigrants. And for me that reality hit home when the INS denied my request for a work visa.

To get a new visa the INS required me to leave America. Zoe said the U.S. consulate in Matamoros was the easiest place to get a visa, according to her grandfather, Dave.

(She said she trusted Dave's judgement because he employed undocumented workers on his farm).

I had no issue with going across the border. But the Mexican consulate in San Francisco refused to give me a tourist visa (because I didn't have one to re-enter America).

"Now you've truly become a man without a country," said Zoe. "Your only choice is to cross the border, illegally."

"That sounds risky. What if I get caught?" I said, my voice laced with panic.

"Don't worry, I'll come with you," she said, smiling.

A Fragile Union

If I were caught (while crossing the border illegally) ... by the U.S. Border patrol or by the Mexican authorities ... Zoe would find herself in a lot of trouble.

But she never once mentioned the risk she was taking on my behalf.

You can call it her devil-may-care attitude if you like ... or paint her as someone who liked to side with the underdog ... but I believe she was hardwired in a genuinely compassionate way, one which made it impossible for her to ignore the call to help someone in distress.

Before we flew to Brownsville, she dyed her hair black. Then she bought me a sombrero, pimped-out with ornaments.

We waited until 3 a.m., before attempting the border crossing at Matamoros.

The Mexican guard looked at us with bored, sleepy eyes.

I lowered my gaze and turned away my face, hidden under the sombrero. But Zoe, her dark hair glowing with glitter and her lips painted a whorish pink, looked him in the eye and said in unaccented Spanish: *"Buenas noches, señor."*

I didn't think he would fall for our guises but he waved us through without checking our passports.

Later that morning, dressed in my best preppy outfit and armed with my rehearsed American accent, I lined up outside the U.S. consulate.

After a torturous interview process, I obtained a new visa stamp on my passport.

The short duration of the tourist visa the consular official had given me was less than ideal, but I was thrilled to be able to re-enter the U.S.

My head, covered by a Stetson as we crossed the border this time, was held high.

———

Fistful of Fog

After we returned to San Francisco, Zoe suggested we celebrate my new visa by bar-hopping.

I shouted an enthusiastic – "yes, let's do this," – but our partying ended prematurely when I dinged a police car, while trying to parallel-park our rented convertible near Folsom Street.

The grey-haired cop surveyed the police-car and, after finding no visible damage, walked over towards our convertible. I panicked because I had an open can of beer in my hand. But as he was walking over, Zoe grabbed the beer can out of my hand and held it in hers. I was bracing myself for immediate deportation but he let me go, after issuing a warning.

"Normally, I would throw your sorry *tuchus* in jail," he said in a strong Brooklyn accent, as he flashed a torch into my eyes. "But because you are here with this *shiksa* goddess, I'll pretend like this shit never happened. Remember, son, this ain't New Orleans during *Mardi Gras*, so don't drink and drive."

After the cop drove away, I said to Zoe: "Thanks but you didn't have to risk getting arrested just to save me."

"But I love you and love means having each other's back at all times," she said.

Misty hills sloped their gentle shadows onto the green earth. Bald eagles circled the cloudless skies, glistening above the peaceful ocean. A lone sailboat turned a corner in the bay and disappeared from sight.

"This is the sort of Bay Area day that makes everyone want to move to San Francisco," said Zoe, as we sat on top of a hill overlooking Green Gulch Farm and took sips out of a bottle of beer.

"The air smells so fresh," I said. "Reminds me of Darjeeling after the monsoon."

"How amazing is this view?" said Zoe. "I could just stand here all day and stare at this slice of heaven."

I looked at the landscape around us.

Down below the Pacific stretched the horizon lines out into an endless blue universe. But as the wispy fog parted and revealed the vista directly north, Mount Tam caught my attention.

"Mount Tam reminds me of the Himalayas sometimes," I said.

"Amazing, isn't it how you can travel half-way across the world and then see something that reminds you of home," she said. "Last year I was in Patagonia and the sunset there had the same tangy violet coloring that you often see in the Bay Area."

"From now on whenever I will look at Mount Tam it will remind me of you," I said. "Isn't it comforting that our association with places often has something to do with memories we build there with people we care about?"

"I agree," she said, as she looked at the blue-grey face of Mount Tam.

She stayed silent for a few seconds, before continuing: "Hey, speaking of mountains, have you heard from Tenzing about our Kanch expedition?"

There it was again: the K-word. In my book, K stood for Killer. Why did Kanchenjunga always seem to come between me and the people I loved?

I considered sharing the circumstances of my father's death and pleading with her to not risk her life by climbing that killer mountain. But wouldn't she brush aside my fear of losing her and reassure me (like she had in the past) about all the safety precautions she would take? Wouldn't my fears about losing her be overcome by her desire to fulfill her mother's dream?

I decided to lie.

"I'm afraid I have some bad news. Tenzing called yesterday. The expedition has been cancelled," I said.

Fistful of Fog

"What do you mean cancelled?" she said, raising her voice above the sound of the foghorn in the background. "Why?"

"Everything had been going along smoothly until a reshuffle of ministers followed the recent elections. The newly elected government officials are staunch Buddhists. They are opposed to mountaineers trampling on their sacred mountain. They said they will not be issuing climbing permits any time soon," I said.

"This is so frustrating," she said. "There is nothing worse than getting your hopes up and then finding out you have been rejected. I guess I will now have to look into climbing Kanch from the Nepal side."

Later, our relationship would pay a price for my lie. But that afternoon, I decided not to expose our embryonic love to a killer mountain.

———

As we stood in line waiting to exit the Shoreline Amphitheater in Mountain View Zoe asked me the meaning of the song – 'Strangelove' – played earlier that evening by Depeche Mode.

She enjoyed decoding the meaning of her favorite songs and we often spent hours debating the interpretation of various lyrics.

"Isn't it about asking permission to sleep around or engage in S&M or something along those lines?" I said.

"I think it's deeper than that," she said. "The song is talking about how hard it is to be perfect in love. Now and again one has to go outside the boundaries to keep the passion alive but that is ok as long as one returns or the other person leaves, if they can't take it any longer."

"That sounds like a risky move," I said. "What if one ends up losing their love?"

"My poor Mowgli," she said. "I guess you are straighter than I'd thought."

My ego hurt. I wanted to prove to her that I could be a badass, sometimes. So, I said: "I shop-lifted a magazine from a Darjeeling bookstore once, after a high school classmate dared me to. That's not so straight is it?"

"You just made that up for my benefit, didn't you?" she said, chuckling.

"No, it's true. I swear it happened," I said.

"Really?" she said, sounding skeptical.

"I love you and I'll never lie to you," I said. "You should know that about me."

"Then prove your love by pinching a book for me," she said, smiling.

Julia had warned me that Zoe could be a prankster sometimes. But I was determined to prove my love for her by being a bad boy.

"All right, I'll do it," I said, in a voice loaded with testosterone and fear.

The next morning, we went to an antique bookstore on Russian Hill. It used to be one of those great old bookstores, tomes scattered everywhere. Literary rock-stars used to drop in occasionally and bless the masses with high-brow readings. But now it was on the verge of closing, bankrupted by the changing city and lost to the whims of tech-savvy times.

After a few minutes inside the bookstore, she pointed to a leather-bound bible and said: "That one will make a nice birthday present for Julia."

She strode up to the check-out counter where a brightly-tattooed girl stood behind the register. She tried to distract the girl by pointing to the cover of Cosmo and asking loudly if the store had any good books on tattoo removal. That gave me an opportunity to stuff the bible into my rucksack. I had almost made my way outside the store when a security guard showed up.

I dropped the bible and ran. But he was faster than me and after a brief sprint caught me and pinned my arms behind my back.

"I'm going to teach you a lesson," said the guard, panting furiously. "You take something from us, we will take something from you. Here, give me this."

He grabbed my watch-band and tried to unfasten the vintage Rolex watch on my wrist. My grandfather had given this watch to Baba upon his graduation from college. And Baba, in turn, had gifted it to me on the day I finished high school. Since that day, the watch had never left my wrist.

"No," I said, terrified and belligerent at the same time. "This watch is a special gift from my father. You will have to kill me before I part with it."

"Get your hands off him or I will spray you," screamed Zoe, who had just caught up with us and was now waving a large can of pepper spray.

How could she be so fearless, when her accomplice (i.e. me) had engaged in a criminal act?

The guard, surprised by Zoe's arrival, released my wrist.

"Here, take this," I said, extracting my wallet out of my hip pocket and handing it to him.

He took my wallet, spat on it, and tossed it on the ground. Then, after saying – "you and your kind disgust me" – he walked away.

I was lucky the bookstore decided not to press charges because that would have meant immediate deportation.

Zoe found the whole thing hilarious. I stayed mad at her for the rest of that day but my anger calmed down when she called that night and rewarded me in bed with a special (backdoor) prize.

Before she left for work the next morning, she chuckled and said: "You've now officially become a badass. And me too!"

A Fragile Union

Like most first fights, ours began unexpectedly.

That evening, Zoe had been more animated than usual because three of her favorite bands – Sonic Youth, Nirvana and Stone Temple Pilots – were scheduled to play. For weeks she had been talking about how she expected a fantastic show, filled with acoustic stunts and physical calisthenics. And now that the day had finally arrived, she couldn't wait to get to The Warfield.

Many relationships have been destroyed by a long-distance phone call and our nascent relationship went through its first major hiccup when Zoe answered the telephone in my apartment.

After hanging-up the phone, she said, angrily: "That was Tenzing. He said the expedition was never canceled but you had asked him to remove my name from the team because, according to you, I'd changed my mind about climbing Kanch. Why did you lie?"

"I'm sorry but I love you and I don't want you to die on Kanchenjunga," I said, my voice trembling with emotion. "Why do you have to risk everything to climb that killer mountain?"

"It is my life. I get to decide what risks I want to take," she said, making no attempt to keep the anger from harshening her voice.

"This may sound crazy but sometimes I wished you believed in God," I said.

"What does God have to do with this?" she said.

"If you believed in God, then you wouldn't throw your life away like this," I said.

"I've accepted who for who you are. Why can't you accept me for who I am?" she said.

"I can accept lots of things. Just not this," I said. "I know you care deeply about your mother but she is dead and I'm still alive. What about me?"

103

"Boy, this was a mistake," she said, as she started heading towards the door. "We should break-up."

"But I love you," I said, as I started to walk fast towards the door in an attempt to use my body as a shield between her and the dreaded door-handle.

"Then you should let me go," she said, getting to the door ahead of me and placing her hand on the handle. "The only way to know if love is true to let the other person go and see if they come back."

"Zoe, please don't leave me. I love you," I said, desperation making my voice screech.

I followed her out as she drew the door open and stepped into the hallway.

"Wait," I screamed, as she got inside the elevator. "There is something I need to tell you about my father."

But she was in no mood to listen to me.

As I watched the elevator door closing, I felt the distance between us growing.

I wondered if I could ever overcome my past.

I didn't think I would hear from Zoe again. But the following week, she called me in the middle of the night.

"Julia tried to kill herself," said Zoe, sounding distraught.

"What?" I said, as I tried to wake-up.

"She slashed her wrists. If her roommate hadn't found her, it would have been curtains for sure. I flew down to Nashville as soon as I heard the news but when I got to the Vanderbilt Medical Center it was still touch and go. She is better now."

"Wow, what happened?" I said, rubbing sleep out of my eye.

"That slime-ball, Mark. Who knew? He has gotten one of his students pregnant. Jeez, what a mess! I needed someone to talk to, so I called you," she said.

"How is she doing?" I said, thrilled that of all the people Zoe could have called, I was the first person she thought of.

"Barely conscious. Can you believe their wedding was scheduled for next month? That Mark is such a loser," she said.

"Shall I fly down to Nashville and join you?" I said.

"No, there is not much you can do here," she said. "Poor Julia! I'll stay on for a couple more days. Then, I'm leaving for Darjeeling."

"What?" I said, surprised to hear she was going to my hometown. Then it dawned on me that she must have called Tenzing and gotten him to include her on his Kanchenjunga expedition team.

I wished Tenzing had consulted me first. He took my advice on many issues but on all matters related to climbing he had always been fiercely independent. And he had always taken the side of any mountaineer looking to realize her/his summit dream.

For him, the lofty wishes of aspiring climbers (who usually arrived in the Himalayas armed with heavenly muscles and bulging wallets) always trumped the head-shaking warnings of naysayers like me, whom he saw as spiritless mortals with their feet bound unimaginatively to the ground.

"Jay, are you still there?" said Zoe, bringing me back to the present.

"Yeah, just thinking," I said.

"Hey, you want to join me on Kanch?" she said in a voice bubbling with sudden excitement. "I promise I won't drag you higher up than base camp. It'll be fun. You should come."

Despite feeling sorry for Julia, I was ecstatic to hear Zoe's invitation.

Zoe had given me another chance. I wasn't going to blow this one!

When I accepted her invitation, she uttered the sweetest 3-letter word in the American lexicon: "Yay!"

Fistful of Fog

The evening she returned to San Francisco, we had great make-up sex.

Afterwards, as she slept, I painted a portrait of her (dressed up as Wonder Woman) attempting to scale Kanchenjunga.

When she woke up and looked at the painting, the golden flecks in her eyes lit up like a dozen tiny suns.

Chapter 6: Death Or Glory

Foreigners either love or hate India; there is no middle ground. I caught Zoe staring out the train window and wondered how she felt about my homeland.

Did she love the tranquil beauty of rural India; its bucolic heart sparkling like an emerald, as the countryside rolled by? Or was she put off by the chaotic ugliness of its towns, many sitting exposed on top of hot, crowded plains, which didn't always showcase my motherland in the best possible light.

"That man is dressed in a pristine, 3-piece suit, but he is peeing in full public view," said Zoe, as the train slowed down to enter yet another decrepit station. "Ugh! Totally gross."

"That act captures a microcosm of the contradiction we call modern India," I said, rubbing my eyes to keep fine particles of coal dust from entering, as smoke from a passing steam engine found its way into our railway compartment.

A few minutes later, the train departed the station and made its way towards the distant foothills. The heat of the Gangetic plains, which had turned our compartment into a sauna on rails, made me take off my shirt. A drop of sweat traced a languid pattern around my torso, slid down my leg and dropped silently down onto the sooty compartment floor.

Jet-lag had finally caught up with Zoe. She began to doze, while sitting upright.

I sat across from her and watched as the fat young boy sitting next to her used his sticky fingers to fondle her hair. Every time he stretched his legs inside our cramped, 3rd class compartment, his knee would bump-up against mine.

From time-to-time the boy would wipe the syrup dripping off of one side of his lip with his fingers, which would then be wiped on the sari worn by his mother, sitting adjacent to him. And then those same boyish fingers would be dispatched to fondle the strands hanging off of Zoe's shoulder.

It struck me, not for the first time, that Zoe didn't need to change her appearance or behavior to be accepted in India, a country long enamored by the pale skin of its European colonizers. She carried the powerful and identifiable card of white privilege. Unlike me, who had to go to great lengths to reinvent myself in America, there was no need for her to be anyone but herself, no matter where she travelled.

During that trip I couldn't help wondering how my countrymen would have reacted to her had she been a non-white American. Would they have been as fascinated? And I? Would I have fallen in love if her skin had been darker than mine?

As soon as Zoe woke up, the boy began to pester me to take a picture of the two of them.

"Never seen hair so yellow, pleez, one photo," he said.

She said – "no problem, kiddo" – and then asked me to oblige with my polaroid camera.

I wished Zoe wouldn't be so obliging all the time. Politeness might work in America. But in India, with a billion eager fingers everywhere, ready to grab everything, it was safer to be unfriendly, sometimes.

Immediately the woman offered Zoe a reward of a *rosogolla*, dripping with syrup (and likely loaded with diarrhea-causing bacteria). It was the sole survivor in her tiffin box, which had been emptied (by the sticky fingers of the boy) of a dozen similar sweets.

I was horrified to see Zoe accepting the offering and depositing it inside her mouth.

After consuming the sweet with visible relish, she turned to me and said: "I love this place. People are so damn friendly here."

Alienation

Dreams seemed more likely to birth in Lavose than in most other places. Whether this illusion was created by the delicate clouds floating in and out of the surrounding mountains or by Lama Pasang's transcendental chanting of hymns at the monastery, I do not know. All I know is that during my high school years, I often hung out here with Tenzing, and heard him talk about his dreams of becoming a rock-climbing star, after he graduated.

There were no metaled roads in Lavose, situated 9,000 feet above the sweltering plains. It remained sleepy year-round, except for a couple of clear-skied months before and after the monsoon. That's when trekkers reared their bandanaed heads to check out the rhododendrons. And mountaineers came to conquer the summits with their ice-axes and their sponsors' logos.

Most tourists who visited Darjeeling didn't make it this far. It could only be reached after a long day's drive through winding hillside death-traps, followed by two days of trekking up and down slippery mountain slopes. The village remained quiet except on Sundays, when the farmer's market brought together peasants and their slaughter animals and turned the square into a chaotic and odiferous spectacle.

It was a typical Himalayan village, with names like the Yeti Bar and the Yak Guest House. Yeti and Yak. Like the East-West paradox that surfaced every time a local and a tourist argued about whether time or money was a more important measure of success. Like the debates that raged between old monks and their young students when talking about whether Lavose should remain tradition-rooted or embrace electricity.

Like many other Sikkimese villages, Lavose consisted of two sections: lower and upper. The few tourists that made it here usually camped out at Lower Lavose, which could be reached by climbing up on the steep trail from Lavo Lake. The Yeti Bar was situated in this lower part of the village.

Fistful of Fog

The houses in the lower part of the village belonged to two ethnic groups: Sherpas and Lepchas. The wealthier families sported stacks of timber on their roof-tops, while the poorer ones dried clusters of red chili peppers on theirs. Locals believed chilies improved blood circulation and purified the soul. As you moved up in altitude and got closer to heaven you could tell from looking at the houses that people uphill had less money but more soul.

Upper Lavose was a half-hour uphill trek from the lower part of the village. In the Himalayas nothing is strictly uphill or downhill, you go up and you come down and, after repeating that sequence a few times, you finally reach your destination. This ethnically distinct section of the village consisted of several new homes, jutting out crookedly from the slopes. These homes had been built by refugees fleeing Tibet.

The Yak Guest House was located on the outskirts of Upper Lavose, near a horseshoe bend from where the silvery-blue silhouette of Kanchenjunga could be seen looming behind the clouds. It was owned by Norbu, a Tibetan schoolmate who had been three grades ahead of me in high school. Since it was open only during tourist season, he often supplemented his income by working as a high-altitude porter on expeditions.

Many believe the ascent of Kangchenjunga, especially from Sikkim, is more challenging than climbing Everest or K2. But Zoe couldn't wait to climb the mountain.

In her state of extreme confidence, which is the sole dominion of exuberant youth, she believed in her ability to conquer the mighty mountain.

Her enthusiasm just could not be subdued. And she wouldn't give up on her dream, even after hearing that the number of dead climbers outnumbered the number of summiteers who had managed to make it back down, alive, on the challenging northeast spur to north ridge route (which Tenzing had chosen for the expedition team to follow) on the Sikkimese side of the mountain.

Alienation

On that trip Zoe was not thinking about failure or death. She was armed with only a few climbing experiences but her enthusiasm to climb this mountain was boundless.

"We will give it the good old college try," she would say often that month.

A vast unruly stretch of wildflowers layered the horizon like a fairy's playground. The immense white face of Kanchenjunga, unburdened by clouds that morning, rose heavenward from amidst a skyline of rocky towers.

Zoe, lying on a deck-chair, turned towards me and said: "I love this story but I haven't been able to figure out what the title means."

I was sitting on the cement ledge of the Guest House porch and feeding Norbu's mastiff, Himal, a dog biscuit but I paused my canine interactions and looked at the book's cover.

It was 'The Name of The Rose' by Umberto Eco. A few weeks earlier, I'd borrowed it from a library in Darjeeling.

"I read somewhere that the author wanted to find a neutral title so readers could focus on his premise that every story tells a story that has been told before and every book speaks of other books," I said.

"But songs have meaning associated with them so why not book titles?" she said.

"Not every song has some deep, philosophical meaning attached to it," I said. "Take a song like 'Hello, Goodbye' by The Beatles. Do you know what it signifies?"

Just then Zoe's tape-recorder came to life, signaling the end of load-shedding, which had descended on the Guest House the previous night. And the stillness around us was assaulted by frenzied verses from the song – 'Death or Glory' – by The Clash.

"This is my favorite song of all time," said Zoe, sitting upright.

"But it glorifies death," I said, appalled at the thought that this track was probably giving her additional inspiration to climb deadly, tall peaks.

"It does not. Listen to the lyrics carefully. In fact, they are saying something quite different," she said.

"I wish people wouldn't risk their lives just to get a bit of glory," I said. "Why don't they think about the loved ones left behind?"

"Jeez, no one is climbing a mountain because they want to die or because they want to hurt a loved one," she said. "We climb so the journey of our life doesn't become another inconsequential speck which disappears into the void of time."

"It's interesting you say that. Last night I was reading 'The Snow Leopard' by Peter Matthiessen. He often uses the phrase – 'comes and goes'. That's probably because he is trying to say everything is impermanent, especially our lives," I said.

"If I die on Kanch then you can say: 'Zoe Comes and Goes'. Otherwise, I'm going to call it: 'Death or Glory – Just Another Kickass Summit Conquering Story'. How do you like that?" she said, smiling.

She paused to feed Himal a dog biscuit.

Then, turning to me, she said in a more serious tone: "But if I die young, don't forget me."

On most Himalayan expeditions, much time is spent waiting around for things to happen: permits to get signed, weather to co-operate, lamas to arrive and bless equipment so the climb can start. That month, we had a lot of free time on our hands. And Zoe spent a lot of that time debating the meaning of songs, books, and movies.

One movie we argued about a fair bit was 'Pretty in Pink'.

Alienation

I never understood why she liked the movie so much, until I realized it was because the girl in that story didn't have to change who she was in order to become worthy of the guy but he had to change his perspective before he could win her over.

In the coming weeks, I would not be able to shake-off my fear of Zoe dying on Kanchenjunga. And neither would she abandon her goal of fulfilling her mother's dream by summitting the deadly mountain. Because I wasn't prepared to change my perspective and see the world through her lens (that of a heartbroken girl willing to go to any lengths to immortalize her mother's name), our relationship would continue to struggle.

That week, Tenzing subjected us to the rigors of training and conditioning. Barely able to differentiate between a crampon and a jumar, my turbulent mind didn't absorb much of his demonstrations or lectures. I tried calming my mind down by chanting some of Lama Pasang's hymns but my fear of scaling up vertical death traps and abseiling down slippery rock faces would not go away.

I wasn't planning on going further than Kanchenjunga Base Camp, so my fears were not solely centered on me. I was also worried about Zoe, because she was planning to climb to the top of Kanchenjunga, a height taller than 20 Empire State buildings, stacked on top of each other.

We spent days learning and practicing how to: fix ropes and ladders on icy slopes; hammer pitons and anchors into mountainside cracks; belay each other across tumbled icefalls; abseil down through knee deep snow.

One day, after we had finished practicing, Zoe turned towards me and said: "Isn't this fun? I could do this 24/7."

Nothing is harder than faking excitement when every cell inside your body is running on fear.

Fistful of Fog

Whenever I faced a vertical wall my breath shortened. Every time that happened, I took a deep breath and tried to expel the fear demons inside my head. But rarely did I succeed in replacing the gut-wrenching fear inside of me with a duller, more acceptable, ache.

I was about to quit one morning when I looked up and saw Zoe's face.

We were dangling from a vertical precipice that had death written across its rocky ledge. But the grimace her face had acquired in the hot Gangetic plains had been replaced in the mountains by a look of intense joy, as if she was creating her own religious experience.

I could tell that it wasn't just her body but her awakened spirit that was flying up the slopes that morning. I tried to feel the same way but when I looked down into the abyss, I saw a vision of my father's fractured face.

I screamed.

———

I took the trail past a small chorten where prayer-flags marked the beginning of 108 steep stone steps. At the top of those steps stood the entrance to the Lavose Monastery.

The monastery looked smaller than I remembered. Like the rest of my childhood memories it seemed to have shrunk. I wondered if my time abroad had somehow diminished the magic of the Himalayas.

The monastery had been built in the 12th century but now it was the exclusive domain of Lama Pasang. Before these stone steps had been built, the vertical setting had allowed monks under siege to remove the ladders that led up into the monastery. The besieged monks would open the central door, painted red to look like a bloodthirsty mouth, and pour boiling oil on the heads of invaders. It was only recently that steps had replaced the ladders.

Alienation

Fragrant juniper smoke rose from a bonfire burning at the monastery's entrance. Beads of smoke floated heavenward like a prayer.

When the lama heard of my arrival, he summoned me into the meditation hall. The morning prayers were over; there weren't many people around. He sat cross-legged on the floor of the hall.

Fishing out a large betel leaf from inside a wooden box resting next to him, he began to load it with betel-nut, tobacco and slaked-lime paste. Then, he offered the fully-loaded package to me.

After refusing his offer, I told him about my love for Zoe. And that I was thinking about proposing to her soon.

"So what's the problem," he said, slipping the loaded betel-leaf into his mouth.

"For the last several months, I've been telling her the idea of summitting Kanchenjunga is fraught with risk. I've made her aware of the mountain's high death-rate. And I've told her that most climber's gain experience on lesser Himalayan peaks, before tackling this deadly one," I said.

He remained silent as he massaged the betel-leaf with delicate dental strokes. His jaw moved behind the folds of his cheek like a well-oiled lawnmower.

"But despite my best efforts to discourage her, Zoe remains determined to join Tenzing's expedition," I said. "And I'm terrified she will die on the mountain, like my father did. What shall I do, lama?"

Pausing his chewing for a moment, he said: "You can't change people or stop them from following their dreams."

"I know but I'm not sure what to do when making the person I love happy means taking the risk of losing her?" I said.

"It is natural to fear losing the person you love but you must learn to let go of this fear," he said.

He paused to swallow a tiny bit of betel juice. Then, grabbing my hand, he said: "Come with me."

Just before we left the meditation hall, he whispered a few words into the hairy ears of an old monk.

Soon, a large cage was produced. A Bar-headed goose sat inside.

I started to speak but the old monk silenced me by putting a finger on his lip.

Lama Pasang grabbed the birdcage with both hands and exited through a side door. I followed him as he went behind the monastery walls and then up a steep uphill path which wound its way to the top of Lavo Hill, partially covered in morning fog.

The hazy sunlight reflected off of a dusting of snow on the path and generated tiny rainbows. From the crackling sounds I heard as we got closer to the top, I could tell there was a bit of electricity in the air.

After we reached the top of the hill, he handed me the cage and said: "Set your fears free, along with this bird."

He helped me release the goose from its cage. The bird flapped its wings, hesitantly at first and then with great gusto. It climbed up into the thin air and rose with the morning jet stream. It continued to climb higher.

After a few minutes, it reached the top of Kanchenjunga. And then it crossed the mighty mountain and disappeared from view.

———

A full-ish moon, surfing on foamy clouds, obviated the need for my flashlight.

I touched the turquoise ring resting in my jacket pocket, as I hurried my way down to the Yeti Bar. Earlier that day, I'd emptied my savings account and bought the ring from the Tibetan refugee center in Upper Lavose.

Alienation

The impromptu party being held at the Yeti that evening was Tenzing's idea. Earlier that day (after I told him about my desire to propose to Zoe) he had offered to host a surprise party. He decided to call it the 'Expedition Kickoff Party', so she wouldn't be tipped-off beforehand. And he asked her to deejay the event, so she wouldn't have any excuse to leave early.

"Thanks, I owe you one," I had said, grateful for his support.

"Don't worry, I'll ask you to return the favor soon," he had said. "If it wasn't for that bastard Salim, I'd be married already."

Like me, Tenzing was in an intercultural relationship. During his junior year in college he had fallen for a Kashmiri girl, Naz, after finding her head covered by a climbing helmet instead of a burqa. They had continued to see each other, even after graduating from college. Her brother, Salim, had warned Tenzing to leave his sister alone, saying religion divided them. But Tenzing had not paid much heed to his warnings. Despite the growing animosity between them, he continued to spend significant time with her.

A few minutes after I entered the Yeti, Zoe showed up.

She looked very desirable that evening: her pouty ruddy lips free of cosmetics, the howdiness in her voice friendly as usual, her glowing gorgeous mane tumbling out of an 'A's baseball cap, her face tanned to perfection by the Himalayan sun.

I felt an overpowering urge to kiss her. But, before I could get in a word with her, Norbu, with more than a hint of *chaang* (barley beer) on his breath, took me by the arm and guided me towards the statue of Green Tara. The statue was housed in a glass case on the far side of the bar, where Tenzing was waiting.

Norbu poured a few drops of barley beer on the statue and started to mumble a prayer.

Reluctantly, I shifted my gaze from Zoe to Tara. The Goddess sat on a stone lotus; her head tilted back; her leg bent; and her body draped in a silken wreath.

I tried to pay attention to what Norbu was chanting but I couldn't keep my gaze away from Zoe: my old lust, my new love, my amazing, All-American dream.

"Oh Tara," I prayed silently, "mother of all Buddhas, miraculous savior of suffering beings, representation of wisdom and love, grant me just one wish; please align Zoe's star with mine tonight."

As the crowd started trickling into the bar, Zoe started off the evening with a Bob Marley song (one of Tenzing's favorites).

A slight, Tibetan girl with a huge nose-ring began spinning around the dance floor. A middle-aged tourist started dancing, Bollywood style, next to her. You could tell from his swagger, and the Pan Parag stuck on his teeth, that he was one of those plainspeople who thought money could buy them anything they wanted on the mountain. But she rebuffed his offer to buy her a drink and he slunk away from the dance floor, his swagger noticeably diminished.

I walked over to the DJ table but Zoe, headphones on her head, seemed lost in her music, so I made my way back over to the dance floor. I nervously fingered the engagement ring concealed inside the pocket of my jacket. I looked at the bar-clock and wondered if my mother was still awake.

After another Marley song, Zoe switched the music from reggae to dance-rock.

Soon, the floor was invaded by a group of female school-teachers from Darjeeling, one of whom dragged Naz into the middle of their dancing circle.

Naz wore a revealing *salwar-kameez* but hid her face behind a Pashmina scarf. I thought about joining them on the dance floor but there is something intimidating about a lone man joining a large group of women who seem to be having fun dancing with each other.

The Yeti started filling up with locals, backpackers and a couple of rich city kids who must have heard about the party and showed up to see if there were any girls who could be had for the price of a pill or a couple of joints.

Salim made a striking entrance. His jeweled Kashmiri dagger swayed like a metallic penis in front of his leather jeans. He stood out with his aquiline, Kashmiri face. Since he didn't have the flat-nosed Sherpa look, nor a pale western-European look, people couldn't always place him. Because of their exotic Eurasian looks, he and Naz were desired by both locals and foreign tourists. Which is why, Salim often swaggered around Lavose, acting like women were going to just fling themselves into his lap.

I finished my barley beer and stepped into the phone booth located on the far side of the bar. After closing the door, I called home.

I hadn't spoken to Ma since arriving in Lavose. I wanted to tell her about my impending engagement and get her blessings. But the servant who answered the phone said Ma was spending the night at the home of her sister, Rama.

When I stepped back outside, I noticed Salim was now standing right next to the deejay booth. He was conversing with Zoe. I couldn't hear what they were saying but from the look on her face I could tell he was up to no good.

I walked towards them. After I engaged her in conversation, he lost interest and left.

"Thank you," she said. "That guy was hitting on me. Such a pain in the ass."

Just then Tenzing's voice floated over the PA system.

Fistful of Fog

"Ladies and Gentlemen, Jay, has a special announcement to make," he said.

Everyone stopped dancing. Their eyes turned towards me.

Grabbing Zoe's hand, I walked over to the dance floor where Naz stood, encircled by her girlfriends.

After a wave of girls parted to let us inside their circle, I got down on one knee.

Taking the turquoise ring out of my pocket, I said: "I know this is sudden but I love you, Zoe-rani. Will you marry me?"

Zoe kept silent for a long nervous minute.

Then, turning towards me, she said, softly: "Oh Mowgli, I wasn't expecting this. I love you too and, yes, I'll marry you but can the wedding wait until the expedition is over?"

Nothing anyone had ever said had made me happier.

I got up from the floor. Holding her hand in mine, I slipped the ring on her finger.

As we kissed, the song – 'One Love' – by Bob Marley' began to play. The cheesiness of the situation made me cringe but I asked her to dance with me anyway.

A few seconds later, I saw Naz grabbing the sleeve of Tenzing's traditional Sherpa jacket and pulling him on to the dance floor.

As they started to slow-dance it appeared as if they were getting ready to kiss. But before their lips met, a shadowy figure moved in from the bar area.

It was Salim. Placing his right hand on the handle of his dagger, he yelled: "Bastard, leave my sister alone."

Tenzing responded by lifting the Pashmina scarf (which partially covered Naz's face like a veil) and kissing her on the center of her lips.

Using a cigarette lighter, Naz set fire to her veil. The scarf crackled loudly as it went up in flames. Someone whistled. A few people clapped.

Salim unsheathed his dagger and waved it menacingly at Tenzing.

Alienation

At this point, Norbu and a few other locals intervened. They wrestled the dagger away from Salim and pinned him to the ground. But soon Salim managed to break-free and landed a punch on Tenzing.

It is hard to imagine a night at the Yeti without some kind of skirmish. Because my engagement had just been announced, I had hoped we would be spared the usual displays of pseudo-Himalayan virility that evening. But no one else seemed to care about maintaining restraint.

Call me chicken if you wish but I'm not one of those macho guys who enjoys trading blows. Usually, I prefer to observe the action from behind the battle lines. But that night, with Zoe watching, I felt more like fighting than I'd ever felt before.

I elbowed my way into the center of the brawl and punched a mouth. It coughed up a column of smoke. A fist scraped my nose and drew blood. My face hurt. But when I retreated to the sidelines, Zoe wiped the blood off my nose. I felt great.

I was about to go back for another round of brawling but then the cops came, with their whistles blowing and their batons charging. Everyone started rushing out of the bar.

I grabbed Zoe's arm. Together, we ran outside.

Equipment had been loaded on yaks and humans. Goodbyes had been whispered to friends and families. And the drinking binge (the previous night) had ensured everyone started the morning with a giant hangover. Now, it was time to go climb a mountain.

I labored behind Norbu, who was guiding two yaks up the trail. Himal, running up and down the path, nipped at their heels, trying to keep the boisterous yaks in check. But the yaks, eager to get to higher pasture-land, dashed uphill, despite the mountain of camping gear balanced precariously on their backs.

Himal would run up toward Zoe one minute and then, the very next minute, come all the way back down, towards the yaks to check on them. One sullen beast took offence to his barks and tried to kick him. But Himal, being a mountain dog, knew how to escape angry creatures, especially giant wooly ones.

When we got to a steep section of the trail I had difficulty keeping pace with Zoe. Her feet seemed to spring-board up the vertical path, barely touching the ground. She didn't slow down, even once, to catch her breath as she strode up the trail, which climbed steeply onto a thicket of moss.

A wandering herd of blue sheep, their large curvy horns forming V-signs against the snowy backdrop of the mountains, appeared in the valley below us. Zoe immediately took her camera out of her backpack and began to snap pictures. That gave me a few minutes to rest my poor blistered feet.

After nine hours on the trail, I'd begun to feel nauseous and light-headed. I could sense altitude sickness kicking-in but I stayed silent. I didn't want Tenzing to lecture me about my lack of fitness, especially in front of Zoe.

After we resumed our trek, the trail forked at a mossy *chorten*. I wished Tenzing hadn't taken the steep uphill branch of the trail. I felt like he was deliberately trying to show Zoe how fit he was and how out of shape I was.

I squatted down on my haunches and tried to catch my breath. Tenzing, lighting another cigarette as he waited impatiently for me to get back up on my feet, said: "Too much masturbation and too little exercise, huh, Jay?"

"Can we rest here for a few more minutes?" I said, haltingly.

I found it difficult to breathe and speak at the same time. Having gained several thousand feet in elevation that day, I was feeling dizzy.

"Are you ok?" said Zoe, with a look of concern on her face. "Why are you mumbling? Are you hallucinating or something?"

Alienation

"Let's make a move," said Tenzing. "We need to get to Base Camp before dark."

I tried to get up but my feet crumpled from under me.

"Here, have a sip of tea," said Pemba, handing me his flask. Pemba was Tenzing's cousin. He was thick-faced and squat-bodied, like a man in a Diego Rivera painting.

"Jay doesn't look good," said Pemba. "There is a trekkers hut around the corner. Let's stop there for the night."

I sat on the rocky ground and warily took a sip of yak-butter tea. I wanted to feel better but the pounding headache (which had started a few minutes earlier) refused to leave.

That evening, I couldn't keep my dinner down.

"How do you feel, honey?" said Zoe, after she watched me throw-up just outside the trekkers hut.

"He is showing signs of altitude," said Tenzing. "Let's keep an eye on him. He may have to go back down."

I felt too exhausted to eat or chat. And when the sun set, I wanted to climb into my sleeping-bag but Tenzing wouldn't allow it. He kept me moving.

Then, when he finally let me lay on one of the hut's bunk beds, my headache wouldn't allow me to sleep.

Tenzing slept through most of the night but Zoe stayed alert. She would wake up from time to time and make sure I was ok. Twice, I had to leave the hut to throw-up. Every time I stepped out, Zoe came with me. The frigid, nasty wind made me cry. I was relieved to climb back into my sleeping bag.

I was still trying to fall asleep, when I found Norbu thrusting a steaming tea-cup into my hands. It was freezing inside the hut. The tea felt great. I was in no hurry to get out of bed that morning.

"We should go right now," said Tenzing. "Lama Pasang is waiting for us at Base Camp."

Fistful of Fog

Slowly, I dragged myself out into the bitter, crackling cold. And, as soon as I felt the icy wind, I warmed myself up by urinating inside my ski-pants.

Tenzing's flashlight guided us in the thick freezing darkness. Overnight frost had brightened up a swath of dark rocks. The trickling stony rivulet from the previous afternoon had been transformed into a slippery glassy strip of cold dirty water. And fresh snow, quilting the trail outside the hut, had turned the bleak landscape into a winter wonderland.

For someone like Tenzing, that morning's trek must have felt like a stroll through a Polynesian playground. But to my feverish mind, the climb up to Base Camp (at 16,000 feet) seemed as demanding as getting to the top of Everest.

Base Camp wasn't far from the trekker's hut, from where we had started that morning. But with my frequent rest stops, brought on by exhaustion and dizziness, progress was laborious.

The howling wind didn't help matters. I clung onto a rope Tenzing had wrapped around our waists, so we didn't get blown off the mountain.

When we got to the top of a hillock, Tenzing pointed to a row of tents in the distance and said: "That's Base Camp; about a mile from here; partly down-hill."

I sat down on the frozen ground.

"Mowgli, are you ok to walk?" said Zoe.

I wasn't ok. I had to throw-up again. After I was done, Norbu loaded me on the back of a yak.

Yaks never like coming down from the high mountains. Something about the heat and crowds below make them ill-tempered on downhill runs.

Norbu held the protesting yak on a short-leash and dragged him down, with me straddling the cranky beast and hanging on for dear life (while trying not to look too far down into the steep ravine below).

Alienation

The valley below us lay entwined by a feathery layer of fog; while rain clouds ruled the sky above. But just before we got to Base Camp, the besieged sun managed to extricate itself from the shackles of angry cloud. And fingers of sunlight drew the cloud curtain aside to reveal the dazzling peaks around us. Like a python drawing a hypnotized deer towards its open jaws, the sparkling summit of Kanchenjunga forced Zoe to lock her eyes on to the mountain. I looked up at its beautiful, inhospitable face and muttered a prayer.

The mountain gods cooperated, and we made it up to Base Camp without any mishaps. Tenzing took me inside a tent, covered on the outside with prayer flags, and made me inhale from an oxygen tank. Soon, the shooting pain in my head dulled down to a milder head-ache. And the sticky feeling between my eyelids disappeared. I was able to keep down a few sips of the hot tea, which Pemba had prepared.

"Some *chaang*, Jay?" said Norbu, whipping out a flask of barley beer from his backpack. "It will make you feel better."

His matted, unwashed hair knot stood up like a bird's nest above his shining crimson eyes, bloodshot by a mixture of *chaang* and the high-altitude sun. His gums, perpetually munching on tobacco, stayed massaged but because he spat constantly, his voice often sounded hoarse.

The thought of drinking alcohol almost made me puke. It was humiliating that Norbu, who drank *chaang* at all hours of day or night, handled the altitude so much better than me. I could barely carry my backpack without having to rest every few feet whereas guys like Norbu went around Base Camp with entire villages loaded on their backs.

It was impossible to hate Norbu for being a true mountain man but I came close to hating him that day. I blamed it on my plain-dwelling ancestors.

Norbu didn't talk much. But what he missed in words he more than made up with his unflagging service on the slopes. Like he did again that afternoon, racing off to Camp I, right after he had served us tea.

"How can he make it up there tonight?" I said. "Doesn't he have to go through the Glacier and Icefall to get there? After all the trekking we've done in the last couple of days, where does he find the energy?"

"He is known as the Icefall doctor around these parts," said Pemba. "Members from another expedition are waiting for him. Tomorrow, they will fix rope above the Zemu Icefall. Norbu is a mountain man; he doesn't tire easily. And he gets paid time and a half for overtime. While climbing may be fun for some of you, for Norbu it is just a job. This is how he feeds his family."

Himal wandered inside. He left his muddy paw-prints all over the tent floor, as he made his way over to Pemba, who was standing by the stove and stir-frying Maggi noodles.

Tenzing, drunk on *chaang*, tried to dance with Himal. But the dog seemed more interested in licking scraps off the floor and ignored him.

A few minutes later, Tenzing picked up a guitar and started to sing lines from 'Girlfriend In A Coma' by The Smiths.

Zoe laughed, saying: "Given Jay's condition shouldn't we sing 'Boyfriend In A Coma' instead?"

Then, turning towards me, she winked and said: "Relax, Mowgli, I'm just pulling your leg."

I was surprised to hear Tenzing play anything other than a Bob Marley tune.

I wondered if Zoe's choice of music had begun to influence him.

Night in the mountains came abruptly.

One moment we shielded the glare of the sun with goggles. The next moment there was just the light of stars.

Alienation

After I'd settled into the protective cocoon of my sleeping bag, Himal came inside and curled up like a jungle cat. Before long, he started to snore, softly. In contrast to my tortured breathing, his was even and gentle. I reached a hand out to touch his comforting, wooly body. It never ceased to amaze me how well adapted he was to his mountain home.

———

I could hear the shuffle of footsteps outside my tent. Morning was alighting but I was in no hurry to leave my sleeping bag. Kanchenjunga Base Camp is a place for both dreamers and undertakers. The memory of my father's death, combined with Zoe's desire to scale the mountain, had resulted in my sleep deprivation. The pounding on my temples had subsided but my mouth still felt dry. I had slept poorly.

By the time I stepped out of my tent, the sun was already covered by dark, thundering clouds. Running uphill, I joined the throng of feet, guided by torchlight, that was making its way up to a hillock overlooking Green Lake.

"Hurry, Jay," said Zoe, grabbing my arm. "The lama said it is bad luck to be late to the *puja* ceremony."

My breathless, sleep-deprived body ached with every step.

"I can't believe two years have passed since your father took his last breath, not far from this spot," said Pemba.

"I miss uncle," said Tenzing, as he handed me a ceremonial Sherpa scarf. "I loved the way he would always share his whisky with us, even though we were underage."

Visibility was restricted to a few feet. But I had to keep my eyes half-shut to block the brutal wind.

"Today is an auspicious day for the ceremony," said Lama Pasang, who was waiting for us at the top of the hillock. "Come, let us say a prayer to benefit the dead."

Fistful of Fog

With closed eyes and folded hands, the lama began to chant. Since my Tibetan vocabulary wasn't as good as Tenzing's, I asked him to translate (for Zoe's benefit).

He translated a few phrases from the lama's prayer: "When Baba saw the signs of an untimely death ... in that moment he clearly saw the light of Protector Amitaba, the destroyer of death. May Baba become an immortal knowledge-holder ... and tirelessly following the path to Buddhahood. May he climb the stairway leading to ultimate enlightenment."

After the prayer service, we began to collect large, circular rocks and stacked them on top of one another to form a cairn. Then, Baba's old ice-axe and crampons were placed next to it. These items were soon joined by offerings of Baba's favorite brand of whisky and a packet of his beloved *chanachur* (Indian snack mix). Finally, I placed the ceremonial Sherpa scarf (which Tenzing had given me) on the largest rock.

Facing the cairn, I said silently: "I miss you, Baba, more than ever. I've waited a long time to say goodbye. I'm finally doing it now, on this mountain where you took your last step."

Prayer flags were tied to the cairn but the wind began to scatter them in all directions. The lama lit incense and chanted a hymn for safe passage of Baba's soul into the next life. Tenzing began to sing. Pemba began to dance. My spirits began to lift. The ceremony ended with the lama tossing barley flour towards the heavens and wishing Baba good luck in his next life by saying "Tashi Delek, Baba".

The cairn was Zoe's idea. She had suggested it after learning about Baba's untimely demise on Kanchenjunga. A memorial dedicated to Baba, she said, would help bring closure. I hoped it would be the last cairn I'd build on Kanchenjunga. Sadly, that turned out not to be the case.

Alienation

As we started our descent down to Base Camp, the dark unfriendly clouds covering the mountains unleashed their full fury on us.

The temperature fell rapidly and the sky began to shower dusty, grey ice. A cyclone, which had originated in the Bay of Bengal, had made its way up into the Kanchenjunga valley. And without any warning, as often happens in the Himalayas, the weather turned toxic.

By the time we got inside the safety of the kitchen tent, a crusty layer of blue-gray ice layered the Base Camp grounds.

The wind threatened to blow us off the mountain. We spent the next few hours holed-up inside our tent, trying not to think of all the things that could go wrong.

And when the storm died, the camp radio screeched to life and delivered terrible news from Camp I. Norbu, who had been fixing rope above the Zemu Icefall when the storm had started, had been killed by a dislodged block of ice.

"Let's go help him," said Zoe, getting up and lacing her boots. "Maybe he is still alive. If we bring oxygen over to him maybe we can breathe life back into him. Otherwise, we can at least bring his body down so he is not all alone up there."

She looked at us for an answer but all she received was stunned silence.

"Fine, if no one wants to come with me, I'll go solo. Just show me on the map where he is located," she said.

Typical of Zoe, she didn't hesitate to put her life on the line for a climber she barely knew. The terrible weather conditions didn't faze her; to her they were just a part of nature that needed to be dealt with. Her heart was entwined with the fallen Norbu and it was only after Tenzing explained how much easier it was for climbers at Camp I to bring his body down, rather than anyone from Base Camp journeying up to his corpse, that she sat back down.

Given the loss of a dear friend, plus the resurgence of the monsoon, it was decided the expedition would be postponed until the following spring.

With tearful eyes, Tenzing said: "I wished Kanchenjunga had spared Norbu. He loved the mountain, treading lightly and respectfully. Too bad, the mountain did not love him back."

"Of all the men I have known, I used to think of Norbu as invincible," said Pemba, his characteristically stoic voice cracking-up. "Once, when Norbu felt he was going to die from a high fever, I gave him an aspirin tablet. He had never taken a pill before. All it took for him to get back on his feet was that one tablet. He recovered quickly because his body was unpolluted by pharmaceuticals."

"The only constant in the Himalayas is that nature can go from being your best friend to your worst enemy in a matter of seconds," said Lama Pasang. "Come, let us go and help him prepare him for the final journey. With the slicing of his impermanent flesh, his immortal soul will be set free. And with the consumption of his body, his mortal fears will be consumed. Soon he will sit on the Heavenly Mountain and his soul will rest in peace."

It was decided Norbu's sky burial was going to be held the following morning on a rocky plateau near Green Lake.

Sky burials had been phased out in Sikkim and were now forbidden in most parts of the state. But where the ground was too hard to dig and when wood was too precious to burn for cremation, said Lama Pasang, it was more environmentally benign to continue this ancient Tibetan ritual.

"My stomach feels a little uneasy," said Zoe. "I guess it's because I don't know what to expect at the sky burial tomorrow."

Alienation

"Here, take a sip of this," said Tenzing, handing Zoe a bottle of rum. "It will settle your stomach."

"After the soul leaves there is no point in keeping the body," said the lama. "Norbu's fate has been decided by karma accumulated through past lives. The birds will help complete part of the life-cycle of death and rebirth."

I looked at Kanchenjunga, barely visible through the layer of evening mist. Closing my eyes, I said, silently: "Make sure you never touch Zoe. I will never forgive you if she dies on your icy slopes."

I took Zoe's hand in mine. The chunk of turquoise straddling her ring finger sparkled like a tiny, blue moon.

Putting my arm around her, I said: "What do you think death feels like? You know, the moment before someone dies, what do you think they think of? Do you think they feel fear? Sadness? Relief?"

"I think death is just a big nothing, some sort of a black hole we slip into, which makes our time on earth irrelevant," she said. "Unless you are a rock star and leave some major records behind no one remembers you, once you are gone. Death sucks."

I would reflect on her words the following day, after she would hand the turquoise ring back to me and return to California. Our relationship, like Norbu's life, would be broken. And (after I would evaluate my options) it would become clear I desired only one vision of the future: a life with Zoe. That realization would make me return to California, where I would try to win her back.

131

Part Three:

Six Miserable Months

(November 1990-April 1991)

Chapter 7: Alienation

Hoping San Francisco would become my muse and heal my wounds, I turned to the city.

Every morning I huff-puffed my way up the breath-busting hills and climbed the slanted city streets that led to my workplace. But that unique silver light, which alighted on the pavement between grey fog and golden day, didn't manage to lift my spirits up like it used to.

During lunch, I kept a Kerouac novel visible on the table at a downtown cafeteria which Zoe used to frequent. She had recently started graduate school at USF, so I didn't expect her to visit our old neighborhood haunts often. But, just in case she turned up at the café, I wanted her to see I was reading 'The Dharma Bums' (her "favorite book of all time").

I liked listening to the sound of underground cable lines. During the day, I heard them groan under the weight of packed cable-cars. But in the evening, with cable-cars and streets emptied of tourists, they chirped.

I visited the Misty Maiden Tavern every evening, hoping Zoe stopped-in during happy hour. But no amount of cheap beer could entice her to visit the tavern that month.

Before going to bed I tuned into cricket commentary on BBC radio. The plummy accents of commentators on Test Match Special sometimes helped me fall asleep.

On those nights when I couldn't sleep, I went outside and walked the city streets again.

Every neighborhood in the city was etched with a memory of Zoe.

I went to bars where we used to dance to live bands. But music only worsened my nostalgia.

Fistful of Fog

The most humiliating day of my life started out sunny. But when the head of HR at GreenEarth said the INS had informed her I'd been working on an expired visa, I wanted the absent Pacific fog to reappear and conceal me, and my shame. She gave me an hour to pack my things and leave.

The actions of the INS made me feel alienated from what America offered to its other residents. And I began to wonder if the word – "alienation" – was created by combing the words – "alien" – with the word "nation".

I spent the rest of that morning making phone-calls. Ron had transferred to the Sydney office of his investment bank, Julia had joined a theological seminary in Nashville, and Zoe didn't return any of my voicemails. Having no one else to turn to in San Francisco, I bought a one-way ticket to Darjeeling.

I was getting ready to leave the country when I ran into Zoe's grandfather, Dave, at the farmer's market in UN Plaza. By the time I arrived, the market was winding down. I found him loading empty crates onto an old pickup truck parked at Civic Center.

"Why don't you stay on my farm while you figure things out?" he said, after I told him about my situation. "I have a lot of experience working with undocumented foreigners. And I can use some extra help on the farm right now."

After I climbed into the cab, he started the truck's engine and coaxed the pickup through the ups and downs of San Francisco traffic. When the stop-n-go traffic starting to block the entrance to the interstate, he got off the main road and began driving along a narrow, coastal road. Surfers, bobbing up-n-down like corks on the shimmering Pacific, appeared in the rearview mirror.

A half-hour later, he steered the pickup off the metaled road and onto a winding dirt track. After driving on the dirt track for a few miles he pulled up alongside a sign that said: "Tailwind Organic Farms; Chemical-Free Produce."

Alienation

Although the farm was small compared to the giant corporate fields that surrounded it, it still required a great deal of work, said Dave.

Farm-work seemed to fuel his existence. He drove his pickup from one end of the farm to another, inspecting artichokes one minute, pruning strawberries the next; always accompanied by a chocolate lab, who answered to the name of Frisbee.

For heavy-duty work he relied on Carlos, and Carlos's wife, Bella. They lived in a retrofitted shed on the southern edge of the property. Occasionally, he would hire other migrant farm-workers to lend a hand.

That afternoon, after showing me his herd of grass-fed beef (an obvious source of pride for him), he said: "I hope you like brisket because we are having a barbeque today."

Ignoring my preference for vegetarian fare, I said: "I love beef. Who doesn't?"

"Glad to hear that son because when I first met you last summer I assumed you were vegetarian, like most Indians. But, as I was about to run out and buy salad dressing, Zoe informed me you were from the Himalayas. And I stopped worrying. Love them big mountains," he said, in a warm voice which put me immediately at ease. "Are you a Sherpa? There are no better people on the planet. I owe my life to one."

I wanted him to think of me as a Sherpa, so I said: "Yeah, I'm from Darjeeling. Lots of Sherpas in my hometown."

"I wouldn't have survived a fall on Dhaulagiri had it not been for a Sherpa named Mingyar, who carried me on his back down to Base Camp. My climbing days ended after that fall but my love for those big mountains lives on. I taught both Zoe and her mother how to climb but now I live vicariously through Zoe alone. I'm thrilled she has summited Denali and Aconcagua but I'm waiting for the day she adds Kanchenjunga to that list. She is the best climber I've seen, even better than her mother, God rest her soul."

With a callused finger he wiped a stray tear which had begun to trickle down his cheek.

"Have you heard from Zoe?" I said, putting-on a nonchalant tone and trying not to sound too needy. "I left her a few voicemails but she hasn't returned any of my calls."

"She left for Cusco last week. She is training in the Andes over winter break," he said. "Too bad you guys broke-up. I was looking forward to welcoming a Sherpa son-in-law into the family."

His words made me feel welcome on the farm but I was disappointed to hear Zoe was going to be out of the country for a while.

We were removing weeds from the artichoke beds when the roar of a jumbo jet, hovering above the fields like a killer whale, shattered the quiet.

Dave looked heavenward at the intruder and shook his head in disapproval.

Walking over to the pickup parked nearby, he fiddled with the knobs on the vintage radio until a Grateful Dead song started to play.

Soon the words – "I will get by ... I will survive" – left the truck's radio and floated out into the afternoon air. But the song failed to cover up the noise from the jet.

"It's way off its flight path. I hate it when SFO puts them on this stupid holding pattern," he said, looking skyward.

"So loud? *Por que*? No manners!" said Bella. "Soon there will be no farm; just freeways and *aeropuertos*."

"That's for goddamn sure," he said. "You know, when we started out at the Farm, SFO felt far away. But now, with all this crazy expansion who knows where it will end up?"

Alienation

The jumbo, having blown smoke circles around the Bay, thrust its carriage wheels out like a set of erupting appendices and faded from view.

After we were done laying down a layer of composted leaves and grass clippings over the weeded beds, Dave walked over to the truck, placed his trowel down on the flatbed of the pickup, and said: "Come on guys, let's take a break."

Removing weeds by hand was tedious work. I was glad to get a breather. Dave passed out cans of lukewarm ice-tea. We sat under an oak tree, adjacent to the beds, and drank ice-tea.

Just as silence was finally settling on the farm, a voice on the radio interrupted, saying: "Gol. Goooooooollll. Gol."

Carlos must have fiddled with the dials on the truck's radio for Spanish language soccer commentary, in a voice alternating between melodramatic and hysterical, was now spilling out of the old pickup.

"What a racket," said Dave. "Can you turn it down a bit?"

"That commentator famous, *señor*," said Carlos, lighting up a cigarillo. "He get big money the way he say 'gol'."

"Who's playing anyway?" said Dave.

"Mexico and Honduras. Revenge match. Those *putas* need a lesson!"

"Give me football any day," said Dave. "This soccer thing just doesn't cut it for me."

The wind started to whistle through the tree's branches. Bella put on her sweatshirt and drew Frisbee close to her chest.

A streak of lightning, accompanied by a drum-roll of thunder, turned the sky into an acoustic gargoyle.

"They have a saying in the Himalayas," I said. "Bad storms mean good dreams."

A few minutes later, the sun staged a comeback through the curdling clouds. Rain was put on hold temporarily as an indistinct rainbow lit up the evening sky with a partial promise of sunshine.

"I saw Hal here this morning, *señor*," said Carlos. "Is everything all right?" (Hal managed a neighboring farm for a consortium headquartered in St. Louis).

"Real-estate prices are sky-rocketing, so Hal decided to pay us a visit," said Dave. "He made a mind-blowing offer but I told him this farm is not for sale."

"No wonder he looked mad; good for you, *señor*," said Bella.

"I must admit I was tempted by his offer," said Dave. "Who knows, someday I may sell this place and move up North. By Eugene, where the hills are greener and people less caught up in this moolah-making frenzy. This place used to be acres of rolling hills with an occasional farmhouse pausing the monotone. And now, look at it. We're constantly fighting those high-tech start-ups for space. I hate computers. Why can't we live the way Thoreau did at Walden?"

Before anyone could respond, the radio, suddenly coming to life, started to wail: "Gol. Gooooooooolll. Gol."

"Turn that down please, Carlos," said Dave. "You can turn it back up again, later. C'mon guys, let's pick it back up. We need to get all of these beds composted by tomorrow."

"We go to Santa Cruz *mañana*, *señor*," said Carlos. "Those *inmigracion* officials are at it again. They are coming to check work permits tomorrow. We'll go hide in mountain like last time. We camp with our cousin, Ramón."

"That's a drag. Specially now. The last time you ran away into the hills, we didn't see you for a week. Can't have that again. Let those goons come. I'll tell them what a fine job you are doing and insist they leave you alone. I pay my taxes; they better listen to me!" said Dave, animatedly.

"Those *putas* no listen," said Carlos. "No permit, then they ship us back to Mexico. My cousin Ramón say those *putas* are getting smarter. We have to be careful."

"What about all those computer geeks from Asia who've camped out in the Valley?" said Dave. "Is anyone checking their permits? They got off the boat a lot later than you guys."

"*Si, señor.* But those *putas* no listen. They forget California used to belong Mexico," said Carlos, pausing to spit cigarillo butt out from between his fractured teeth. "Last time they look for us many days. But they no find. But this time—"

"How would they know to look here?" said Dave.

"*Como?* Oh, they saw me at Miguel's restaurant last week. Got suspicious. Asked me all sort of questions," said Carlos.

"That sucks," said Dave. "You guys are needed on the farm more than most. The borders of our world are so screwed up."

Dave used a free hand to reposition his straw hat, angled to keep the sun from entering his eyes. Then, turning to me, he used a line from a Bob Marley song and said: "And how about you, bad boy? Whatcha gonna do when they come for you?"

I flew to New Jersey to see Mr. Jacob, the attorney who had executed my father's will. His office was situated on the second floor of a rundown office building in Princeton, not far from the cemetery on Greenview Avenue.

"Can you please help me get a green card? You are the only connection I have to my father's life," I said. "I hope you still in touch with Angela. She must have my father's papers."

He was a tall balding man with stooping shoulders and a boxed beard. After asking his secretary to get me a cup of tea, he said: "Your father wouldn't have left your mother if he hadn't fallen in love with Angela. He told me his marriage to your mother had been arranged purely to fulfil familial obligations. Angela was younger than him but she shared his passion for *Hatha* yoga. It is unfortunate you and your mother had to suffer the consequences of his elopement but it is not my role to judge my client's morals."

A wave of sympathy for Ma forced its way up my throat and dried-up my mouth, making me take a sip from the teacup.

"Everything went fine for the first few years," he said. "Then Angela left your father and he fell to pieces."

An image of my father scratching his yellowy skin and cracking it up into a thousand tiny pieces, as the winter of his life descended on him, entered my brain.

I tried, unsuccessfully, to keep a tear from rolling down my cheek.

Mr. Jacob forwarded me a box of tissue. Then, he continued: "A few months before he passed away, your dad showed up at my office. He sat in the same chair where you are sitting today and asked me to draft his will. He had tried to reinvent himself but without an American college degree he didn't have much success here. He wanted you to go to college in the U.S. so you could have a better life than he did."

He paused to answer the phone, which had started to ring.

"I'm sorry but I have to run now," he said, after he had hung up the phone. "That was my wife. She needs me to pick up candles for the Shabbat dinner she is hosting tonight. Don't worry, son, I'll provide you with an affidavit outlining your relationship to your father. That should help you get a green card. But you need to return to Darjeeling immediately. Don't let the INS catch you staying here illegally because then they will deport you and you won't be able to come back."

The next morning, as I drove on the twisting back roads, south of Princeton, I could see why my father had settled here.

New Jersey, away from the grime of the turn-pike, looked gorgeous: fields of fragrant herbs scenting the morning air; wings of colorful mallards unzipping the summer sky; dedicated varsity rowers caressing the Delaware River with gentle paddle strokes.

I wondered how different my life would have been had I lived here with my father. Would it have been better or worse than Darjeeling? And would it have made Zoe look at me with different eyes?

Alienation

When I got to the cemetery it took me a while to locate my father's grave. Only after I scraped the stubborn mold off the tombstone could I decipher his name on the epitaph. It read: "Here lies a butterfly that flew from a distant shore; charmed us briefly until heaven knocked on his door".

Afterwards, as I drove towards Newark airport, I noticed the malls and condos had reappeared, as had the poisonous refinery smoke, which garlanded the turn-pike. There were no mountains or trees to be seen anywhere on the horizon. The landscape was overrun by concrete flatlands, built over a few dabs of struggling grass – nature entombed in an endless asphalt mausoleum.

I was overcome with a heavy, heart-wrenching sadness.

As evening receded into the dark abyss of the Tenderloin, and the assorted homeless fought each other for possession of precious footpath real-estate, I finished my dinner at the 'Flavors of Himalaya' restaurant on Turk Street.

The restaurant wasn't fancy. But the steamed *momo*s here always packed a juicy mouthful. And the spicy dipping sauce never failed to induce tears of familiar comfort.

As I started the slow, lonely walk back towards my apartment, a poster that caught my attention. Nine Inch Nails was playing at The Warfield that night.

I wondered if Zoe was attending the concert.

The lights from the downtown skyscrapers bobbed in and out of the late-night mist as I walked into The Warfield.

By the time I pushed and shoved my way up to the dance floor, Trent Reznor was singing the last song ('Head Like a Hole') from his setlist.

It was the same song Zoe and I had slam-danced to at the I-Beam, nine months earlier.

143

Fistful of Fog

    A tall girl sporting an "Om" symbol tattooed in Sanskrit alphabet on her cheek stood next to me. From the way she was moving, in slow motion and completely out-of-synch with the band's beat, I guessed she was high on a mish-mash of drugs.
    I stood on my tippy-toes and looked for Zoe but I couldn't locate her on the dance floor. I made my way over to the bar. She wasn't there. I ran upstairs. And then downstairs.
    I combed the entirety of the historic music hall, as I looked to remake the history of my love life.
    Then, just before the band was finishing up for the night, I saw her standing in line outside the restroom. Although her back was facing me, I could tell from the partially visible logo that she was wearing a Dominican University sweatshirt.
    I wished she hadn't cut her hair short. I used to love its fullness; its shiny, bouncy pizazz, the first sighting of which had triggered an incurable addiction to blondes for a Bengali boy (a.k.a. me) unaccustomed to seeing fair hair.
    But it wasn't the shortness of her mane I had a problem with that night. My issue was that she was kissing a man. The sight of his long, blonde dreadlocks birthed a miserable, jealous monster inside of me. And even before I saw his face, as he came up for air after a long kiss, I knew it was Hayden.
    The sight of them made me nauseous but, like an animal staring at a hunter's torch, I couldn't look away. Not wanting to be recognized, I pulled my sweatshirt over my head. But it was too late. I saw him whispering into Zoe's ear.
    When she turned to look towards me, I ran.
    Fighting the exodus of people moving in the opposite direction, I hastily exited through a side-entrance. As I stepped into the still foggy night, I felt the music in my life fading into silence. Not the good meditative kind of quiet but the terrifying stillness of loss.

Alienation

As Valentine's Day approached, the dreaded claws of loneliness began to scratch inside my mind again.

The best way to forget a girl, said Ron, was by sleeping with someone else. Seeing her with Hayden had been the final straw for me. I decided to erase Zoe from my mind.

With my feet aching with quiet desperation, I rummaged through the hills of San Francisco and began to look for a new love. I approached tourists in cable-cars and flirted with off-duty stewardesses at hotel bars. But no one seemed inclined to start any sort of relationship with me. I even signed up as a volunteer at the Asian Art Museum but the docents there sought a level of sophistication I just couldn't fake. I hit my lowest point while riding the cable-car when a man with sagging jowls asked me to come home with him. Even as I told him I wasn't into guys, I wondered if I would ever again find the kind of love I'd once experienced with Zoe.

Loneliness drove me to an 'Evening of Rabindra Sangeet', hosted by the Bengali Society of San Francisco. The event was being held at a music hall near Van Ness Avenue. It featured a well-known male singer, who was visiting from Calcutta. According to the program, the evening's setlist featured only songs of Rabindranath Tagore, my favorite poet.

I had paid extra to attend a cocktail reception after the show. But everyone must have had the same idea for the event was packed with patrons. A large number of single Indian men, mostly young engineers who worked in Silicon Valley, converged on the lone Caucasian girl at the reception.

She was the only one in the gathering whose hair wasn't dark but blonde, a color I'd begun to associate with love (after meeting Zoe). And she wasn't dressed in a staid dress but in a vibrant Murshidabadi silk sari, which gave me hope that there might be a colorful soul hidden between those silken folds.

It took me a while to break through the herd and start a conversation with her. She talked while she grazed, using her perfectly proportional teeth to crunch on crispy *samosas*.

Fistful of Fog

Her name was Sofie. She was pursuing a graduate program in South Asian Studies at UC Berkeley. She was an international student from Holland and had spent the previous semester in Calcutta, researching the love poems of Tagore.

She spoke English in throaty, hesitant sentences. The struggle of vowels inside the depths of her throat excited me tremendously. My English was not much better than hers but when I offered to help with her ESL assignments she rewarded me with a hypnotizing smile.

To help her deal with a painful divorce, she had recently begun to practice Buddhism. And when I discovered we admired the same Dharma Teacher at the Zen Center, I suggested we sign-up for that teacher's Vipassana course.

She had a slender frame; boyish everywhere except at the hips, wide and meaty. I wondered if she had experienced childbirth. And, unlike many of the smooth legs strutting around San Francisco in high heels, hers were unshaven and encased in short socks and flat Birkenstocks.

("Homely but will do if in a pinch," was how Ron described her the next morning. He was visiting from Sydney and staying in my apartment that week).

Her face hinted at one too many seasons spent outdoors. Despite her attempts to hide the beginnings of her laugh lines behind oversized sunglasses, no one asked for her ID at the reception that evening.

I felt good vibes emanating from her. When the reception ended, I invited her to come with me to the Misty Maiden Tavern. Given our obvious age difference, I was surprised when she accepted my invitation.

After the tavern closed, she said she didn't want to risk a DUI by driving back to Berkeley. And she asked me if she could spend the night in my apartment.

My walk back to my apartment building had less the swagger of a triumphant victory march and more the tired limp of an obligatory service that was underway.

Alienation

It was almost dawn by the time we got near my building but a family of tourists was lining up to take photos of Crooked Street. It never ceases to amaze me that there is not an hour that goes by in San Francisco, when some tourist is not taking a photo of some city landmark somewhere.

Once we got inside my room, Sofie hurriedly took her clothes off and jumped straight into my bed. A few seconds later, we were naked and entwined in each other's arms.

As we turned and twisted, and wrestled with positions that would minimize the hair on my legs tangling up with the hair on hers, I wondered whether we would find a stance that would work for both. But before we could resolve that issue, I caught Sofie looking at me with maternal eyes. An image of my mother flashed quickly before my eyes and I lost my erection.

I moved my eyes away from Sofie's face and aimed downwards, towards her breasts, as I tried to regain my erection. But my mind started to wander. Now that her jeans had come off, did her hips look larger? She hadn't mentioned a child but did she have one with her ex-husband? And where was that child now?

I closed my eyes and tried to think sexy thoughts but I heard Ma's voice saying: "*Chi-chi*, how can you do this with a woman old enough to be your mother? Your soul will burn in hell."

I panicked and opened my eyes. Sofie's eyes were closed but her legs were open.

"Please hurry, I need to leave for Berkeley soon," she said.

I closed my eyes again and tried to channel leggy porn stars. But that didn't work. So, I turned my thoughts to Zoe.

I forced my brain to replay an image of Zoe's long tanned legs spinning around in mad circles to the music of Sonic Youth as her flaming hair sent waves of light shimmering through Forest Meadows during dance-night. After replaying that vision a few times in my head, I was able to regain my erection.

Fistful of Fog

It wasn't the best of orgasms for me but when Sofie was finished I uttered a silent sigh of relief. She had been my first sexual partner since Zoe. I'd thought a sexual encounter with another girl would help erase Zoe from my mind. But now I felt more miserable than before.

That evening of disappointing sex ushered in a serious gloom. Did my unsatisfactory tryst with Sofie signify I still harbored strong feelings for Zoe? And would I ever enjoy sex with another girl the way I once had with Zoe?

I was still feeling awful when I went jogging in the Presidio the next morning. It was a beautiful day with fog dancing on the trail and sunlight flirting on tree-tops.

After I finished my run, I picked a few blackberries from a wild bush close to the trail. The berries tasted like spring, with a hint of newness and a dash of tartness. At first, I enjoyed the way the seeds stuck inside my mouth: in between my teeth; to my gums; on my tongue. Then, when I couldn't spit them out without inserting my fingers inside my mouth and scraping them off, they left a sour taste.

I decided to return to Darjeeling.

Life is made up of different emotional threads strung into one messy bundle, my father had once said. For two people to fall in love their dream threads must connect. Threads formed during a puritanical childhood are the most difficult to deal with. Pull too hard at a few of these guilt threads and life comes apart. Tie too many of these strict ends together and life becomes a noose.

The threads of my life began to unravel when an immigration official at San Francisco Airport stamped my passport with an inky blue sign that read – "deported".

Was God punishing me for breaking my vows? Or was it because (after meeting Zoe) I'd stopped praying?

Alienation

That old familiar feeling of guilt began to resurrect itself.

I had treated my emotional threads as if they ran through parallel lives, with distinct boundaries between them. So, I had kept my Darjeeling past separate from my life with Zoe. But now that my past had caught up with my present, and I felt alienated from both, I realized these threads were interconnected in my circle of life.

"Does this mean I can never return to the U.S. again?" I said, in a shrill, panicked voice.

"I don't know," said the official, tapping the keys on her computer with rhythmic precision. "You shouldn't have overstayed your visa. Before we let you go, we need to ask you a few questions and make some additional background checks."

"But I'm in love with a girl who lives here," I said, desperation and guilt transforming my face into a strange mixture of defiance and fear. "Whatever you do, please make sure I'm able to come back here. I'm sure you been in love, you must understand."

But the official did not relent. After punching a few more keys on her computer, followed by a phone call, her colleague escorted me out of the airport. A few minutes later, a police car transported me to a detention cell, near the airport.

That evening, I sat alone in my cell, located in the great western city of San Francisco – where technology ruled, and destiny was self-made – and I wondered if I would ever be able to control my fate.

My cell was painted a bright shade of white but it felt soulless. I sat on a chair facing the window and peered outside. The darkness outside was thick, like sediment trapped at the bottom of a pond. Occasionally, the darkness glowed as the landing lights of an airplane chiseled a moving luminescent strip into the heavy motionless night. The action on the flight path was slowing down. From the height of the moon in the night sky, I guessed it was around midnight.

Fistful of Fog

In a few hours, I would leave this cell and start my journey back east to my birthplace, half a globe away. To an ancient land, where the great Himalayas separated the hot plains from the cold plateaus, and where tradition dictated that destiny be pre-ordained. A place whose only similarity to San Francisco was that its landscape was painted with the same dual brush-strokes of sun and fog.

I loved both places but why did my history have to be so complicated?

17 months earlier, I had started my journey to America from the Himalayas, a place where change happened slowly. So slowly that in a monastery tucked away 10,000 feet above the frenzied plains, I had once been summoned by a lama to come and change a light bulb. I was the only one who could do it, said the lama, because everyone else was afraid of electricity, which had just arrived in the village.

Family and friends had journeyed with me to Calcutta, where I was planning to board the plane bound for San Francisco. I confided to my uncle, Kaku, that I felt a bit nervous. After all, I told Kaku, I'd never been on an airplane, or used a soda machine, or taken cash out from an ATM, or experienced any of those other wonderful shiny gadgets which I'd seen photographed in every U.S. university brochure.

On our way over to the airport, Kaku took me to see the escalator at the Metro station. It had been installed a few years prior but I had never used it. Calcutta was in the throes of a wave of power-cuts and load-shedding had rendered the escalator immobile that day. But Kaku showed me how to walk up and down the stationary escalator until I got a feel for how my feet would move on the steely staircase.

Many people had come to see me off at the airport. There were lots of garlands, food packed in tiffin-carriers, last-minute gifts. And a few tears, shed by my mother.

After I landed at San Francisco airport and saw a moving escalator for the first time, I was surprised to find that my hands had gotten a bit clammy.

Alienation

I waited and observed how people got on and off the escalator. Then I stepped on the machine gingerly, as if I was stepping on quicksand. I panicked when my suitcase wouldn't come off at the end of the ride but I managed to yank it off at the last second with a huge heave.

And now, a year later, I sat in my detention cell and stared at an old photograph of Zoe. The photo had been extracted from that same suitcase which I'd carried with me on that first trip to California. But the suitcase was no longer new; its edges were bruised; and its fabric was coming apart at the seams.

In the dim light of the night-lamp, I stared at the photo. It was shot in the dual colors of a departed era – black and white. Dressed in well-worn hiking boots and a shiny 'Sonic Youth' T-shirt, the photo displayed Zoe posing on top of Twin Peaks. Parts of the photo seemed to be fading, like my relationship with her.

I dreaded the night would soon end. And then I would have to board an airplane which would fly me across many high seas and over many high mountains before depositing me back to my lonely, single state.

I got down on my knees and prayed: "I know You are punishing me for my past sins but if You can find it in your heart to forgive me and reunite me with Zoe, dear God, I promise I will never cross You again."

Clutching my passport, I rode an airport escalator the following morning.

Moving a half-step ahead of the immigration official (who had escorted me from my detention cell to the airport), I looked closely at the escalator.

It was the same escalator I'd encountered 17 months earlier but it had lost its shine and it was scratched in several places.

Chapter 8: Homecoming

A 6-hour drive from Darjeeling, the Subirpur Wildlife Sanctuary was located on the banks of the Sheelanadi, a subtropical river that originated near the glaciers of Kanchenjunga.

The Subirpur Conservancy, a non-profit organization, was charged with managing the sanctuary, spread over 300 square miles of grassy jungle, with elevations ranging from 540 feet to 4,908 feet. The sanctuary used to be the former hunting grounds of the Maharaja of Subirpur. Shrinking forest cover as well as hunting and poaching had decimated tigers to below endangered levels. Conservationists, opposed by politicians incensed at the loss of timber revenues, had finally won the battle, enabling them to declare the reserve as protected.

Successful re-introduction of tigers bred in captivity had significantly boosted their population in the sanctuary. But poachers had made a recent comeback. Tigers had been hunted to the point where they were rarely seen in the sanctuary. And rhinos, once numbering in the hundreds, had dropped down to less than a dozen. Rhino horns were prized for their aphrodisiac and curative properties since the days of Marco Polo who, legend said, had once mistakenly identified the rhinoceros as a unicorn. During my first few jungle days, made miserable by Zoe's absence, I often wished for a unicorn to magically appear and close the distance between us.

By the time I arrived at the Conservancy's forest bungalow, situated on a hill-top near the northern entrance to the sanctuary, the tender green brought on by the last monsoon had matriculated into jungle grass tall enough to hide an elephant.

One morning, I discovered a three-foot monitor lizard in my closet and panicked. Unseasonal, storm showers had washed the reptile out of its jungle hole. Harboring no desire to share my bedroom with a reptile, I had the bungalow fumigated.

The giant lizard left my closet and made a new home on a banyan tree branch across from my bedroom window. A family of monkeys that lived on the tree screeched relentlessly at the lizard but the reptile didn't budge. The monkeys were forced to move up a few branches higher. Rain had forced prey to reluctantly share home with predator.

During my first week at the sanctuary, it rained every day. Heat made way for humidity. Roads became rivers and these new tributaries flowed into the Sheelanadi, which ran through the middle of the sanctuary. And the Sheelanadi, in return, overflowed its muddy bounty back into the forest.

During those initial weeks in the jungle, I would endeavor to capture the turbulent Sheelanadi on a drawing-pad. Assisted by a pencil, a paintbrush, and a few tubes of water-color, I would sit on the balcony of the bungalow and paint the river at different times of the day. My mood would change to reflect the constantly changing river: raging during the rains; pensive in the evening; lethargic during the middle of the day. While sketching the swollen river, I often wondered if my life would ever rise above the flood-waters of loneliness unleashed by my separation from Zoe.

The only permanence, in the middle of this constantly changing jungle landscape was Kanchenjunga, whose distant peak was sometimes visible on clear days from the balcony of the bungalow. On those days when the mountain showed its icy face, I made sure to not sit outside. There was nothing I wanted to see less of than that giant cold slab of killer rock.

When the rain departed, the heat returned and the humidity sapped the life-force out of everyone. It became so unbearable that time seemed to stop moving between the mid-day hours. Nothing ever got done; no amount of shade or sun-tan lotion could protect anyone during those hours.

Homecoming

Joseph (a tribal man who had been assigned to me as an attendant) and I worked primarily after sun-fall. He worked cheerfully and tirelessly, often doing double-duty as cook and animal-tracker.

Without his rustic companionship my jungle stay would have been intolerable.

Our work involved attaching radio-collars on tigers and tracking their movements. We hadn't caught a poacher yet but I couldn't wait to get my hands on one.

Tribal people had been living in this jungle since prehistoric times. They were the original inhabitants of this land. Most still hunted with bow and arrow. They lived off of the forest, only taking what they needed. Some had tried to live in cities but most had eventually returned, saying they could not survive anywhere but here. They spoke Ongthali, an Austroasiatic language that predated the arrival of Hinduism on the subcontinent.

Since the beginning of recorded history, tribals had been racially persecuted by every group of sub-continental invaders (including my Aryan ancestors). Their plight reminded me of the terrible suffering of African Americans in the U.S. And it highlighted the issue of race as an often insurmountable barrier in relationships.

The difference in skin color between Joseph (black) and me (brown) was as striking as the difference in skin color between me and Zoe (cream). Now that she and I were no longer a couple, I sometimes consoled myself that maybe our break-up was for the best because our respective families would have had a hard time accepting our racial, cultural, and religious differences.

Many tribals followed an animistic religion revolving around sacrifices to please various gods. To my critical mind, tribal faith stemmed primarily from superstitious belief, so I had a hard time accepting the validity of their religion.

Fistful of Fog

If you had asked Zoe's opinion about my religious practices, she would likely have expressed similar sentiments about my beliefs. So, who was I to pass judgement on their tribal beliefs? Was the animism practiced by them any worse than the Hindu traditions practiced by my family or any better than Zoe's enduring belief in atheism? In the months Zoe and I had spent together, we had been unable to reconcile our religious differences. So, who was I to think that, after just a few weeks in the jungle, I could address questions pertaining to the difference between my religion and that practiced by the tribals?

Some tribals, lured by economic enticements, had been recently converted to Christianity by missionaries. Resentment against conversions, including veiled death-threats from local priests, was growing.

What wasn't growing here was money; after the opulence of San Francisco I found the poverty here sobering.

Living in Subirpur made me starkly aware of the differences between Zoe's rich homeland and my poverty-stricken one. And it made me wonder if she were to ever live in my homeland would she be able to adjust to living in India, like I had to in America?

―

Early one morning, a wild dog that often scavenged outside our bungalow dragged in a half-eaten human head.

Joseph said the head used to belong to Sarah, a young tribal woman, who had recently passed away. After being diagnosed with leprosy, she had been ostracized by her family, who lived on the outskirts of the sanctuary. She had not left behind enough money to ensure a proper burial. And the recent rain had made it easy for scavengers to dig up her body.

Homecoming

After I paid for a coffin, Joseph recruited four tribal men. They helped us bury her remains inside a limestone pit, located on the left bank of the Sheelanadi.

As I caught one last look at her partially-eaten face, a vision of vultures feasting on Norbu's eyes (during his sky burial) flashed through my brain. I pulled my eyes away from her coffin and looked up. I couldn't see any vultures but soaring in the distance was Kanchenjunga, its summit deathly-white against a background of clear, tropical sky.

"Sarah was only 21," said Joseph. "Her entire life she lived in this forest and helped this community but her disease made everyone around here act like she didn't exist."

"Let's host a memorial service and make sure she is not forgotten," I said.

Sarah's memorial service was conducted by Father Ian, a missionary with the weather-damaged look of a middle-aged English man surviving the tropics on faith and whisky.

After the service, he placed a candle on a boat stitched out of banana-leaves and set it afloat on the Sheelanadi.

We watched it meander its way downstream for a few yards, before the life-force of the river extinguished the candle.

As soon as I got back to the bungalow, I called my mother and told her how much I missed her.

"Jayanta," she said. "I've been thinking about you. It must be hard living in the jungle. You should come back to Darjeeling and enjoy the comforts of home cooking."

"I will come home soon, Ma," I said. "But I need to save a few tigers first."

In the evening, when the heat let-up a bit, I would sometimes drive the jeep deep into the forest and look for signs of poachers.

Fistful of Fog

Usually, it was difficult to spot anything in the tall grass but one night I chanced upon a young tigress wading through the Sheelanadi. She appeared like a furry galleon, sailing silently through the darkness. I sat silently in the jeep. Using my infrared binoculars, I peered at her until she moved out of sight.

After dark, crickets clamored and lightning bugs shimmered through the syrupy air, thick with humidity. The bungalow was often without electricity (because of load-shedding). Most nights, I tossed and turned on the moist sheets.

I missed the cool of San Francisco. I tried not to think of Zoe: jogging through the morning fog on Baker Beach; chugging down pitchers of brain-freeze beer after a softball game in Golden Gate Park; tossing a snowball at me after she finished a snowboarding run on the slopes of Heavenly Mountain Resort near Lake Tahoe. Nothing seemed further away from this jungle than San Francisco.

The road climbed through forests of Sal and Rosewood, up red-blue hills, and into denser woods of eucalyptus and bamboo. After a few miles, the dark canopy of trees gave way to a grassy clearing on the banks of the river, stretching like a muddy rope through the grassland, with innumerous tributaries spawned by the recent rain thickening its girth as it advanced downstream.

The eucalyptus trees reminded me of the ones growing in the Presidio of San Francisco. I suppressed a wave of nostalgia that mushroomed out of nowhere. The Presidio this wasn't, that was for sure!

As we charted our way through the jungle, the sun cooked any piece of exposed skin. I hated the discomforts and dangers of the jungle: its unbearable heat and humidity; venomous creatures crawling everywhere; and the lack of a reliable source of electricity.

Homecoming

What was I doing with my life? And who was I kidding by playing the role of a conservationist? Was this my true passion? Shouldn't I be pursuing the only vocation that mattered to me: art? But did I want to risk become a struggling artist and leading a life of poverty?

Despite the inconveniences of working in this uncomfortable jungle, the job at the sanctuary guaranteed a steady pay-check. And that, for now, would have to do – I rationalized to myself.

My high school had been filled with rich kids, who reveled in showing off their wealth. One bright winter morning spent smoking cigarette butts behind the school dumpster, a wealthy classmate offered to hand-me-down his blazer. He had noticed that mine showed less wool and more daylight, which was filtering through my jacket's threadbare patches. That day, I vowed to make sure I made decent money when I grew up, so no one would treat me like a kid on welfare.

While growing up, I used to hate living in our decrepit neighborhood. Often there was no electricity and roads had potholes so deep that they sometimes doubled as manholes during the monsoon and spewed sewage back onto the street.

When I was in tenth grade, Baba mailed me photos of his big house in New Jersey and of highways wider than any river I'd seen. The best part of America, he wrote in a letter, was that there they never ran out of Coca Cola, electricity or gasoline. Once I tasted American coke, I didn't care for the taste of any of the local colas anymore.

"We now in core area, sahib," announced Joseph, jolting me back to the present as he brought the jeep to a sudden halt on the banks of the Sheelanadi.

He leapt out to inspect, what looked like, paw-prints. Taking a twisted piece of string from his jacket pocket, he measured the diameter of the prints. I followed him as he made his way up the muddy tracks into a grassy area upstream. Beads of sweat lined his brow as he swatted mosquitoes, which attacked the skin exposed below his khaki shorts.

Fistful of Fog

Dry leaves crackled beneath our feet as we made our way up the path.

The dirt path soon disappeared into the elephant grass, which lined the mouth of the coffee-colored river. Strategically placed on the banks of the stream were two watch-towers, called *machans*.

These *machans*, standing on spindly bamboo poles, functioned as viewing platforms. They were camouflaged with eucalyptus branches and made to look like a tree.

Joseph and I climbed on-board the near-sided tower.

"I hope at least one tiger will come there for a drink," said Joseph, pointing to a riverine location by raising his arms, blissfully unaware of the assault he launched on my nose every time his deodorant-free armpits were exposed. "They sleep through heat of day and then come here at night."

"What about the other streams?" I said.

"Tigers prefer this one because it has less crocodiles," he said.

"So, we will not be taking a dip before dinner then, eh?" I said, jokingly.

Joseph didn't laugh. Instead, he put a finger to his lip and motioned me to be silent.

We used hand signals until visibility declined and stillness reigned.

Balmy shadows lengthened and then disappeared into the darkness. He took out his infra-red binoculars and peered into the blackness.

The night sky turned into a star-spangled quilt.

I had felt relatively safe in the forest during the day but now I had an eerie feeling of being watched.

Flashing my torch into the undergrowth, I squinted for evidence of glowing eyes.

Unable to find any signs of animal presence, I settled back into an uncomfortable squatting position.

A few minutes later, I returned to my favorite jungle pastime of wallowing in nostalgic thought. Trying to bring back lost time, I replayed in my mind those precious and fantastic moments I'd spent with Zoe over the last 18 months. Then, I attempted to permanently etch those precious memories, which now seemed like a mirage, deep inside my brain.

As we drove back to the bungalow, electric tongues of lightning lit up the tinderbox of a sky. Rain began to thunder down. The air began to smell new again, as if someone had sprayed a giant can of freshener.

The telephone was ringing when I entered the forest bungalow. I picked up the old-fashioned handset.

"Your mother is in the hospital," said Kaku, on the phone.

"What happened?" I said, panic creeping into my voice and making it squeak, like the static across the telephone wires.

"At first, we thought it was because of her heartburn, from the large plate of chili *pakoras* she had for dinner last night. But when we took her to the hospital the doctor confirmed she had suffered a heart attack," he said.

I had broken her heart. Guilt erupted all over me like an invisible rash.

After calling my supervisor and telling her I was taking an extended leave of absence from work, I drove to Darjeeling.

When I got to the hospital, I knelt by my mother's bedside and said: "I'm sorry, Ma."

"The doctor said I may not live much longer," said Ma, her voice sounding woozy from the effects of medication, a stack of which stood next to her bed. "So, promise me you will marry soon. Nothing will please me more than having a grandson."

After reaching over to wipe a silent tear rolling down her chin, I said: "I promise."

Fistful of Fog

After she fell asleep, I went outside.

It was a clear night with a pinkish moon shining on the south face of Kanchenjunga.

I sat enjoying the quiet nocturnal landscape for a few minutes before the silence was disrupted by the unforgiving sound of a walking stick, scraping against the cement floor of the hospital's porch.

I turned around. It was Kaku.

"You did the right thing," he said. "You've made your Ma very happy."

After returning to India, the vast differences (in race, religion and nationality) between Zoe and me became more obvious to me. These differences (combined with the fact that she had broken up with me and I had no way of returning to her homeland) made me agree to Ma's proposal.

Soon, I would regret my decision.

But that night, with the Himalayan moon shining on my conscience and memories from my glorious California summer with Zoe fading, I made a confused and hasty compromise.

As the U.S. was finalizing martial plans against Iraq, I found myself making marital peace with my mother. She had just returned home from the hospital. And Kaku warned me to not do anything that could antagonize her heart.

"You will like Rita," said Ma. "She wears jeans and keeps her hair short, like those American girls you admire. And she just got her degree from Loreto College in Calcutta, so her English is better than yours. But she is a *Kulin* Brahmin. And her father owns one of the largest tea estates in Darjeeling. The head-priest at the Shiva temple has assured me your stars are perfectly aligned."

Homecoming

A few days later, I found myself at the Sherpa Bar in Darjeeling, waiting for Rita to show up. And when she did, I looked hard but I couldn't find any show-stoppers.

I could see why Ma had chosen Rita – she had all the characteristics that allowed Ma to check off her prerequisites for marital suitability: amber complexion, which passes for 'fair skin' in India; no perm or coloring in her hair, which fell straight down to her waist like a black velvety drape; no visible tattoos; she was skilled at reciting Tagore; and she could play the sitar.

From my perspective, I was impressed that Rita: smelt less of coconut oil and more of complexion-lightening creams; knew the lyrics to 'True Faith' by New Order; was an expert at mixing cocktails (a handy skill to have amongst members of the Darjeeling club circuit elite).

Her arm showcased a long rubbery scar, which snaked around in the dim light of the bar as she stirred, vigorously, her second glass of gin and tonic that evening. The scar had been acquired during a childhood tree climbing misadventure, she said. And it ran counter to what was expected behavior from a typical Brahmin girl, which pleased me.

"I want to make a few things clear," Rita said, as she continued to stir her drink with a straw. "First, I'm not a virgin. Second, I want to work after marriage. So, if you are one of those Darjeeling boys looking for a virginal housewife, then I'm definitely not your girl."

Had Darjeeling changed in my absence?

Or had I become more open-minded during my time abroad?

Regardless, I liked Rita's attitude and her aspirations.

Was that because her liberated attitude reminded me of Zoe? Maybe.

Fistful of Fog

My mother chose the festival of *Poila Baisakh* to announce my engagement to Rita. This festival marks the first day of the Bengali New Year. And it is considered the ideal day to start new ventures.

Since Ma focused primarily on the religious end of our engagement ceremony (held earlier that morning), Kaku recruited my cousin, Bhagwat, to orchestrate festivities at the dinner party (planned for that evening).

Bhagwat's primary role was to ensure alcoholic relief was available to those guests (like Rita's father) who wished to counter some of Ma's puritanical, vegetarian excesses.

"Jayanta," said Ma, "we will use this auspicious evening to announce your engagement to Rita. All of Darjeeling's VIPs will be coming, so please make sure you don't drink Bhagwat's whisky or engage in any other foolish acts. You need to make a good impression on Rita's family, ok?"

A Nepali doorman, Bahadur, had been hired to help with the engagement festivities. He was strategically positioned at the entrance with a tray loaded with jasmine flowers, sandalwood, basil, betel, and vermillion. He sported a necklace of jasmine and marigold and his task was to: salute and open the car door when the important guests arrived (anyone who arrived on foot was not worthy of his attention); take them to their assigned seat at a huge tent which had been erected on the lawns outside our house (several hundred guests were expected that evening); and keep the riff-raff away.

Next to him stood a white horse which Ma wanted me to mount (so I could make a grand entrance, timed to coincide with the arrival of Rita's family). When firecrackers were exploded to announce the arrival of the guest of honor, the perplexed horse dropped two steaming turds. Bahadur said that was a good sign because horse-droppings (which was sometimes used by locals as fertilizer) meant my marriage would be fertile.

Homecoming

Every little thing in the Himalayas is considered an omen, every material is designated as pure or impure. I was lucky, said Bahadur, that it was a horse which had pooped and not a dog, because that would have meant my marriage would be doomed to die a dog's death.

Bhagwat, who was a major in the Indian Army, was dressed in military uniform. He greeted Rita, and her family, as they arrived (fashionably late) in a car wrapped in strands of marigold and jasmine. And before Ma could intervene, he took them straight to the bar (manned by one of his army orderlies) and left her shaking her head in disapproval.

Soon, an announcement was made on the PA system that dinner had been served.

The first batch of diners left gossip behind as they elbowed people out of the way and made their way over to the dining area.

Caught-up in this throng, I tried to make my way towards Rita but a fuzzy-lipped woman, swinging a designer handbag, stopped me.

"From Amereeka? I knew it!" she said, as she swung the handbag around like a lasso. "My brother is famous tycoon in Silicon Valley. You must know him. His name is Kumar! I'm Mona, by the way."

I shook my head, partly to assure her that I'd never heard of Kumar, and partly to end the meaningless small talk that I knew would quickly turn into questions about how soon I planned to have kids and whether I would eventually work for Rita's dad or not.

"When Kumar left India, he said he only wanted to make a million. Then, after the first million, he said he'd stop at ten. Now he's shooting for a billion. They call him a serial entrepreneur – just like a serial killer, only richer," she said, chortling at her own joke.

Fistful of Fog

I remained silent, hoping she would take the hint and go away. But she remained immobile and continued to tell me more about Kumar.

"He's a genius. Even the President can't get to see him, he's that busy," she said. "He married a beautiful girl from Siliguri. She would have come to the wedding but she has to go to the consulate tomorrow to interview for her green card. Isn't it terrible how your government separates husbands from wives for several years just because of that stupid green card?"

I was about to tell her that I also hated U.S. immigration rules, when she looked at me conspiratorially and said: "Kumar is trying to find a husband for me. You see, he wants me to move to Amereeka."

Mona, pausing in anticipation of being congratulated. But after encountering my stiff upper-lips (preoccupied with filing an errant fingernail), she continued: "You look nothing like your mother. You must have taken after your father. By the way, where is he? Can't say I've met him."

Unsuccessful in deflecting her verbal volleys, I was saved by Bahadur. He was sprinting down the hallway. The horse must have taken a few bites out of his jasmine-and-marigold necklace for it was now dangling around his neck with only a few flowers remaining.

"Sir, telephone," he said. "Tenzing is on the line in the drawing room. He says it is urgent."

I said to Mona: "Excuse me, I have an urgent call. Nice talking to you."

"Wait, wait. I know a man from—" said Mona, but I'd had already spring-boarded to safety, before her entwining handbag could snarl my progress.

Walking briskly, I disappeared amidst the throng of revelers, leaving Mona to hunt for more conversationally-inclined game.

Homecoming

Tenzing's voice sounded scratchy over the telephone.

"Congrats, Jay! Sorry I couldn't come today but you know how it is with getting an expedition started. You can count on me making it to your wedding though," he said.

After we had exchanged a few pleasantries, he said: "Look, I need your help. Zoe showed up unexpectedly yesterday. She was planning to climb from the Nepal side but when she found out Marija Frantar is climbing with a Slovenian team over there, she came to Sikkim. She wants to join our expedition, but you know how it is with these army guys. They don't want foreigners on their team, so the army leader refused to let her join. Now, she is stranded here in Lavose. Doesn't your cousin have high-level connections in the army? Can you get him to help her?"

I felt the dual forces of guilt and euphoria sprouting inside me. Soon, they began to rage unchecked, like two emotional fires, separated only by a strip of apprehension.

"Of course, I will help Zoe," I said. "Tell her I'll be in Lavose as soon as possible. Also, can you include my name on the expedition list? Then Zoe and I can train for Kanchenjunga, together."

"Don't let her know I contacted you," said Tenzing. "She asked me to not tell you that she is over here. By the way, what's going on between the two of you? Did you not tell her that you are engaged to Rita?"

Before I could reply, I felt a tap on my shoulder. I turned around to find my mother standing behind me.

"If you get back together with that American girl then you are dead to me," said Ma, her voice rising above the static on the phone line attached to my other ear.

"Ma, please be reasonable. Zoe is a nice girl," I said.

"First your father and now you? What's wrong with our Bengali girls? Aren't they good enough for you? Why can't you be normal?" she said.

Fistful of Fog

"Ma, stop," I said, as I placed the telephone handset back into the cradle. "I'm sure you will like Zoe once you get to know her. I just need some time to—"

"If you plan to be with her then you should leave this house and never come back," she said, as she left the drawing room and walked out into the courtyard.

As I followed Ma outside, I noticed that Kanchenjunga was now blanketed by purplish rain clouds.

Part Four:
Another Memorable Year
(April 1991 - April 1992)

Chapter 9: A Second Chance

Zoe took off her climbing boots and dunked her feet into the grey blue waters of Lavo Lake.

Although I'd last seen her under trying circumstances, she instantaneously took me back to a happier time. When your college love shows up at your doorstep it brings along a few good memories, which, like good songs, never get buried.

A gentle breeze rippled the lake, causing the water to move up and down her ankles. Some of the blueness from the water seemed to transfer itself and flow, like ink, upward through her feet and color her pupils a bright shade of purple.

After putting her boots back on, she started to throw a handful of pebbles across the lake.

They skipped across the surface of the water a few times, before sinking into its depths.

I'd been grieving since our break-up. But now that she was in my part of the world, I didn't want to make the wrong move.

I began to walk, hesitantly, towards her.

"I see you haven't lost the ability to make things dance around you," I said, when I got within earshot.

"Oh, hi Jay," she said, pausing her pebble-flinging. "Didn't see you coming."

"Pemba said you did very well in training today," I said.

"That is because he is a terrific instructor," she said, using her hands to keep the wind from blowing her hair into her eyes.

Pemba, who was busy untying rope from a stony ledge, paid no attention to us. Although he was employed by the Indian Army, he was more likely to be found at high altitude camps during expedition months (working as a 'climbing Sherpa') than at the district army barracks.

"I'm sorry about what I said to you on our last expedition," I said to Zoe. "Will you please forgive me?"

"No worries, all that's water under the bridge. Now I'm focused solely on climbing this mountain," she said. "By the way, Tenzing tells me you are engaged. Congratulations!"

I could have killed Tenzing. I'd asked him not to tell Zoe about my engagement to Rita. But I should've known he couldn't keep a secret.

I said, awkwardly: "I'm sorry, I was planning on telling you but—"

"It is probably for the best," she said. "We had a great summer together and now I have a mountain to climb. Thanks, by the way, for helping me secure me a spot on the expedition team."

"No problem, I have a cousin who is well connected with army bigwigs," I said. "Anyway, I'm so glad you are here. It is so great to see you."

"Me too," she said.

"Guys, we need to make a move," shouted Pemba, as he made his way towards us. "Lama Pasang is conducting a special *puja* for us. We have to get to the monastery before sunset."

Even though the mid-day temperature at the lake was near freezing, Zoe's presence warmed me up. As we began our uphill trek to the monastery, I took my shirt off and enjoyed the feeble sunrays bouncing off my back. And I thanked my old enemy, Kanchenjunga, sparkling in the distance, for reuniting Zoe and me.

Zoe's arrival in the Himalayas flung me into the middle of a familiar dilemma, that age-old hackneyed plot-line of Bollywood movies, of choosing between love and family expectations. Sure, my engagement to Rita gave me a few sleepless nights. But I was more stressed-out by the fear that Zoe didn't harbor any feelings for me any longer.

My muddled passions emerged again that evening, as we sat roasting marshmallows in the kitchen-fire roaring inside the Guest House.

The song – 'There Is A Light That Never Goes Out' by The Smiths – was playing on Zoe's tape-recorder. Smoke mingled with song and danced around in circles around the toasty kitchen. As Zoe sucked slowly on a stick of marshmallow, the memory of our lusty nights from the previous year got resuscitated.

Stop, I said to myself. You are seeing her after a gap of several months. You don't even know if she has a new boyfriend. So, cool your jets, will you?

A few minutes later, Himal, walked inside. He left his muddy paw-prints on the wooden floor as he made his way over to the stove and licked at a few strands of stale, stir-fried Maggi noodles that were stuck to the floor.

No yak-rustler came anywhere near us while Himal was around. He was perfectly at home in the high mountains, feeling neither cold nor altitude and fearing neither man nor beast.

After slurping up the fallen noodles from the floor, Himal went out onto the porch. Zoe wrapped a blanket around her shoulders and went outside. I followed her.

She squatted next to Himal and (pulling him close) hugged him for warmth.

Soon, Lavose succumbed to load-shedding.

As the stars began to glow brighter, she marveled at the magic of an electricity-free night. And I reminisced about my high school years, with summers often spent at Lavose.

Memories came alive.

"I could live in a place like this," she said, "where beauty and inspiration surrounds us at every turn."

"Yeah, the Himalaya is a pretty special place," I said, thrilled that she liked being in my part of the world.

"This afternoon I walked across a meadow where wildflowers created a floral rainbow. And there were mountains everywhere I looked, all the way to Tibet. I love it up here," she said.

I couldn't control myself any longer. I leaned over and attempted to kiss her.

"Stop, what are you doing?" she said, pulling away from me.

"Why are you acting like we barely know each other?" I said, frustrated. "Have you forgotten we were engaged not so long ago?"

"But you are engaged to another girl now," she said.

"But I still love you," I said, hope adding volume to my voice.

"Whoa, slow down cowboy," she said. "We haven't seen each other for six months. And I need to focus all my energy on climbing Kanch. Can we not rush into anything right now?"

I felt like a passenger sitting in an airplane which had just hit an air-pocket.

"Trust me, we can make it work if we want to," I said, trying not to sound desperate.

"This is all too much for me to process right now," she said. "I'm going to turn in for the night. We'll talk tomorrow. Goodnight."

Kanchenjunga looked breathtaking in the starlight but that evening I couldn't bear to look at it.

As I turned my back to the mountain, it occurred to me that the past few days had caused me to lose the respect of the two people (Zoe and my mother) whose opinion mattered the most to me. Both romantic love and familial relationship had taken a back seat. And Kanchenjunga, now front and center in my life, had won.

A Second Chance

The trail from the Guest House climbed steeply until it ended at a small *chorten* where prayer-flags marked the beginning of 108 steep stone steps. After climbing those steps, I paused to catch my breath.

The whitewashed walls of Lavose monastery gleamed in the slate light of the morning. The walls hugged a ledge on Lavo Hill. And behind that hill stood Kanchenjunga, icy and tall.

As I reached the monastery's entrance, the sun dipped into the fog-filled valley below. The young monk at the gate asked me to wait. Lama Pasang was busy teaching students how to use the monastery's newly acquired computer (a gift from a former student, who had started a successful IT company in Bangalore), he said. I parked myself on a quiet corner bench in the monastery's courtyard and looked at the tube lights illuminating the courtyard.

My thoughts flashed back to my visit just before leaving for Dominican, two years earlier, when electricity had just arrived at the monastery. Now light bulbs garlanded the village but back then Lavose had been powered by kerosene lamps and candles. Lama Pasang, who had been told by the authorities that none of the villages in Kanchenjunga region were scheduled to get electricity, had started a holy fast which ended only when the power minister came down from the capital and inaugurated the new electric line. As soon as the first light bulb was lit the lama had ended his fast, declaring that the miracle of electricity had finally blessed their village. A feast had been prepared for the entire village; yaks had been sacrificed and the stream running through the village had turned red.

"What's the matter," said Lama Pasang, interrupting my reverie. "I heard you need to discuss an urgent problem."

Typical of the man he had somehow managed to seat himself, unnoticed by me. The rumor-mill at the monastery said he didn't walk but glided, sometimes invisible, because all those nights spent meditating had given him powers of concentration beyond the reach of most humans.

Fistful of Fog

It was comforting to see his familiar, betel-chewing face. Every time he opened his mouth he revealed large, betel-stained teeth which managed to dull some of the shine emanating from his hairless scalp and made him look more human, less divine.

From inside his vest he fished out a heart-shaped box. It was loaded with betel leaves, tobacco and slaked-lime paste. He took his time packaging the ingredients into a leafy mouthful and then offered it to me.

After refusing his offer, I said: "Those feelings I've had for Zoe and which I have tried to bury for the last several months, have resurfaced. I want to break-off my engagement to Rita but I worry my mother will lose face in Darjeeling. What shall I do, lama?"

He slipped the betel-leaf into his mouth. Chewing on it loudly, he said: "Who do you spend more time thinking about, Rita or Zoe?"

"Zoe, of course, but the problem is I'm not sure that she has feelings for me anymore," I said. "All she seems to care about right now is summitting Kanchenjunga. Can I risk losing a sure thing with Rita for an uncertain future with Zoe? If it was my destiny to be with Zoe, don't you think it would have happened by now?"

Drops of betel-juice started to ooze out from his mouth and paint his lips. He spat a mouthful of the gooey, red juice out into the far side of the courtyard. The projectile of liquid flew in a perfect arc and landed near a juniper tree, whose base had been painted a rusty-orange color by generations of betel-users.

He cleared his throat, twice. Then he said: "The worst thing you can do when you love someone is play it safe."

A Second Chance

When Zoe woke up and saw fresh snow lining the Guest House lawns, she broke-out into her version of a Native American rain-dance. But when Tenzing came by and said her climbing permit had been denied, that news stopped her in her tracks.

We had requested permission to follow the northeast spur to the north ridge route that had first been climbed in 1977 by an Indian Army team led by Colonel Narendra Kumar. The locals considered Kanchenjunga a holy mountain, so it was difficult to obtain permits to climb the mountain from Sikkim.

Most mountaineers climbed from the Nepal side, but that spring a 36-member Indo-Japanese team had finally received permission to pursue the north ridge route. By the time Tenzing applied for our permits, several members from the Indo-Japanese team were already on their way to Base Camp. This made the minister in-charge of issuing permits decide that the mountain was too crowded to host any more foreigners that season. And he turned down Zoe's permit application.

Tenzing had filed a petition to overturn the decision but with monsoon fast approaching we needed to get her permit situation sorted out quick.

"Welcome to the Indian bureaucracy. If the sluggishness doesn't kill you then red tape will," said Tenzing to Zoe. "The Union Home Minister in Delhi is the only person who can help you now."

"This sucks. I fly half-way across the world only to find out I have been rejected," said Zoe, with her hands on her hips. "Tell me, how do I get to Delhi?"

"I'll take you there," I said, thrilled at the possibility of spending time alone with Zoe, away from Kanchenjunga.

I desperately wanted to win her back. And a journey half-way across the country would allow plenty of time for us to reconnect. For once, Kanchenjunga seemed to be on my side.

Fistful of Fog

A few hours after arriving in Delhi we were ushered into a cavernous government office that housed one of the deputy home secretaries, Mr. Sinha.

(We had asked to see the home minister but we were told he was away on a three-week tour of Europe).

Sinha asked his orderly to get us tea. Then, speaking in Hindi, he turned to me and said: "To what do I owe this honor, Mr. Acharya?"

I explained why we had come to see him.

When I had finished, he said, in an unnaturally sweet voice that dripped with false humility: "Mr. Acharya, I am also a Brahmin. So, I consider you part of my extended family. I would be delighted to do you a favor. But my hands are tied. Mr. Bhandari is highly regarded. It is not possible to go against his wishes unless …"

He paused and stretched his lips into a smarmy smile.

Zoe widened her eyes and asked: "What is he saying? I wish he would speak English."

"Your missus probably doesn't understand how we do business here," he said. "I think it will be best if she excuses us gents, so we can talk business."

Not wanting Zoe to figure out that Sinha wanted a bribe, I whispered into her ear: "Why don't you wait outside? It will only take a minute. I will explain later."

After she left the room, he pointed to the vintage Rolex watch on my wrist. The watch, a graduation gift from my father, was my most cherished possession.

"No, I'm sorry; you can't have that," I said, angrily.

"As you wish," said Sinha, making no move to get up from his chair. His pseudo-friendliness evaporated, along with the syrup in his voice. As I was exiting his office, he yelled: "Good luck, getting that permit."

I knew I would regret it later but I turned around and made my way back towards him. Depositing the Rolex on his desk, I said: "Here, you can have it."

A Second Chance

On the train ride back to Darjeeling, Zoe noticed my bare wrist and said: "Oh Mowgli, you shouldn't have. How can I ever repay you?"

"Hearing you call me Mowgli again is reward enough, my dear Zoe-rani," I said.

After arriving in Darjeeling, we rented a shared-taxi that was heading in the direction of Lavose.

We had barely left the train station when the driver of a stalled Land Rover signaled for the taxi to pull over.

After the grueling train journey, I wanted to get to Lavose as quickly as possible. So, I was annoyed with the taxi-driver for making an unscheduled stop. But after I saw my mother's sister, Rama, climb into the taxi, my mild irritation turned into full-blown panic.

"Surprised to see you here, Jayanta," she said. "Your Ma mentioned you were not going to be home for a while. And who is that girl sitting next to you? Is this that the girl from Amereeka you left Rita for? *Chi-chi*, gallivanting all over town so everyone can see your blonde trophy? Mark my words, one day you will regret this. Choosing love over family can only bring shame."

My aunt rode with us only a short distance but before getting out of the taxi she handed me a plastic box filled with cashew *burfees*, sparkling with ghee.

"Take this with you," she said. "This is special *prasad* from the Shiva temple. You may have abandoned the Lord, but he hasn't forgotten you. Make sure you wash your hands before eating this *prasad*."

As I watched her depart, I tried not to think about how my mother would react after Rama informed her that she had seen me in Darjeeling with my "blonde trophy".

Fistful of Fog

We continued our drive on the bumpy, dusty road which featured many hairpin turns. After few more switchbacks, the great icy face of Kanchenjunga, towering above the silvery fir trees, reappeared. Earlier, I'd been delighted to have secured a climbing permit for Zoe. But now as I looked at the imposing, icy slopes of the mountain, I wondered if I'd handed her a death sentence.

The worst part of any Himalayan expedition is the amount of time wasted waiting for permits to get approved and for the weather to cooperate. Officialdom rules most expeditions and ours was no exception. Even though Sinha had approved Zoe's permit, it had to go through another set of approvals at the state level, before she could climb Kanchenjunga.

As we waited for Zoe's permit to arrive, Tenzing suggested we practice our climbing skills on a nearby peak, called Tinchenkhang.

"Let's do it," said Zoe. "I'm ready for Tinch-whatever."

"How high is the summit?" I said, trying not to sound fearful.

"Much lower than Kanchenjunga," said Tenzing. "It's considered a trekking peak. Pretty easy but we will camp at a higher altitude than Lavose, so our bodies can acclimatize."

I guess with a name like Tenzing he couldn't help but make Tinchenkhang sound like a hillock. But its summit, located at 19,718 feet, was tall enough to give me sleepless nights.

Being a Sherpa, he moved as easily at Base Camp as I did on a beach. He leapt effortlessly up Himalayan slopes, rarely panting, while my breathing sounded like the dying gasp of a fish from coastal Bengal, one that had been hung out to dry on a piece of Himalayan rock. Add to that my fear of heights and you can understand why I cursed my Bengali ancestors that day.

A Second Chance

I hated that I had to overcome generations of plain-dwelling genes, whereas his ancestors had been flying up these mountains for centuries, scarcely breaking a sweat.

After we returned to the safety of our tents, Tenzing handed Zoe a cup of tea. Taking a sip, Zoe screwed her face up and said: "Wow, this tea tastes pretty strong. What's in it?"

"It is Sherpa-tea," said Tenzing. "Ingredients are secret so I'm afraid I can't reveal them to you. But trust me, this tea will help you feel good on the slopes."

Tenzing never disclosed the ingredients of his tea to anyone but I knew it was a mix of Darjeeling-tea and-rum, a recipe he had learnt from an army cook. The tea-leaves could be any from among the plethora of the varietals grown in and around Darjeeling but the rum always had to be at least 80-proof.

Like his father and grandfather before him, Tenzing had joined the Gorkha Regiment as a solider. This regiment, comprising of ethnic Sherpas, Gorkhas, and other Nepalese hill-tribes, who were highly in demand by the Indian Army (and the British Army before them). These soldiers knew no fear and charged ahead, even when they had a limb or organ missing. Whether that courage came from the rarefied air of their birthplace or from the rum flowing through their arteries I did not know. All I know is that the same tea-rum-blend had taken the bite out of many a wintry morning, spent with Tenzing, during our high school days.

"I know the ingredients," I said, smiling. "But that's because I'm an honorary Sherpa."

Tenzing laughed and said to Zoe: "There are a lot of customs here but there is one sure way to tell who is truly from the mountains and who is not. Come with me and I'll show you how you can tell the difference."

Fistful of Fog

I knew what he was going to do and I hated him for doing it. Every time I'd pretend to be a Sherpa, he would find a way to out me. He could never accept me as a Himalayan local because my ancestors hailed not from the mountains but from the coastal plains of Bengal.

It can be confusing to keep track of the various hill tribes but if one goes back far enough in Himalayan history, Buddhism united most people and their customs remained essentially the same, irrespective of tribal affiliations. What was common, however, was their dislike for plains-people, who they saw as weak, money-grubbing scoundrels.

During my high school days, I had tried to copy local ways, like chewing *chhurpi* (a rock-hard Nepali yak-cheese) rather than gum, so it wasn't obvious that my ancestors had originated from the lowlands. But, no matter how hard I tried, there were some customs that I could never fool the locals with. The hardest local custom to imitate was the act of spitting cleanly over a steep slope while running down a hillside. The substance you spat out didn't matter: some spat betel juice; others chewing tobacco. What mattered was the way you executed the act: bending your knees slightly to lower your center of gravity but without slowing down your pace much and then forcing the spit out from deep within your throat, much like projectile vomiting or Tibetan throat-singing. It looked easy but my spit always landed on my feet because (not wanting to fall off the mountain) I would invariably slow down my pace. Tenzing, on the other hand, was a pro at racing down slopes while spitting out a perfect arc of liquid. He demonstrated his expertise again that afternoon by taking a mouthful of water from my bottle and spitting it out clean, while running down the sloped hill in front of our tent.

There are ways to tell who is native to the Himalayas and who isn't. I've wished on many occasions that I'd had Tenzing's Sherpa genes. Then no one would doubt that I truly belonged on these mountains.

A Second Chance

Norbu and I tried our luck but it was Zoe who came closest to spitting like a Sherpa that day.

She received a ceremonial Sherpa scarf from Tenzing.

"You spit like a Sherpa and you also climb like one," said Tenzing, clapping his hands. "There aren't that many women who can climb well at these altitudes. So, I was worried when you wanted to join our expedition. But after seeing you in action on Tinchenkhang, I can confidently say you are one of the best climbers, man or woman, I've ever seen. I have no doubt you will be standing on top of Kanchenjunga very soon."

"Thanks, Tenzing, that is high praise, coming from you," said Zoe.

"Now Jay is a different matter altogether," said Tenzing, jabbing a finger into my ribs. "He climbs as if he is walking on rotten eggshells."

Normally, I would have been upset at Tenzing for putting me down in front of Zoe. But that day I felt a great sense of relief. Guilt had dogged me since the day I'd gotten Zoe her permit (I could not bear the thought of losing her on the mountain). But Tenzing's vote of confidence in her climbing skills made me feel better (there was no better judge of a climber's ability to tackle Kanchenjunga than him).

I left them to reminisce about their Tinchenkhang summit conquest and I walked back up the trail, carrying a sketch-book in my backpack.

A few minutes later I turned a bend and there she was: Kanchenjunga: Zoe's dream, my old nemesis. The summit glowed silver against a rippling sea of sky-blue.

Sitting down on a slab of rock, I began to sketch the outline of the mountain with a drawing pen. Slowly, the angst I'd felt earlier was replaced by a sense of wellbeing.

Fistful of Fog

Prayer flags whispered in the incense-scented breeze, as we continued our climb down. But we managed to progress only a few yards before a giant, fallen rock brought the two yaks (who were carrying our camping gear on their backs) to a sudden halt.

Pemba, swirling tobacco cud around in his mouth and balancing the juices on the tip of his tongue, as if he was tasting fine wine, shook his head. "There is no way the yaks can go over this," he said, slurring his words a bit. "There is too much snow and ice."

"We need to dig a new path around one side," said Tenzing.

We took turns chipping and digging our way around the rock with an ice-ax and a shovel. I stood as far away from the edge of the cliff as possible. After an hour of labor, we managed to create an alternate path, on the edge of a sheer slope, made slippery by melting ice.

Pemba inspected the rock. It appeared unlikely to slide off the slope and fly down so he didn't bother securing it in place. Instead, he tied ropes around the horns of the two yaks and then, holding onto a piece of rope tied around the horns of the first animal, he prepared to scramble around the rock.

Even though he had crampons fitted onto his boots, he stepped gingerly on the icy slope. One little stumble by the giant beast could have taken Pemba down the mountain but he handled the slope with the dexterity of a Pashmina goat. And when he shouted – "I made it" – from the other side of the rock, we clapped.

Tenzing, then repeated the exercise, taking the second yak across.

Now it was my turn. I tried not to think of the several hundred feet of freefall that awaited me below the rock.

"Are you ok, Jay?" said Zoe.

"I'm fine," I said.

But soon she realized I was not fine.

She tied a rope around my waist and then secured it around hers.

Taking the leading edge of the rope and tying it around her fingers in the shape of a "figure 8" knot, she said: "Don't worry, I got you covered. We will go together as a rope team. Lean on your ice-axe and walk sideways with your crampons. And, whatever you do, don't look down."

Holding my ice-ax in one hand and the polyester rope Zoe had tied around my waist in my other hand, I inched forward. Despite the cold mountain air, I felt sweat drip down my palms and coat the rope, my lifeline.

To calm my galloping heart I closed my eyes, partially, and began to chant a hymn which Lama Pasang had taught me. Then, I started to take baby-steps on the freshly dug path.

Time moved with suffocating lethargy. And I had to remind myself to breathe with every step.

Because I had been listening to the stream of instructions coming from Zoe, I could tell when we had managed to make it over to the other side. But it was only after she untied the rope around my waist, that I opened my eyes fully. And then I thanked her.

There was barely any foot-traffic on the trail after we resumed our trek. The only human we met was a maroon-garbed monk, who raced downhill singing a Nepali song. He had the trademark gait of a local going downhill – short, brisk, steps – half-run, half-walk.

These mountain folks walked the slopes any which way they wanted. That was because locals knew one couldn't fall off a mountain, as long as one kept a foot firmly planted on the ground, said Tenzing.

Fistful of Fog

On a day characterized by cyclonic winds, my father had fallen to his death on the Zemu Icefall. Since that day, I've had difficulty climbing anything taller than a ladder.

I had not shared my fear of heights with Zoe. But after seeing me freeze on the slopes, she decided to coach me on a technique she believed would help me overcome my fear.

For my training, she chose a sheer rock-face, that rose straight-up from the middle of Lavo Lake. This technique (similar to deep-water soloing used by rock-climbers) ensured that if I fell, there would be a body of water to protect me from serious injury.

"In order to get rid of the fear of falling from a mountain one has to fall first," she said. "We need to make your fears manageable. Training and reasoning has to triumph over nervous response. This will involve some safe falling, with ropes and without. We will make sure nothing, other than your ego, gets seriously hurt. We will repeat these exercises so many times that through systematic exposure you will gradually get desensitized. Trust your equipment and your physical abilities. So, the next time you feel the onset of a panic attack you will stay calm, instead of freezing up or throwing in the towel. Every time you hear your heart pounding, take a deep breath. Be patient with yourself. The fear will go away but it will take some time."

As I began my exercise, I looked up at a house perched on a sloping hill, near the shoreline. Its reflection swayed tipsily in the pulsating waters of the lake. I tried to stop my mind from wondering if its owners ever worried about the house sliding off the mountain and disappearing into the depths of the lake.

After the sun had extricated itself out of from behind the mountains, I started climbing the rock-face. When I stood ten feet above the water, she instructed me to fall down, backwards, into the water. The cold water numbed me. This was part of her plan. She wanted to take my mind off of falling and focus it on something else.

We repeated the exercise several times, from different heights and using different angles of fall. My fear of falling never went away; it just simmered down to a lower level.

For my final exercise, Zoe took an egg out of her rucksack and handed it to me.

"You must climb up the rock face with this egg in your mouth. If you get up to the top of this cliff without dropping the egg, then you will be better prepared to tackle vertical sections on Kanchenjunga. Are you ready?" she said.

Like a bird carrying its young inside its beak I held the future of my love-life in my mouth. Only when I'd made it to the top did I release the egg and let out a joyous yell. My cry bounced off of the cliff walls and mingled with the chimes of the monastery bell before disappearing into the calm green waters of the lake.

Thin powdery snowflakes fell from a semi-clear sky. Carrying snowboards in our hands, we trudged through knee-deep snow, covering a slope behind the Guest House.

Zoe was an advanced freestyler but I had snowboarded only once before. She showed me a few moves. Her balance was extraordinary. I had a hard time getting the hang of it until she readjusted the bindings and showed me how to ride goofy.

"Ready for a real slope?" she said. "Let's go find one that has more of a runway."

We walked around until she found a slope she liked. I completed the run, with many stops necessitated by my inability to stay upright on my snowboard.

Walking uphill through fresh snow was exhausting. My snowboard felt heavier than a Himalayan boulder. The altitude didn't seem to bother her, like it did me. She looked energetic enough to compete in a triathlon but my lungs screeched and my knees hurt.

Fistful of Fog

As I stumbled my way downhill, I lost my balance and plunged face-first into the thick snow near the bottom of the slope. Before I could get up on my feet, she pointed behind me and said: "Look, there it is."

"What?" I said, too exhausted to get-up and look around.

"Kanch," she said. "What a gorgeous sight."

The five summits of Kanchenjunga stuck out like giant icy fingers, glowing silver against an undulating sea of powder-blue. The main peak towered above other Himalayan ice-queens, most covered in cloud. There were many mountains surrounding Kanchenjunga and even more mountains behind those mountains. We were in the land of a thousand mountains, where many stone-n-ice gods stood tall.

"The Kanch massif looks ginormous," she said. "Maybe that is why the lama called it the mother of all mountains. Can you imagine what it would feel like to get up top and then snowboard down? Every time I see the mountain, I feel like its peak is calling out to me."

"You know what they say about the call of the mountains – once they beckon there is no turning back," I said, hesitantly. I liked admiring mountains from a distance but I was in no rush to climb one of these killer peaks.

We sat on a rocky ledge at the bottom of the slope and watched the gorgeous glowing sun settle slowly on the large rocky face of Kanchenjunga, shining above us. Snow continued to fall in light scaly flurries.

"I could live like this," she said. "Climb every peak around here and never have to go back to civilization."

"I feel at peace with the world also," I said. "For once, I haven't thought about Darjeeling and all the problems I've been having with my family. I'm happy just to be here with you. Maybe, this is what life is all about. Living day-to-day and not stressing out about things we have no control over."

A Second Chance

"I really dig this place," she said. "Being out in nature like this renews my appreciation for the simple things in life, like food."

The wind blew a little powder down from an adjacent pine-tree branch and dumped it onto her ski-boots. She shivered. Taking a container of yak-noodle soup out from a thermos box inside my backpack, I said: "Here, have some of this. It will warm you up."

As soon as she opened the container, Himal appeared and inserted his nose inside. After tossing a few noodle-strands towards the dog, she held the bowl in her hands and slurped hungrily at its contents.

"Boy, I never thought I'd say this about Pemba's noodle soup but out here in the freezing cold even yak-meat tastes good," she said, pausing to wipe her lips with the sleeve of her ski-jacket.

"Isn't it amazing how much weather influences our diets?" I said. "My mother told me that vegetarians live longer. But the other day I picked up this book on traditional Tibetan medicine, written by Lama Pasang. Guess what he prescribes for various illnesses? Different types of meat!"

"Vegetarianism suits the heat of the plains where your ancestors grew up," she said. "Here, yak *momo* and barley beer is the way to go. Like the beef and beer my European ancestors grew up with. Diet just happens to reflect the environment folks find themselves in. And everyone is trying to be happy and make do with what their surroundings provide them."

"I guess there is no better path to happiness than being one with your environment," I said. "A college professor of mine, who loved to talk in equations, once said: 'Happiness equals fulfillment divided by desire.' In the west, you believe in maximizing fulfillment. Here in the east, we have trained ourselves to minimize desire."

"In either case, no one is striving to be unhappy," she said.

189

Fistful of Fog

"You can say that again," I said, putting my arm around her shoulder and drawing her closer towards me. "I'm anything but unhappy right now."

"Me too," she said.

Then, after a brief pause, she said: "I think I'm developing feelings for you again."

"Me too," I said, ecstatic upon hearing her words. "I love you, Zoe-rani."

"I love you, Mowgli," she said.

We kissed.

A few minutes later, the sky gurgled loudly, shattering the calm. You could tell a storm was imminent from the way the horizon was turning purple. Icy rain started falling in big, heavy flakes. We repacked our backpacks. Then we ran up the hill towards the monastery with the treasured snowboards grasped tightly in our hands.

The scenery on the trail was spectacular but I had a hard time keeping up with Zoe. She skipped up mountain slopes effortlessly, with the lazy, muscular ease of a greyhound racing with lesser breeds. Her legs worked in perfect unison, much like a catapult, sending the rest of her body hurtling up the slopes. Her calves pulsated like twin pistons, pumping energy into every corner of her body. And her breathing never got irregular, not even once. The only way I could have kept up with her on the mountain is if I'd received a transfusion of Sherpa genes from Tenzing.

When I sat down to catch my breath on a sunlight-drenched ridge, Zoe came back down and sat next to me.

"Everything ok, Jay?" she said.

"Yes, just a bit short of breath, that's all," I said.

A Second Chance

She offered me tea from her flask. After a few sips of tea, my aches began to melt away. And my spirit began to revive. "Thanks, I feel better now," I said.

"There is something very Zen about trekking," she said, with one hand on her sunhat, which the wind was threatening to blow into the mountainside. "Same here as in the Sierras. Sure, the altitude and the cold can get to you sometimes but if you shut out the blisters and concentrate on putting feet forward, one at a time, it can be magical. But you've got to be Zen about it."

"Lama Pasang says walking in the Himalayas is like meditation," I said. "Focus not on the result but on the pilgrimage. Every step is its own reward. Enjoy the lifting of one leg; the steadying of the other; feel blood pumping through your calves; taste your breath; relish the beads of sweat playing in between layers of clothing; sense the rubbing of blistered feet on leather; breathe in the crispy clean air; and then, when you are ready, plant your leg back on the slope."

"That is so true," she said. "Because when you make it to your destination, everything becomes clear. Why you had to go through all that perspiration in the first place. And, it's not just the view or the ambiance. Food tastes better. Friends feel closer."

"Life feels so much simpler in the mountains, doesn't it?" she said.

"It sure does," I said. "You should stay here a while, after the expedition is over."

"But what would I do here?" she said.

"Oh, I don't know," I said. "Raise yaks and make cheese. Maybe find a spring to bottle water and sell to the masses down below."

"Bottling water is a crazy good idea," she said. "Once, Grampa and I found a mineral spring near Cathedral Lakes. The water tasted fresher than mint. We camped out near there and didn't feel like coming down."

Fistful of Fog

"Sit on top of a mountain and chill out? That sounds wonderful," I said.

I took another sip of tea. Normally I didn't care for yak-butter tea but the fog that afternoon felt colder than usual and the fatty tea warmed me up. The day had started clear, no hint of any cloud or mist anywhere but now we suddenly found ourselves in Himalayan fog, thick like oatmeal.

"I keep seeing things here that remind me of San Francisco," I said. "This morning, when the sun came out of the mist, I saw a yak rolling-around in the snow. It reminded me of bison rolling-around in the fog in Golden Gate Park. Isn't it odd how similar phenomenon can occur at two very different places, half a globe apart?"

"I know what you mean," she said. "I think the French have a word for it but I can't remember it now."

"Maybe this sort of stuff is happening because I'm confused about which place to call home," I said.

"The only way to know whether you can call a place home is to leave and see if you get goosebumps when you return," she said.

"And how about you?" I said. "Could you see yourself living here in the Himalayas?"

"I wouldn't mind living here if I could follow in the footsteps of the great Messner," she said, getting up to resume the hike. "Starting with Kanchenjunga in the east, I could work my way up to Nanga Parbat in the west. Climbing all these amazing 8,000-meter peaks? Now, wouldn't that be a blast?"

Her words sucked the warmth out of my body and replaced it with a bone-numbing chill. Climbing deadly tall Himalayan peaks was not my idea of fun. How could Zoe not fear death's logo, which seemed to be invisibly imprinted on every Himalayan expedition flag?

A Second Chance

When we got back to the Guest House, we found Pemba standing next to the kitchen-stove. He was furiously stirring a pot. How he'd managed to leave the Yeti at the same time as us and get a pot of noodles cooked before we arrived was a mystery to me.

"Boy, did noodles ever taste so good," said Zoe, slurping a mouthful straight out of the bowl that Pemba handed her. "I love the way the fried egg straddles the top of the bowl like a noodle-mountain conqueror."

"When you're real hungry after a big night of drinking, a bowl of Pemba's noodles, chased down with some *chaang*, sits in the stomach like a happy Buddha," I said.

Himal, stretched out on the floor by the stove, got up and came over to Zoe. Standing on his hind-legs he tried to lick her plate with his tongue.

"One of my favorite things about going up and down mountains is the appetite it creates after," she said, working a long noodle strand into Himal's pliant mouth. "These noodles taste like heaven. Thanks, Pemba."

As dawn broke, the tireless Pemba untied his yaks from a tree-stump and set-off uphill again. Something in his genes allowed him to mix a head full of *chaang* and no sleep with an ease that made me jealous.

When Zoe carried her bamboo-mug of *chaang* out onto the porch, I followed her.

As a sliver of sun liberated itself from the foggy vale below, Zoe said, abruptly: "I need to make a pit stop. But stay right here. I'll be back soon."

Several minutes passed. When she didn't return, I went inside to look for her. The bathroom door was open. She was doubled up next to the toilet bowl.

"You ok?" I said.

As she looked up at me, I noticed a ring of vomit coating one side of her upper lip. "My poor stomach," she said. "It feels like a bullet train is running non-stop through my gut."

"The *chaang* must have been contaminated," I said. "Don't worry, I have antibiotics to fight any kind of diarrhea. You will be fine in a few hours."

She tried to sleep it off. But when she didn't feel any better that afternoon, I decided to take her to the army hospital, located in lower Lavose. Pemba loaned us one of his yaks (but not before complaining to me, privately, that he was tired of weak tourist stomachs not being able to handle something as pure and beautiful as *chaang*).

I placed Zoe on top of a yak. We made it all the way to the Lavose market, before Zoe threw up again, not far from a tethered mountain goat, who looked back at her with fuzzy eyes. I sat her down on a roadside bench (upwind from the smell of blood and guts in the air). Locals, dressed up in their finest for the Sunday market (which drew villagers and their animals from neighboring hillsides), looked at her with open curiosity as they walked past us.

After arriving at the out-patient clinic, we joined the line of people standing outside. We waited an hour before Naz, who worked as a part-time nurse at the clinic, could meet with us.

"Give me a stool specimen," said Naz to Zoe. "The army helicopter is flying to Darjeeling this evening. The lab there will be able to tell us what kind of bug is living inside you."

When the army doctor arrived, Zoe said to him: "Give me some strong meds and get me out of here. I need to rejoin the Kanchenjunga expedition team as soon as possible."

"You might have amoebic liver abscess but we won't know until the lab results are back," said the doctor, a cherubic, middle-aged man. "The disease has made you weak. Why don't you rest here for a few days? Kanchenjunga isn't going anywhere."

"But my climbing permit will be arriving soon," she said. "I need to get back to the Guest House now."

A Second Chance

"Then make sure someone is available to look after you at the Guest House," he said. "You will need help, in case you need to come back here."

"Don't worry, doctor," I said. "I'll look after her."

"Oh, Mowgli," said Zoe. "You are my rock."

I was thrilled to hear her call me Mowgli again.

With Zoe fighting the fever that raged within her, I slept on the living room couch. But the howls of scavenging dogs kept me awake.

I got off the couch and turned on the lights. Walking up to the front door of the Guest House, I made sure that the locks were still securely in place.

I had no desire to set my sights on any wild canines that night. There is no sight more terrifying in the Himalayas than a pack of wild Tibetan mastiffs on the prowl. These packs can be a fearsome force and the drunk who (usually after a big night of drinking) made the mistake of messing with them never drank again.

It was almost dawn. I decided to check-up on Zoe.

Pushing open the door to the bedroom, I walked inside. She lay passed out on her bed, naked, except for the sandals on her feet. An arc of light coming in from the living room highlighted her stomach, its whiteness standing out in contrast to the darkness of the bedroom. Her robe lay disheveled on the smooth wooden floor. A portion of her robe (having absorbed the contents of an open bottle of Pepto-Bismol) had turned pink.

I tried not to stare at her at her naked body but she took me back to a warm collegiate night, when both of us had been drunk on music and lust.

I looked at her delicate sleeping body; sweaty and delirious. And my feelings resurfaced, like a hibernating bear waking up from winter's slumber, with a hunger greater than before.

I sat down next to her. I wanted to extend a finger and feel the softness of her breast but I stopped myself in time.

Stop behaving so despicably, I said to myself. Can't you see that she is not feeling well? You are supposed to look after her, not start touching her in sensitive places.

I was about to get up and return to the living room, when she opened her eyes. Her pupils looking blank and distant.

"Mowgli, is that you," she said,

"My dear Zoe-rani, are you all right?" I said.

"Yeah, just tired," she said, closing her eyes and opening her lips slightly as she breathed in deeply through her mouth.

"I love you, Zoe-rani," I said.

I couldn't resist bending down and kissing her gently on her lips. They tasted chalky and felt chapped but I didn't mind.

"I love you too, Mowgli," she said, kissing me back.

I was still savoring the chalky medicinal taste on her lips when I heard a voice behind me say: "What in God's name do you think you are doing?"

I didn't have to turn around to know the voice belonged to Rita.

After extracting my tongue from inside Zoe's mouth, I said to Rita: "I was going to call and tell you our engagement is over. I'm sorry you had to find out this way."

Lights from Lavose monastery disappeared from view, as we began our trek up towards Kanchenjunga Base Camp. Zoe's climbing permit had finally arrived and she raced uphill, desperate to make up for lost time. She was worried that either Marija, or the monsoon, would get to the summit before her.

A Second Chance

The heavy, root-beer-like scent of rhododendron flowers hung around in the predawn air. A smattering of snow-crystals, shining like stars on patches of black rock, revealed themselves in the arc of our flashlights. The moisture in my breath coalesced into a gentle, grey cloud and floated slowly up into the fading night sky.

The rhododendrons and pines made way for lichen and moss as we went uphill.

I could barely make out the blurry shapes of Zoe and Tenzing, up ahead in the distance.

Just ahead of me, Pemba steered two fully-loaded yaks. Their hoof-patches made secure toeholds for our boots, but the steep terrain made me breathless. From the way the yaks excitedly flared their nostrils as they smelt fresh snow, you could tell they wanted to get up to the high mountain pastures as quickly as possible. And once yaks got that crazed look in their eyes, there was no stopping their relentless march uphill.

"Zoe should have waited a couple more days," said Pemba, as I caught up to him. "It takes a while to recover from amoebic dysentery and the last thing you want during a high-altitude expedition is to climb while sick."

"She doesn't want to slow down because of Marija," I said. "Apparently, she and Joze have already reached Camp II."

(Zoe wouldn't slow down, even after hearing, a few days later, that expert Slovenian climber, Marija Frantar, had breathed her last on the mountain. Like Zoe, Marija was attempting to become the first woman to summit Kanchenjunga. But Marija and her climbing companion, Joze Rozman, fell while climbing from the Nepal side in gusty conditions).

Despite having been recently diagnosed with severe amoebic dysentery (which she had tried to down-play by calling it a "just an upset tummy"), she had raced up to Base Camp, powered by antibiotics and an unshakeable faith in her ability to overcome adversity.

"Her enemy is not the Slovenians but a small bug known as Entamoeba Histolytica," said Pemba. "An uncompromised body is critical to survival at high altitude. Her disease will make it difficult for her to function in an oxygen deficient environment."

"I'm carrying a cannister of oxygen with me," I said, reaching behind and patting my backpack. "I hope she is not too proud to use it."

"In her current state she will need more than a few of those if she wants to get to the top," he said.

The horizon lightened up with a hint of sharp purple, as we continued our trek. A flock of geese took loudly to the skies. Rising quickly from dark dense trees they ascended overhead, a moving curtain of wings beating swiftly to migratory currents pulling them back to their Tibetan homeland, on the other side of the Himalayas.

Within minutes the birds became a distant grey wave, surfing over Kanchenjunga and blending into the northern horizon, repatriated briefly, until the inhospitable hand of winter pushed them back south again.

The bells of the Tibetan monastery below us heralded the arrival of another day in Buddhadom.

Zoe tried to increase her pace, but I heard the fury of her lungs and the agony of her backpack (which was carrying a fresh canister of oxygen that morning) express themselves with every panting step.

I unbuttoned her jacket and let the cold air slow down the sweat beads running loose between layers of her clothing.

Tenzing, who had lit another cigarette as he waited for us to catch-up, said: "Can we speed things up a bit? We need to get to Base Camp before dark."

A Second Chance

Her breathing sounded heavy. I would have liked her to have taken a longer break. But she signaled she was ready to resume.

I unlatched the pack from her back and fastened it across my chest. As we began to walk, the rising sun lengthened her craggy shadow on the mountainside and made her look ragged.

"Are you ok?" said Tenzing, with a look of concern on his face.

She looked up at him and said: "I'm fine. It's just diarrhea. Not being able to control my bowel movements on the mountain sucks but it's not going to kill me."

She didn't seem ok. The mountains must have started to spin around her because she sat down abruptly on the ground. I wondered if she had tasted a few drops of bile on her tongue because she spat a large amount of fluid onto the ground.

"I don't think you will be able to make it to camp today," said Tenzing. "Let's pitch our tent here for the night. Tomorrow, we will get an early start."

I handed her my mineral water bottle. Holding onto the string of prayer flags tied to a *chorten*, she took a sip from the bottle and gargled her mouth with water.

"No, let's keep moving," she said, after spitting out a mouthful of water. "I'm sure the Slovenians aren't taking any breaks."

Fresh snow and hard icy rubble surrounded us. Dozens of shiny ice fragments formed a spiny ice wall. Sunlight reflected off the ice and flooded the area with a hypnotic blinding light.

Zoe's stomach bug had resulted in a smelly, bloody diarrhea, which required frequent stops. And her painful, abdominal cramps forced intermittent grunts from her. It appeared as if her body was squeaking and leaking with every step up the mountain.

Fistful of Fog

The climb up to Advanced Base Camp, according to Tenzing, was one of the more manageable sections of the Kanchenjunga summit climb. But with our frequent rest stops, necessitated by Zoe's gasping and feverish body, progress was laborious. The gale-force wind made her cling onto the rope Pemba had wrapped around our waists, so we didn't get blown off the mountain.

I was carrying a canister of oxygen for Zoe. When we finally made it to camp, I switched out her old canister and gave her the fresh one.

Pemba delivered a bowl of steaming ramen noodles. It took me several minutes to coax a few spoons down Zoe's reluctant throat. That was a mistake because soon she went outside the tent and threw-up.

"She is not well," said Pemba. "In addition to dysentery, it is obvious she is suffering from altitude sickness. She needs to go back down tomorrow."

"I'm sure I'll be fine," said Zoe, her face puffed-up with the effects of altitude. "Just need to rest for a bit."

"You need to recover at a lower altitude," said Pemba. "Tenzing, why don't you take her and Jay down to Base Camp tomorrow. I have to go now. I promised Colonel Thapa I'd make it up to Camp I tonight. The rest of the team is waiting."

After saying goodbye, the diligent Pemba, left us.

She wanted to climb into her sleeping-bag right away but Tenzing wouldn't allow it. He kept her moving.

"Most people suffering from AMS die in their sleep," he whispered to me. "Make sure she doesn't fall asleep too soon."

I gave her a Diamox tablet and an aspirin but neither seemed to help her much. When she went outside to throw-up again, I went with her. After a few heaves, she aborted her attempt to retch and came back inside.

"Promise me you will come down to Base Camp with me tomorrow morning," I said to Zoe.

A Second Chance

"All I need is a night's rest and I will be as good as new," she said. "We must get to Camp I tomorrow. The Slovenians aren't slowing down for anyone."

"Honey, let's discuss tomorrow, ok?" I said. "Now, will you please put your oxygen tube back on?"

I was disappointed that the possibility of Slovenian success had catalyzed Zoe into ignoring her body's warning signals. All she wanted to do was to continue moving up the mountain and into the record books.

The cold bitter dawn forced me to embrace the downy comfort of my sleeping bag. A pounding overnight headache (caused by the altitude) had turned my body into a feverish orchestra of aches and pains that morning. Outside, the whistling wind sounded like a killer whale.

After shaking me awake, Tenzing thrust a hand-written note in my face. "Read this," he said, dusting frost off the ear-flaps on his woolen Sherpa hat. "She is on her way to Camp I, alone. Pemba will kill us when he hears about this. Let's go find her."

I stepped outside out my frost-covered tent and into the sharp crackling cold.

Before joining him, I poked my head inside the other tent, just to make sure. But there was no sign of Zoe or her sleeping-bag.

Thick relentless snow continued to fall as Tenzing and I trudged through knee-deep powder. Our faces were bundled up in woolen scarves and our googles reflected the great white summits surrounding us. Dark clouds overhead served an ominous reminder that the monsoon was not over yet.

With the help of the hazy grey light of dawn he peered at the slopes with a binocular. But there was no sign of any movement.

Fistful of Fog

"We need to hurry," said Tenzing, looking up at the grey-black sky. "Those clouds don't look friendly."

The ice-storm descended on us just as we were leaving camp. It was a thick storm that hung around the mountainside like an icy sentinel. Soon everything turned dark. Not wanting to get buried under an avalanche, we rushed back to camp. Once we were inside our tent, I closed my eyes and prayed for Zoe's safety.

As soon as the storm ended, we called Camp I on VHF radio. The fog had lifted. The sun was now shining over the mountains, their icy summits visible in the mid-morning sky.

When I told Pemba about Zoe and asked him if she had made it to Camp I, there was silence on the other end. I thought the radio had died but a few seconds later he said: "She isn't here. How could you let her climb in her weakened condition? You guys need to go find her. I will descend to the Icefall and also look for her. I doubt she will survive a night out on the mountain, in this sort of weather."

I felt as if someone had suddenly taken all the air out of the tent. Despite the warm glow radiating from the tea-cup I was holding, a deathly chill began to spread through me.

The return of cyclonic clouds forced us to pick up our pace. We were in a mad race against the possibility of another ice storm descending. After putting on crampons, we tackled the treacherous moraine awaiting us at the junction of the Zemu Glacier and the Twins Glacier. Those glaciers sucked up my energy and attention. It was only after we had finished navigating that tricky passage that I noticed that Tenzing's chin had begun to grow a beard of frost.

A Second Chance

As my steps got heavier, my breath got shorter. I could have used a break but Zoe's life was at stake. I kept marching upwards. The climb up towards Camp I was excruciating. But my physical woes were overshadowed by the sickening angst birthed by Zoe's disappearance.

I worried because she was close to 20,000 feet, the Yeti demon's playground, where the angry wind and falling blocks of ice, caused strange deadly things to happen.

Skirting through the maze of the Zemu Glacier while trying to avoid fallen boulders was treacherous and disorienting. Twice, I lost my way through this maze of ice, not the wholesome color of milk but a drab grey, the color of depression. And then, when we finally got to base of the Icefall – a frozen coliseum of ice-n-rock larger than any waterfall I'd ever seen – it felt as if the cold face of death itself was staring back at me.

From time to time I heard Tenzing shouting Zoe's name. The echo of his voice, bouncing off the solid walls of ice, sounded much like the soulful trumpets at Norbu's sky burial.

I waited for the reciprocal sound of Zoe's voice to come floating down from the upper reaches of the Icefall. But all I heard was silence – not the soothing tranquility one associates with the Himalayas but the harsh chilling quiet of death.

I began to hallucinate. When scarlet-tinged sunrays fell on the Icefall, my tired overactive mind imagined I was walking through a frozen river of Zoe's blood. I slapped my face to stop the hallucinations.

I summoned all my strength and climbed halfway through the Icefall. But then I saw a large island of rock and I sat down.

Tenzing, with concern written all over his sunburnt face, sat down next to me and said: "Jay, are you ok?"

"Oh, sure," I lied. "Just a bit tired, that's all."

"Well, rest for a bit then," he said. "You will need all your strength to climb this section of the Icefall."

Fistful of Fog

A chunk of overhanging ice on a nearby rock broke off and tumbled down the mountain. It made a frightening sound.

I looked around the ice coliseum. Large caves hung like icy balconies off rocks. Tiny, glacial ponds surrounded us like a halo of crystal. Huge, frozen boulders rested precariously on narrow, melting ice stems.

We were in a magical icy wonderland but I was in my own personal bone-chilling hell: exhausted; numb with cold; dizzy with altitude; trying not to throw-up; and petrified that Zoe was lost forever.

Sitting in the center of the Icefall, I heard the crackling groaning ice, a sound that still haunts my nightmares. It was an ice-fairy's paradise but dangerous for tropical mortals like me. Even with the fixed-rope that had been left behind for us, the path was hazardous going up. I tried not to think how much worse it would be coming back down this icy labyrinth.

The remainder of the route proved to be extremely challenging. We inched our way slowly through walls of ice, using the fixed ladders that had been left behind for us by other members of the expedition. And every time I looked down from an ice-ridge on the glacier, I screamed.

Occasionally, we would be forced to squeeze into a crevasse, narrower than a coffin. And then we would climb out of that crevasse, only to come face-to-face with an ice block larger than a fire-truck. I tried to stop my mind from wondering whether one of these ice blocks had fallen on Zoe.

It started to snow again. Fresh powder built up on top of blank ice. Every now and again, snow would peel off the rocks and come barreling down the incline, making a frightful, roaring sound. One such mini-avalanche buried us up to our waists. To my mind, weary from battling the elements, it felt like we were not just in a war-zone but in death's front yard.

A Second Chance

After more torturous ice-climbing we came upon a vertical wall of icy rock. It stood in front of me like an icy colossus and resurrected my fear of heights.

"We need to scale-up this rock face and then abseil down to Camp I, which lies on the other side of the rock," said Tenzing. "Then, we can connect with Pemba and continue our search."

"Don't do it, Jayanta. Don't climb this monster," I heard my father's voice, ringing inside my head, say softly. "A deathtrap like this ended my life and it could end yours as well. And then who will rescue Zoe?"

Tenzing, who was preparing to jumar up the rock, saw my hesitation and stopped. Taking his goggles off he looked down towards me and said: "Jay, do you think you can do this?"

"Yes," I said, my voice betraying my lack of conviction.

"Ok, let's do this then!" he said, putting his goggles back on.

I tried calming my mind by chanting one of Lama Pasang's hymns. But instead of feeling confident, I started having visions of falling off of the slippery, vertical face and landing inside a hidden, icy ravine; my body lying undiscovered for centuries.

A kernel of fear started to grow inside my stomach. And by the time Tenzing had roped me up, it had swelled to the size of a football. I peed in my ski-pants. The warmth of the liquid made me feel a bit better.

A few minutes later, our bodies were dangling down from the rocky, deadly cliff. And when I faced that vertical wall, my breath shortened again.

I took a deep breath and tried to expel the fear demons wreaking havoc inside my head. But the gut-wrenching terror persisted.

The tired sun, struggling to cast off the blanket of grey fog rolling in from the valley below, flirted briefly with the Icefall before moving up to the silvery summits adjacent.

I saw Tenzing, hanging un-roped several feet above me, use his ice-axes like claws to hold on to the rock face. His face had a look of calm determination.

I tried to channel his calmness but when I saw the mouth of a giant icy ravine below I had to pee again.

I heard him asking me to come up beside him and hand him the length of rope that lay in my hand so he could negotiate a crevasse above him.

As I began to slowly crampon my way up towards him, I tried not to look past the slippery rock face down to the blackness below, where I knew the icicled mouth of a ravine was waiting.

The freezing air made everything go in and out of focus.

I fought the rising waves of terror and tried to inch upwards but my feet remained frozen.

Afraid to breathe, I said (silently) to my tired cold feet: "Just a few more steps up and you will be able to hand Tenzing the rope."

But I couldn't do it. The more I tried to get my feet to move up the more they refused to cooperate.

"Jay?" shouted Tenzing, hovering several feet above my head. "What's going on?"

His voice echoed off the rock face and floated down towards me.

I wanted to respond but I couldn't summon the energy.

"You obviously don't have the strength to climb anymore, so wait for me here," he said. "I need to get to a place with a better signal so I can contact Pemba again. I'll keep looking for Zoe but I think it may be too late to save her."

Leaving me with those incredibly depressing words, he scaled-up the rock face.

And then he disappeared from view.

———

A Second Chance

Coming down the rock was harder than going up.

Every few steps I would slip and slide on the hellish, icy slopes. While navigating a particularly tricky stretch, I fell into a bed of sharp pebbles.

But I didn't get up. What was the point? Zoe was dead. And my life didn't carry meaning any more.

I sat on the bed of pebbles and thought back to what Zoe had once said: Why do all the good rock stars die so young?

I had fallen off the soft mountain of Zoe's love only to land hard in the netherworld of grief. But I knew it would be useless to try and climb back up to the surface of normalcy too soon. I thought about praying but I didn't feel like talking to God that day. Instead, I played some of Zoe's favorite songs in my head. I didn't expect the lyrics to lift me up from my painful, Zoe-less existence but I just couldn't deal with the stony silence.

Trying to prepare myself for the many lonely days to follow this one, I rationalized that grief would inhabit my body much like a parasite, hanging around only for a little while, sucking all the joy out of my life for a limited time before finding a different host and moving on. But, as the painful minutes rolled by and there was no relief in sight, I began to realize that my grief was going to be more like the missing part of an amputated leg, an enormous hole which would constantly remind me of how I used to be able to waltz through life, before the blade of separation came down and sliced-off a crucial part of me.

The mountains began to spin around me.

I closed my eyes and saw Zoe: dancing the fertility dance at the Burning Man festival; singing-along with The Mighty Lemon Drops at Shoreline Amphitheatre; joining Norbu at his sky burial and soaring magical far above the hot, madding plains and into the astral realm of a thousand Buddhas, where days and nights blended endlessly, and the great sky reflected the hopes and dreams of a thousand tomorrows.

Zoe: my love, my guilt, my loss.

I called her name out loud and then mine, repeating the exercise several times. I wanted to become her; I wanted her to become me; I wanted us to become one.

Time seemed to move both slow and fast. Slow, whenever I forced myself to exist in the present, for time stretched endlessly on then. Fast, when I thought back to my prior life with Zoe, for then it appeared as if our months together had barely taken any time to live.

I must have dozed-off because I woke-up to find Tenzing shaking me vigorously by the shoulder.

"I just heard from Pemba," said Tenzing. "He has found Zoe. She is alive but we need to get her to a hospital as soon as possible. She is suffering from frostbite and pulmonary edema. He has radioed for an army helicopter."

I heard the angst in Tenzing's voice but I was ecstatic. Zoe was alive. Despite my exhaustion I found the strength to let out a victory yell. My scream rode up the mountain on the wings of relief and then disappeared into the thin blue sky.

———

I washed Zoe's hair in a hospital bowl filled with warm water. A few renegade strands of warm hair got tangled up with the cold plastic tubes which connected her nose to an oxygen tank. Only a tiny bit of sunshine remained in her tangled strands.

Visible through the window in the hospital room was Kanchenjunga. As I got up to draw the curtains shut, Zoe opened her eyes. They were the only part of her face that still had any color left.

"I'm so glad you came, Mowgli," said Zoe, slowly raising her head up from the pillow. "Tenzing said you risked your life to save me. Thanks, I owe you."

She had lost two toes to frostbite. And she was constantly short of breath because of fluid build-up in her lungs. But those weren't the only problems I worried about. She had also been diagnosed with amoebic liver abscess. Although the doctor had assured me he was going to use a combination of surgical drainage and intravenous antibiotics to treat her liver, he had warned me this disease was associated with a high mortality rate. And that made me nervous.

"I love you so much, Zoe-rani," I said, biting my lip to prevent tears from escaping.

"I love you too, Mowgli," said Zoe, softly.

"I wish we had found you earlier so you wouldn't have had to suffer so much pain," I said.

"Hey, stop feeling so guilty," she said. "And don't be sad. Love never dies; it only pauses to rest."

"Let us pray," I said. "I'm sure God will make sure you get better."

"But I don't believe in God," she said.

"Not even now?" I said, astonished.

"Nope, but cheer up," she said. "I promise I will get better soon. And, before you know it, I'll be climbing again."

Even though her life was hanging by two plastic tubes, she was thinking about her next expedition. Typical of Zoe.

"I've had a hankering for lavender ice-cream," she said. "Boy, I can't wait to get out of this bed."

I tried to not think about what would happen to my world if she never made it out of that hospital bed.

"The morphine has been giving me vivid dreams," she said. "Last night I dreamt we were living inside a treehouse built on top of Maggie."

The act of speaking seemed to have exhausted her. She lay her head back on the pillow.

The tape-recorder on the bed-side table finished auto-rewinding and a Sonic Youth song – 'Tunic' – started to play.

Midway through the song Zoe tried to sit up and sing along to words – "don't be sad, the band doesn't sound half bad" – but she gave-up a few seconds later and collapsed onto the bed.

"Hey, if I make it out of here alive, can I join you at the wildlife sanctuary?" she said slowly, her voice laced with sleep. "I think I'm ready to take a break from the mountains and go play in the jungle for a bit."

Her words sounded sweeter than any music I'd ever heard. I switched-off the tape-recorder.

After making sure I didn't step on her bandaged toes, I climbed into the bed. As we lay together sideways (with our knees lined up together front-to-back to form a close fit), I cradled her head in my arm.

Chapter 10: The Jungle Blues

We missed the cool of the Himalayas. The Subirpur Conservancy's forest bungalow suffered from perennial power cuts. Most nights, we lay tossing and turning to avoid the damp sweat patches triggered by the silent air-conditioner, and wondered whether we would die from malarial mosquito bites or if heat-stroke would get us first.

Zoe enjoyed the early morning hours, when the air was still cool. She would wake up leisurely to the sounds of the jungle and then start her day by stretching her limbs into various yoga asanas. Like mercury on a chipped mirror, drops of sweat collected on her forehead, as she levered herself up on her elbows and lowered her stomach onto the bungalow floor, before exhaling into a 'downward dog' pose.

On her first morning in the jungle, Zoe discovered a dead cockroach jammed inside her mineral water bottle. How the insect had sneaked past the sealed cap was a mystery to everyone but Joseph.

"Memsahib, cockroach like bubbly water for bathing," Joseph, after blowing a puff of aromatic *bidi* smoke in our direction. "Bubbles clean their skin."

"Welcome to the jungle; a place where mineral water bottles get filled with tap water and resold. So much for not drinking tap water; we will end up drinking it one way or another; might as well get used to it. And don't mind Joseph's theory about cockroach behavior; he has an overactive imagination," I said.

Zoe pried the insect out of the bottle with a fork. But the weight of the wet cockroach proved too much for the plastic fork. The carcass landed on her foot, with a piece of fork jutting out of its belly like a spear.

"Glad there are no poachers here to witness my ineptitude," she said. "I can't even save a cockroach, how will I save a tiger? But I'm so excited. When do we start work, Joseph? I can't wait to see a tiger."

Fistful of Fog

That afternoon, we rode on elephant-back through the tall grass that surrounded the sanctuary.

Zoe had never seen a tiger in its natural habitat before. With her forty-proof sun-block and khaki safari hat, she looked like she was auditioning for a role in an 'Out of Africa' type of movie.

"Are conservation efforts working?" she asked.

"We do the best we can, memsahib," said Joseph, in a resigned voice. "But there is a large demand for tiger bones in China. I hope we can save these magnificent animals."

"One of my high school friends from Assam had the same problem in Kaziranga," I said. "Rhinos killed for their horns. Damn, I hate those poachers."

"Don't hate these people, sahib, hate the corrupt system," said Joseph. "These poor people are just trying to earn a living."

"Well, we are here now," I said. "We will fix the system. No more of this nonsense. We will bring those poachers down on their knees. Justice will prevail in the jungle."

Silly me. As if the jungle could be tamed. In the coming weeks, my naïve notions about jungle justice would be turned on its head.

The red earth drew a hot, dusty curtain over the jungle. A strong wind blew fine red dust into everything – the trees, the elephant grass on the river banks, inside our ears and even into parts of our body that never saw any daylight.

In the heat some creatures in the sanctuary wilted while others flourished. Flying squirrels, refusing to live up to their names in such heat, stayed riveted on tree-tops. In direct contrast, chameleons, enjoying the sauna-like conditions, swayed rhythmically on rocks.

The Jungle Blues

When thunderstorms cracked open the heavens, we received temporary relief from the heat. The Sheelanadi, engorged by the rain, overflowed some of its muddy bounty back into the forest. But the storms disappeared as quickly as they had arrived. And the parched jungle earth, which had briefly acquired a tinge of green, returned once again to its dry dusty state.

After our last Himalayan expedition, we'd brought Himal back with us to the jungle. He had lost his ferocious bark and remained silent at all times. I couldn't tell whether that was because he missed Norbu or because (like most mountain dogs) he suffered from the heat and humidity of the jungle.

One morning we drove over a large log that lay on the dusty road. Himal jumped out of the jeep and bit the log. The log moved. That's when I realized it wasn't a log but a python. The snake didn't show any signs of injury and slithered away behind the jeep, leaving Himal licking his lips. Joseph said he'd never seen a dog who acted more like a wolf.

Our earlier forays into the jungle had not been productive. That month, Joseph recruited his cousin, John, to help us track those elusive tigers.

"Sahib, we will not come back today without attaching a collar on at least one tiger," Joseph said to me. "John is an expert with gun, as well as bow and arrow. He knows the forest like a farmer knows the monsoon."

The jeep's shock absorbers creaked as Joseph drove over a pothole large enough to induce whiplash. John had his eyeballs fixed onto a dusty binocular, as he scoured the shrubbery for signs of animal life. After a long and bumpy drive, we arrived at the two watch-towers, placed on the banks of the river, hundred yards apart.

Zoe and I took the nearest tower. John, carrying the tranquilizer gun with him, climbed up the other tower, along with Joseph.

Fistful of Fog

I pulled the cloak of darkness around me and turned to the task at hand. Collaring tigers with radio-transmitters was tricky. First, we would use a dart gun to tranquilize the tiger. Once the animal was immobilized, we would fit it with a radio collar. Then we would inject the animal with an antidote and hope we could leave before it regained consciousness. Tranquilizing the animal prior to collaring would require steady nerves.

Peering through my binoculars I looked at John, seated inside the other watch-tower. He was sucking on a plastic straw, placed inside a bamboo mug. I hoped shooting narcotic bullets came as easily to him as drinking palm toddy.

A hint of a breeze wafted in through the elephant grass. An owl pierced the nocturnal silence with a hoot. A few clouds drifted into the night sky. I felt I was forging a grudging kinship with the forest.

I fixed my eyes on the moat of darkness that surrounded me. Circling my toes inside my boots to rid them of cramps, I checked the dial on my watch. I wriggled my toes again to prevent them from falling asleep. The tower would have been a tight squeeze for two children; two adults made the space stifling. I wondered how I'd pass the night without having my legs cramp-up every few minutes.

The repellent-cream made little impact on the mosquitoes. I stretched my shirt to reduce exposure but the thin cotton didn't deter their raids much. Even taking a swig from my water bottle, without hitting Zoe, was proving to be a challenge. My crouched legs kept falling asleep. Trying to massage them without throwing her overboard, I almost gave myself a hernia.

Joseph flashed his torchlight in the other tower across the stream. I trained my infrareds onto the watchtower and followed the torchlight. It was an elephant, bathing in ankle-deep water. I would never have detected the gentle giant in the moon-less darkness without Joseph's flashlight. So much for my acclimatization to the jungle!

The Jungle Blues

"Locating a tiger in this blackness is going to be extremely challenging," I whispered to Zoe.

For the first time since I'd been in the forest I realized it was us that was in the cage, and not the animals. They came and went freely, undetected, for the most part, in the darkness, while we sat uncomfortably penned in our tower. It was a sort of a reverse zoo, where animals could watch the humans.

The mosquito repellent was wearing off. Gnats, the size of hummingbirds, dug into any hint of exposed flesh.

I felt a drop of rain on my arm.

Feeling restless, I asked Zoe for a piece of chewing gum.

The stream mirrored the night sky which was now speckled with clouds. And then I saw the tiger glistening like a polar bear in the early light, its immersed head lapping up the glassy stream.

Afraid to breathe, I nudged Zoe, who had started to doze.

A single shot shattered the cocoon weaved by daybreak.

John's tranquilizing bullet had found its target.

The tiger crumpled down into the ground.

The gunshot galvanized the forest. Screeching monkeys and squeaking birds protested this rudest of wake-up calls.

Zoe and I climbed down to the ground clasping several radio-collars in our sweaty palms.

Photos and measurements were taken.

Soon it was all over. And we stepped back into the security of the jeep, with the extra collars clutched in our hands like trophies.

When we arrived back at the bungalow, Himal surprised us with a bark.

The dog that had stayed silent so long seemed to know that the time had come to celebrate.

Fistful of Fog

The Subirpur police station was housed in a battered government building which reeked of urine on the outside and Phenyle disinfectant on the inside. The peeling, blue walls were stained with a mixture of betel-juice, spit and neglect.

The town of Subirpur was located few miles outside the tiger sanctuary. It housed a narrow-gauge railway station, a run-down hospital and a school run by Christian missionaries.

It was a typical hinterland town, with daily scenes unfolding no different than in other villages that dotted the Indian plains: bangle-covered mothers stuffing sweets into wailing infants while potty-training them on greasy rail-tracks; unhappy porters haggling with a merchant for more money; an urchin (sporting a Nike T-shirt proclaiming "Just Do It") administering CPR to a dilapidated dog.

When the Superintendent of Police, Mr. Roy, saw us standing in line outside, he had an orderly call us into his office.

He greeted us with folded hands that ended in extended fingernails. His middle fingernail was curved inward, like the beak of a scavenging bird. Years of finger-licking curry and cigarette-smoke had imparted a golden hue to its scaly surface.

In a voice made hoarse by a lifetime of chain-smoking, he said: "What can I do for you, Mr. Acharya? It is my duty to help a high-caste Brahmin like you."

I wasn't surprised he knew my name because Subirpur, like most small Indian towns, was notoriously gossipy. But (because he was being too nice to me) I wondered if he was expecting a bribe for any services we would require from him.

"I'm here on her behalf," I said, pointing to Zoe. "Her Indian visa requires her to register with the police. Can you help us?"

"Yes, that is the law," he said, scratching his mustache with his middle fingernail. "That way we keep track of foreigners, in case something happens to them. You just need to fill out some forms for your missus."

The Jungle Blues

"We are not married," I said. "Where can we get these forms."

"I see," he said, raising his eyebrows in obvious disapproval. "So just friends, then?"

Like most men of his background, it was apparent he didn't approve of a Brahmin bachelor like me hanging out with an unmarried foreigner like Zoe.

"I'm in a bit of a rush. Where can we get the forms?" said Zoe.

He ignored her.

Then, turning towards me, he said: "There is something I need to ask you first, Mr. Acharya. This weekend we have our *Nag Panchami* festival at the Subirpur temple. I'm Chairman of the Fund-raising Committee. I know it is inauspicious to ask a Brahmin money for *puja* but we are in a desperate situation. Without donations, there will be no *Nag Panchami* this year."

Joseph had warned me about Roy. Apparently, the Superintendent took a percentage off of any activity in Subirpur that required his approval. I wondered if part of the *Nag Panchami* donations were also getting funneled back into Roy's bank account.

"I don't have time to attend *Nag Panchami* this year, maybe next time," I said, hoping to cut the conversation short. "Can we please get those forms? We need to get going."

"Please, Mr. Acharya, don't forget your duty as a Brahmin," he said. "I know you have returned from Amereeka with your fancy degree. But believe me it is not good to do away with tradition so quick. Our ancestors have been following these ancient rituals for thousands of years. Who are we to turn our backs on them? We need to respect local customs."

"I don't want to be part of any superstitious nonsense," I said, impatiently. "Can we please get the forms?"

"*Chi-Chi*, don't let people hear you talk like this, Mr. Acharya," he said, wagging his finger.

"But we don't believe in this superstitious jungle nonsense," said Zoe. "Don't you understand?"

He ignored her, once more.

Turning to me, he said: "*Nag Panchami* is an annual festival held in honor of the serpent god. Snakes are believed to keep evil away from homes, protect people from the elements and bring favorable monsoons. You don't want to ever offend the serpent god, and certainly not in the jungle. Bad things can happen. It is important you come."

Only after I reluctantly agreed to go to his *Nag Panchami* festival did he call his orderly and ask him to get Zoe the necessary forms.

As the sun set over Kanchenjunga, shining cloud-free in the distance, a peacock on the lawn of our forest bungalow began to dance circles around a peahen. Slowly, as he dazzled her with his plumage, she began to pay attention to him. And when the first drop of rain landed on my arm, the birds began to mate.

The peacock's determined efforts made me finger the turquoise ring inside my *kurta* pocket. I took the ring out of my pocket. As I looked at it, I wondered if the moment to propose had arrived. But when I heard footsteps, I hid the ring inside my palm.

A few seconds later, Zoe walked out onto the porch and said: "I'm having so much fun in the jungle that Tenzing had to remind me why I'd come to India in the first place. He called a few minutes ago. He wants to know when I'm returning to Lavose because he plans to begin training for our next expedition."

I cursed the mountain, shining unencumbered in the rain-free skies. I'd never hated (or feared) any inanimate object as much as I hated Kanchenjunga. I wished it would get the hell out of Zoe's life and leave me alone with her.

The Jungle Blues

"Why do you have to risk our happiness just to climb that killer mountain?" I said. "There are other, easier 8000-meter peaks you could become the first woman to summit. Why not try Cho Oyu or some other less dangerous mountain?"

As I felt the late afternoon shadow of Kanchenjunga creeping in between us, I wondered if we were going to have a protracted argument.

But, instead of saying anything, she looked at me with compassionate eyes, before walking away.

I slid the ring back into my pocket.

In my collegiate days, I used to believe in my ability to change my value system. Back then, the naïveté of my extreme inexperience had allowed me to believe blindly in the forgiving power of love and the new adventures it promised, as it revealed some of life's greatest mysteries.

But now, with a painful, post-collegiate year behind me, I saw myself more clearly for who I was: shaped by my genes as well as my environment; these shapes and counter-shapes constantly battling inside me; able to accept some changes but unable to accept others.

No one caused me the same amount of joy and heart-ache as Zoe. And I loved her more than anyone or anything else in the world.

But could I accept that the girl I wanted to marry was prepared to risk her life and my happiness for the uncertain glory that comes with being the first to summit a challenging peak?

I had to live with the aftermath of my father's death on Kanchenjunga. I wasn't sure I wanted to go through that again.

There was no denying that my initial attraction to Zoe had been purely physical: her glowing skin, her dazzling hair, her toned body. But over the course of our relationship much of that superficial attraction had evolved into loving who she was as a person – free-spirited, mischievous and fearless.

Fistful of Fog

In the beginning I'd been afraid to love someone who was so different to me. So, I'd hidden behind cultural barriers, using the obvious differences between our races, nationalities and religions as an excuse to justify our break-up. But hiding behind these pseudo-barriers had not allowed me to face the real obstacle – my fear of her dying on an expedition, which had left little room in my mind for entertaining the possibility of having a long-term relationship.

The irony of the situation was this: while each of us may be divided by our differences (race, religion, etc.) we are all united in our fear of death, and by extension, our fear of losing a loved one.

I understood her reasons for wanting to summit Kanchenjunga. But did I agree with them? Shouldn't the wishes of the living trump those of the dead?

The more time Zoe spent with me in India, the more it became obvious to her that we had grown up in very different cultures. But no place brought our cultural differences to the forefront like the jungle did. And this became apparent, once again, on *Nag Panchami*, when hundreds of vermilion-painted foreheads congregated in the temple courtyard.

As soon as we arrived at the crumbling temple complex, located in the heart of the sanctuary, a police constable ushered us past the chanting multitudes and into the sacred area of the outdoor shrine. A few minutes later, we were seated in the VIP section, near the large stone *lingam* of Lord Shiva.

A stone statue of the five-headed serpent god was suspended over the *lingam* of Lord Shiva. Towering over the stone statue, stood a huge banyan tree. A singing hill mynah sat on the top branch of that tree and whistled, like a jilted lover, the same tune over and over.

The Jungle Blues

"Looks like a scene straight out of an *Indiana Jones* movie," whispered Zoe.

I didn't say anything to her but to me this scene was not more shocking than what I had experienced when I'd visited my first cathedral in America, filled with mummified saints, some of who I feared would creep out of their tombs at night and climb into my nightmares.

Across from the *lingam*, a hymn-reciting priest sat, Indian-style, on the stone floor. He wore only a loin-cloth and his bare chest sported a piece of sacred thread that is customary for Brahmins to wear. Roy arrived decked out in a medal-adorned police uniform. As he sat down in an empty chair next to me, he waved his hand, signaling for the priest to begin the ceremony.

The priest smeared the stone statues with delicate dabs of vermilion. Then, he placed offerings of milk, honey and vermilion around the shrine.

From time to time, he would pause his chanting and pour drops of clarified butter into the fire burning in front of him. Smoke from the fire, as well as from the numerous marijuana pipes, redlined a sea of devotional eyes.

The arrival of a large wooden cage slowed the priest's chanting into an audible whisper. Panchnag, the temple's king cobra, had arrived.

Blowing a mouthful of cigarette-smoke into my ear, Roy said: "His venom is as potent as that of five ordinary cobras."

The priest stood up and made way for Bansi, the temple's snake-charmer. Bansi had discovered the snake, coiled on the temple doorstep, one monsoon morning, said Roy. Because Panchnag's hood sported an auspicious birthmark that resembled Lord Shiva's trident, Bansi had convinced the priest to let the cobra remain in the temple.

Smoke and heat from the fire made the place stifling. Zoe began to fan her forehead with a newspaper.

Bansi squatted on the floor-space which the priest had just evacuated and started playing a flute. Like the priest, Bansi's chest was bare except for a silver chain necklace hanging loosely from his neck. The necklace held a large silver pendant, which was shaped in the form of a trident.

For a few moments, all that was heard was the sonorous vibrations of Bansi's wooded flute. Then, a gentle movement inside the cage signaled the presence of the cobra. The hush heightened to an anticipatory hum. With a shortish cane that looked like an extension of his spindly arm, Bansi opened the lid of the cage. The hum modulated back down to a hush.

The cobra raised his membranous hood out of the cage, as if to acknowledge the gathering. He flicked his tongue out and slowly lowered all twelve feet of himself down onto the stone floor. He moved a few paces, before realizing that it took too much effort to glide across the stone floor. Languidly, he settled his silvery frame into a muscular coil and rested at the far end of the statue, away from the fire. Soon, his hood began to sway to Bansi's flute, and everyone breathed again.

"Animal instinct," said Roy. "He can't hear the sound but he can feel vibrations with his tongue. Let that tongue not fool you. He's deadly poisonous. Instantaneous death if he breathes on you."

"I'll rest easier, when he's safely back in his box," said Zoe.

A large bowl of honey-laced milk was forwarded to the coiled cobra. Bansi used his cane to place the rim as close to Panchnag's hood as prudence allowed. Stage fright appeared to have robbed the snake of his appetite – he chose not to drink.

The crowd waited anxiously for the cobra to bless them by accepting the sacred milk but no one, not even Bansi, seemed inclined to coax a drop through those formidable fangs.

Sensing Panchnag's reluctance, Bansi changed his tune to a drowsier beat, as he delicately maneuvered the cobra back into the cage with the help of his cane.

The Jungle Blues

Once the snake was locked securely in his wooden prison, the crowd came back to life. They raced each other in an attempt to out-smear the cage with vermilion, treating the box like an extension of the cobra. An urchin picked up the bowl of milk and started to drink it quickly. The festivities now started in full force. Amidst much bell ringing and chanting, the throngs in the courtyard were now let inside the shrine area.

A stampede of devotees entered the temple complex, as Zoe and I rushed for the exit.

The clouds erupted. It looked like someone had slashed heaven's bladder open with lightning. Gummy-bear sized raindrops made mud-pie out of carpets of dust. Pent-up heat left the ground in steamy pockets as water rushed inside.

I gazed outside and wondered if we'd be able to change batteries on tiger collars that morning.

"Do you think we can make it to the *machan* today?" I asked Joseph, who was kneeling on the balcony floor, offering an over-ripe banana to a wet monkey.

The monkey, shaking rain out of its fur, sat on the railing and bared its teeth at me.

"No *machan* today, sir, too wet," said Joseph, "But we will look for tigers on elephant-back. Deer like to eat this new grass. And tigers love to hide in the tall grass and prey on deer."

By the time the rain took a breather, it was almost evening. We on-boarded equipment and humans safely onto a large, male elephant. The elephant sported two kerosene lanterns that glowed like a miner's lamp against his dark forehead. The lanterns tunneled dual luminescent strips through the swarthy canvas of still grass.

The citrusy smell of eucalyptus hung around in the humid air like a menthol bouquet. The elephant grunted frequently but clamorous crickets soon buried his grunts.

Fistful of Fog

We spent a futile hour on elephant-back looking for tigers. Then, just as we were about to give up and return to the bungalow, the flight of Zoe's circling flashlight was arrested by a fallen tigress.

I peered deep into my infrared binoculars. On a shallow pit of wet leaves the tigress lay still, incapable of harming even a blade of grass. A large gash, where her face used to be, had transfigured her face into a grotesque clotted mess.

Zoe kicked her legs free from the saddle and slithered off the elephant. She started to walk towards the pit, but Joseph screamed, saying: "Stop, madam! Don't move."

He got off the elephant and ran after her. I followed suit, running as quickly through the shoulder high grass, as my legs would allow.

"There's an animal dying over there," said Zoe, her voice shrill with angst. "We got to do something! It must have gotten into a fight with another tiger or something."

"It's no accident, madam. Electric wire killed tigress. It can also kill you!" said Joseph.

I couldn't see what Joseph was pointing to. But Zoe seemed increasingly annoyed at his persistent tugging of her shirt, as he tried to stop her from advancing.

"What the hell are you talking about?" she said.

"Poachers, madam," he said. "They put current in the grass. Don't you see that half-eaten goat inside the pit? That's how they got the tigress inside. Poor thing!"

When I saw the wire strung across the pit, it dawned on me that poachers had dug a shallow trap, tossed in a live goat and then strung live-wires across the pit. The tigress has been electrocuted with high voltage.

In an attempt to save the tigress, Zoe moved closer towards the pit but Joseph said: "No use, madam. Can't you smell the hyenas? She is as good as finished. Please, madam, let's go."

I flashed my torch to see if I could spot any hyenas waiting. All I saw was the tigress lying still on a grave of leaves.

Stunned, I sat down on the edge of the pit and stared at the still tigress lying on her electrically-charged coffin.

Had she had been too feeble to walk out of the pit before being swallowed up in the humid stillness? And when were these cruel men planning to return and get a piece of their precious flesh? How could they have so callously ended another regal life in the forest?

Zoe started taking photographs with her camera. The jungle glowed every time the camera's flashlight went on but my spirit darkened with rage and resentment.

As we headed back to the jeep, Zoe shone her flashlight down into a grassless patch of earth. A silver chain necklace, with its trident pendant face-up, lay shining on the ground. It looked like a carbon copy of the necklace Bansi, the snake-charmer, had worn while playing the flute at the *Naga Puja*.

"Those bastards," she screamed, as she snapped a few more photos. "We must find them and put their sorry asses in jail. Let's go to the police station and file a report against these criminals."

Too upset to drive, she handed Joseph the keys to the jeep. Silence prevailed as we journeyed homeward.

Thoughts flashed through my mind like bush-fire but one sticky thought refused to leave. And that thought centered around our future in Subirpur.

Sitting in the middle of nowhere, unwilling witness to a gruesome crime, I felt terrified. What if they came after Zoe? What would I do then?

I shut my eyes and tried to erase the torturous scenes. My mind was still erasing when the jeep pulled up at the police station.

Fistful of Fog

When we returned to the police station again the following afternoon, there was a crowd of people standing around the entrance.

"Oh, Mr. Acharya," said Roy, walking over to us and ushering us into his office. "I was just about to call you. There seems to have been a terrible misunderstanding."

As he augmented his decibel range, a faint odor of whisky sprang from his breath.

"This is no misunderstanding," said Zoe. "I saw with my own eyes. They killed the tigress. I have photos."

"No, madam," said Roy, shaking his head vigorously. "I know these men. Bansi and his three friends. My team has finished making inquiries. These men are not poachers but protectors. They killed a blood-thirsty tigress to protect the villagers. The tigress was terrorizing villagers. It's understandable that you were mistaken madam, their tribal language can be tricky–"

"Nonsense!" said Zoe. "They killed a perfectly innocent tigress. Protecting villagers, my foot! All they were protecting was their bone trade."

"Bansi's story has been confirmed by the village headman," said Roy. "I've asked the town council to cancel all your charges against these men. The people of Subirpur consider Bansi and his men heroes."

"I don't believe this!" said Zoe, angrily. "Are you going to just sit back, and let them get away with this? You know they are lying. Wait a second, did they pay you?"

"There is no need to get excited, madam," said Roy, lowering his voice down to a conspiratorial whisper. "It's your word against theirs. My hands are tied. The entire town is behind them. You tell me if you were in my situation–"

"I'll tell you what I'm going to do," said Zoe. "I'm going to call the U.S. Consulate in Calcutta. And then the Chief Minister of Bengal. I have photos!"

"Your words don't scare me madam," he said. "Neither do your photos."

"I'm going to courier these photos to The Telegraph," she said. "They will make sure this grisly truth gets printed in all local newspapers tomorrow. And then I will write to the National Geographic. We will throw all your sorry asses in jail."

"This is not your America, madam," said Roy. "Your threats don't frighten me. My advice is to let sleeping dogs lie. That would be the best for all concerned. Do not say I didn't warn you."

Just as we were leaving Roy's office a mustachioed constable brought in a young woman, feet shackled in cast-iron chains. "What the hell is going on?" Zoe asked the constable.

"*Arre*, that poor woman is the widow of a man who died recently when their hut caught fire," answered Roy. "The woman's in-laws are insisting that she had finished-off her husband through witchery. They got the villagers to go against her. Men broke into her brother's hut, where she was hiding and raped her. They lit a fire and tried to throw her in. Somehow, she escaped. What could she do, poor woman? She called me and begged me to take her into my custody."

"Doesn't she have any place to go?" said Zoe.

"This is how it is here with the tribals and their complicated beliefs, madam," said Roy. "The thugs you see gathering outside now want her released so they can get their hands on her again. They plan to make speeches outside my office today. What jokers, as if all this sloganeering can frighten me?"

He paused the drumming of his fingers on the desk, as if expecting applause.

"These are tribal people," said Roy. "You have to understand their customs, madam. Tribal justice is different from ours. They believe in black and white, no gray allowed. It is best to leave them alone, madam. Do not meddle in their business."

Fistful of Fog

An actual witch-hunt in this day and age? I left the Superintendent's office feeling nauseous.

That evening Tenzing called. The expedition was about to restart. He wanted to know how soon Zoe could get to Lavose.

Between murderous poachers in the jungle and the killing slopes of Kanchenjunga, I wondered if Zoe would have any respite from the shadow of death that seemed to follow her everywhere that year.

———

On weekends, we often played cricket with students from the Subirpur School.

Father Ian, the English missionary who ran the school sometimes joined us for these matches.

One afternoon, Zoe bruised her thumb trying to defend a delivery that reared awkwardly off a good length.

After the game, the Father took us back to his place to ice her thumb.

After pouring us a beer, he handed me a packet of Marlboros.

I took a cigarette out from the packet and lit up. I hadn't smoked since my boarding school days. It felt good to inhale.

"How are things?" I asked him.

"Getting better," said Father Ian. "For a while I thought about packing up my bags and heading back to England. But this is home. My work is here. I will find the people who killed Charlene and bring them to justice."

The mission had been going through a rough time since the murder of a young missionary from Perth the previous year. The culprit had not been found.

It was widely believed that the Superintendent of Police, Mr. Roy (who had made angry speeches about losing locals to the religion of the white devil), had had a hand in the murder.

Father Ian paused to clear his throat with a swig of beer. "And you? How has it been for you?" he asked Zoe.

"Tough," she said. "I've provided photographic evidence but those darn poachers are still walking around freely. There is so much corruption here. Some days I miss San Francisco."

"Well, you're certainly taking a lot on your shoulders, young lady," he said. "I'd be careful if I were you. That article you published in The Telegraph has set tongues wagging. It doesn't pay to make enemies here."

I was glad to hear Father Ian cautioning her.

For the past few days, I'd been terrified her detective work could lead to unwanted consequences. Zoe was the bravest person I knew, completely fearless, but honesty and bravery don't always fare well against politically-connected thugs and corrupt policemen.

"He is right," I said. "Best to not get involved in this mess. I think it is time for us to move on. Better safe than sorry, as they say."

"Don't be such a wuss," she said angrily. "I'm not going to let them get away with this, just because this is the third world. This is not the dark ages! If this was America, one court date would have sent their sorry asses off to jail."

"In most places in the third world you can get away with some corruption and law-bending, as long as business gets done eventually," said Father Ian. "But here the law of the jungle – might is right – is the operative mantra. Criminals play politicians and vice-versa. You can get away with murder in Subirpur as easily as you can get away with not returning a library book in San Francisco. There is no crime here, only punishment. The cardinal sin in this world is not in committing a crime, but in getting caught. This is the world we are living in now. Here, there is no law, no power of the press, no morals. Life is wretched for most and there isn't a smidgeon of hope for those who persevere in trying to get justice. I call this the Lost World."

Father Ian's voice took on evangelical fervor, as he painted a stark picture of Subirpur. I suppressed an involuntary tremor and exhaled a mouthful of smoke. I hoped the smoke from my first-world cigarette would blow away the third-world terror that had suddenly alighted on to my shoulders from a clear evening sky.

The monsoon was in full flow. It got so humid that sometimes I would feel drops of moisture land on my arm every time a bird flying overhead flapped its wings. Armies of red ants left their burrows and climbed into our bedroom. They chewed up the gum on the inside pad of the keyboard on Zoe's lap-top computer, rendering the keys useless.

"Welcome to Subirpur; a place where computers get eaten by ants and criminals hobnob with the police," she said, unable to keep the frustration out of her voice. "Without a computer, how will I get my article over to the National Geographic? And without outside intervention, how will we get those damn poachers locked up? They will continue to walk freely, no matter how many court dates we have. Father Ian was right: there is no justice here and the rule of the jungle prevails."

Humidity wasn't the only thing the monsoon carried. Tropical germs infested the waters, mosquitoes ruled the air, and reptiles took over any available piece of dry real estate. Before long, the monsoon turned me into a shivering piece of feverish flesh, which was deposited into the unsanitary innards of the Subirpur Hospital.

As I waited to get diagnosed, I inspected my new surroundings with great trepidation. This place was no San Francisco General Hospital, that was for sure.

The hospital doubled as a polling station, during election years. Inside, the hallway was plastered with faded campaign posters partially covering "stick-no-bill" signs.

The Jungle Blues

At the end of the hallway was a high-ceilinged room with grease-splotched walls, where a male nurse stuck a thermometer into the mouth of one patient first, and then into another, without sterilizing the thermometer in between patients.

When I had to use the restroom, I held my nose as I squatted over the cavernous toilet, which did not appear to have a flushing mechanism installed.

Gripping the railing on the side-wall, I tried not to look down at the pile of turds resting at the base of the toilet, six feet below my bottom. I had no desire to slip and fall inside the giant hole and go for an involuntary swim with feces deposited by other patients.

"I'd rather die than stay here," I said to Zoe, after returning from the restroom.

"There are no other hospitals within a 50-mile radius, I checked," she said. "Just wait a few minutes longer. Let's see what the doctor discovers from the tests."

When the doctor arrived, he said: "You have malaria. From the color of your eyes it appears as if you may also have malarial jaundice. You need to stay in the hospital for a while. We need to run some more tests."

"But I have a lot of stuff to take care of back at the tiger sanctuary," I said. "Can't you give me some medication that I can take home with me?"

"You need to stay here," he said. "If you don't get treated, you can die."

"He will stay here as long as needed, doctor," said Zoe, in a stern voice.

Before I could protest, I heard my name called on the PA system. A few seconds later, a male nurse handed me a telephone receiver.

I was surprised to hear my mother's voice on the phone. How had she found out about my condition?

The pace at which Subirpur gossip operated continued to astound me.

"I'm coming to take care of you, Jayanta and I won't take no for an answer," she said in a voice accompanied by a stream of static. "I'll bring *prasad* from the Shiva temple and some home-made yogurt. The yogurt will help displace the bad bugs in your stomach with good ones."

"I'm fine mother, no need to come down here," I said, desperately wishing she hadn't found out about my illness. "Besides, there aren't any good hotels in Subirpur for you to stay in."

"Hotel, what hotel?" she said. "I will stay at your bungalow, of course."

"But there isn't enough room in our bungalow," I said.

"Don't worry," she said. "I'll make sure my path doesn't cross with that American hussy of yours. Just so you know, I will sleep in the room furthest away from her."

That evening when I heard the distant ring of temple bells, I wondered if those chimes signaled my mother's arrival into Subirpur.

I came home to a dead dog and a bisected snake. Himal lay on the front yard, fangs visible through open mouth, dead eyes haunted with a crazed look. The severed head of a king cobra, its silver hood birth-marked with the symbol of a trident, lay next to him.

A lump, starting at the base of my throat, raced its roots down to the pit of my stomach. And a bead of sweat goose-bumped its way down to the small of my back.

Frantic searching of the Bungalow's premises unearthed an incoherent Joseph.

I heard him speaking in Ongthali, but I didn't understand a word of what he was saying.

The Jungle Blues

"Speak English, Joseph," I shouted, "I do not speak your language, remember?"

He finally mumbled a few words that I could decipher: "...Ma and memsahib hospital...snake, no good, no good..." Then, he lapsed back into speaking in Ongthali.

I raced my bicycle to the hospital, furious with myself for having left Zoe alone in the jungle. During her time in India, I'd been so preoccupied with the possibility of her dying on the slopes of Kanchenjunga that I'd never spent any time thinking about the risks of her living in the jungle. Didn't many more people die from snake-bite every year than mountaineering?

"God, you must save Zoe's life, else I will never talk to you again," I screamed out to the sullen clouds hovering above the jungle canopy.

The uniformed orderly at the security desk seemed to know exactly why I was there. Without a word he steered me into a ward, where Zoe sat on a chair, stationed next to the bed where my mother lay.

"Thank God, you are all right," I said to Zoe. Then, after hugging and kissing her, I asked: "What happened?"

"I was slicing a coconut in the kitchen when I heard your mom scream," said Zoe. "They had planted the temple cobra in our bedroom. I was able to fling the machete at the cobra but it had already bitten Himal. Your mom hit her head on the bedpost, when she fainted and fell. She has a concussion. The doctor doesn't think it is serious but he is waiting for her X-Rays to come back. Poor Himal, I will miss him. Let's make sure those rascals go to jail."

"Jayanta," said my mother, startling me by sitting up on the bed. "This wonderful girl risked her life to save mine. She is the bravest person I know. I will be in her debt, forever."

Fistful of Fog

We put Himal's carcass in a large duffel bag and filled it with ice. Then we drove out of the jungle.

The heat of the plains receded as the jeep made its way uphill, through the many hairpin bends that knotted the road, as it climbed up into the misty Himalayan countryside.

After an exhausting day's drive, plus another three days filled with strenuous hiking, we arrived at a rocky plateau, near Green Lake.

Twelve months earlier, Norbu's corpse had been fed to the vultures on this same plateau.

A group of vultures began to assemble. The body-breakers began to sharpen their knives. I wondered if the faint remnants of Norbu's bones still remained inside their stomachs.

Tenzing looked up from the photograph he held in the palm of his hand and said: "The dog from the mountains has come back home to the Himalayas. His spirit is now flying high over Kanchenjunga. He will never have to go back down to those life-sapping plains again."

The slightly-faded photo showed Norbu sitting on top of a yak. He was cradling a very young Himal in his arms. In that picture Himal appeared to be a newly-born puppy, with his eyes still closed.

Lama Pasang lit an incense stick and said: "The faithful dog will soon be united with his master. Resting together inside the body of these giant birds they will fly high up and dance on the astral plains, where night and day, as well as life and death, are one and the same."

Zoe, paying no attention to what the lama was saying, stood on a ledge and stared at Kanchenjunga.

The great rocky face of the mountain seemed to make every fiber in her being come alive. I could tell she wasn't moved simply because of how imposing the summits looked or because she could see an endless chain of gorgeous glassy mountains hiding behind it.

The Jungle Blues

She was dancing inside because she was back in the land of the mighty mountains, where the great forces of nature ruled, and where Kanchenjunga, the center-piece of her ultimate dream, shone brighter than everything else.

Kanchenjunga: that magnificent icy tall piece of rock that sometimes reflects the courage of the human spirit and the beauty of the natural world; and at other times reflects the frailty of the human body and the terrifying force of nature. I realized the futility of directing my grieving emotions at a giant slab of rock but I couldn't bear to look at the mountain that day.

"Time to get the ceremony started," said Tenzing to Zoe.

After Zoe had placed rhododendron flowers on top of the duffel bag containing Himal's remains, I took the turquoise ring out of my jacket pocket and got down on my right knee.

It wasn't as if I'd been able to completely turn-off the incubus which resided inside my head and filled it with fearful thoughts. It was more a grudging acceptance that life was like a porcelain canoe wobbling across rocky rapids; the journey could end anytime. And it didn't matter whether death came in the form of a cobra's fangs, or the slopes of Kanchenjunga, or something else, like cancer. When life presented only terrifying choices, like it did to me that year, all that mattered was living in the present and enjoying every minute with the person I loved.

Holding the ring with two fingers of my left hand, I uttered four words no girl expects to hear at a funeral: "Zoe, will you marry me?"

When she said – "yes" – my world blossomed, like never before.

Chapter 11: A Brief, Mostly Happy Reunion

It was the last day of *Durga Puja*, the most important festival in the Bengali calendar and the best time to win a Bengali mother-in-law's heart. This *Puja* is a ten-day long festival which celebrates the Goddess' victory over the demon. As the warrior goddess, Durga represents the feminine power in the universe. She is another representation of Kali, the consort of Lord Shiva, my mother's patron deity. The festival is often marked by animal sacrifices. In the high Himalayas herds of yaks are sacrificed; streams run red for days and the meat feeds families through winter. My family, having originated from the coastal plains, sacrificed goats instead of yaks.

My mother always went overboard with religious and culinary overdoing during the 10-day long festival. According to my family's tradition, alcohol and other carnal indulgences were allowed only on the last day of the festival. Kaku made sure the day of my wedding coincided with that day of lenience.

I wasn't sure how Zoe would cope with the wedding my mother had planned. Even the most charming Bengali wedding can be overwhelming for the uninitiated. The crowds, the drums, the incense, the chanting and the endless ceremonies can make one's head spin for days.

Zoe spent the day before our wedding: playing poker with my high school friends from Darjeeling; sipping tea with my aunts and drinking whisky with my uncles; winning everyone over by saying she preferred tea to coffee.

Our wedding day began with a trip to the *puja pandal* at the Kanchenjunga temple. In the middle of the flower-festooned *pandal* stood a large clay statue of goddess Durga. Firmly planted on a terra-cotta lion, Durga looked down at the vanquished demon, his ruddy eyes wide open as he lay impaled on a plastic spear resting on one of her arms. Diverse weapons of war rested on her other arms, as well as on the arms of the various other gods and goddesses.

We exchanged vows at a ceremony presided by Kaku. Ma had dressed Zoe in a *Benarasi* silk sari and had loaded as much of the family jewelry as her ears, neck and wrists could tolerate.

Afterwards, as Kaku chanted Sanskrit hymns which he said sanctified our union, my mind began to wander. I wondered how the Goddess would look straddling a Harley on Polk Street – if she were to come to San Francisco and play Avenging Angel in leathers and a Stetson. And what if her hair was not black but blonde, like Zoe's? How ravishing would the Goddess look then?

Stop, I silently chided myself, have you lost all sense of decency?

After apologizing to the goddess, I turned my head slightly and looked at Zoe. With her eyes closed and a partial smile across her lips, she seemed absorbed in meditation.

Our house that evening was a mixture of voices, aromas, and colors. People bubbled out of packed rooms, their vacuous laughter inflating the egos of both giver and receiver.

Tenzing, who was doubling as bar-tender and deejay for our wedding reception, blasted shake-a-leggy music out of ancient speakers inside the house. Outside, one had to yell to be heard as the drums went: *"Dhinaka dhimdhim ... Dhikita thumthum ... Dhikipa thupthup ... Dhimika dhumdhum."*

Heat and spice, as well as sweet-n-sour, drifted in from the kitchen tables. Disappearing waiters, glowing in white uniforms, played hide-n-seek with snack-trays that nimbly avoided grabby fingers. Large pegs of military-strength rum and chalky gin lubricated tongues. Psychedelic saris triggered hallucinatory fantasies in corpulent men and jealous rage in their less-inebriated spouses.

Zoe was loving every minute of it, until she heard the goat being slaughtered and made the mistake of peeking behind the kitchen tent. She did not eat any of Pemba's goat curry at the wedding reception that evening.

Later that night, we went out with a group of friends to listen to a Bangla-rock band playing at the Sherpa Bar in Darjeeling.

When the band took a break, Tenzing jumped on-stage and announced he was going to sing a "special song to welcome my newly married friends."

Strumming a Spanish guitar, he sang just one line – "come on it's a nice day for a white wedding" (from the song 'White Wedding' by Billy Idol) – repeatedly.

Zoe leaned toward me and said: "Doesn't have a clue, does he, that white wedding is being used purely as irony in this song?"

"It's the only line from that song he knows," I said. "He thinks he is paying you a compliment."

Before we left the bar, I surprised Zoe by showing her my green card, which had recently arrived in the mail.

"Oh, Mowgli, that is the best wedding present you could have given me," she said, throwing an arm around me and giving me a kiss. "Now, all I have to do is get a lifelong Indian visa and then we can divide our time between California and the Himalayas as we please. Come, this calls for a celebratory wedding dance."

Gripping my arm, she hobbled her way until we made it to the edge of the dance floor. (A few days earlier, she had had reconstructive surgery performed on the toes she had lost to frostbite).

Turning her crutches upside down, she converted them into make-shift stilts by placing her plastered feet on the handgrips and her hands on the shoulder rests.

She tried to dance on her stilts. But soon she fell onto the floor, laughing as tears rolled down her cheeks.

Everyone at the bar cheered, as I helped her get back on her feet.

Fistful of Fog

Two days after Christmas, Zoe and I repeated our marriage vows in front of family and friends gathered at her grandfather's farmhouse near Half Moon Bay.

The day started clear but by the time guests began to arrive, a thin finger of afternoon fog had wrapped itself lightly around the farm.

Smoke from the charcoal-pit barbeque split the sunlight and created a hazy rainbow of sorts. A slight breeze ushered in a bit of relief to the grill worshipers, as I joined their ranks.

The reception was a loud messy affair with people everywhere, inside the house and outside. I was reminded of our Darjeeling house during *Durga Puja*.

Three dozen of Zoe's relatives arrived from various parts of the country, along with several of our Dominican classmates.

Having come without a date, Ron tried, unsuccessfully, to hook-up with one of Zoe's cousin, a redhead, attractive if one overlooked the thin red line of fine hair growing on her upper lip.

Turning to me, he said: "Dude, tell her I'm the real deal. God, she has such amazing fun bags. Reminds me of that sensational Irish stripper from The Foxxxy Kitty. God, she always makes me come like a tidal wave. Too bad this is your last night as a bachelor. God, I'm never getting married."

Ron claimed he was an atheist, but he never failed to take God's name when he thought about sex.

Julia, sporting an off-white bridesmaid dress, showed up late. She was accompanied by her new boyfriend, Scott, a dentist-turned-pastor from Tennessee.

When Ron (in his usual tactless manner) asked Julia why she had broken off her engagement to Mark, she sighed and said: "You can only tango with your first love for so long, before it is time to move onto the next dance."

"Been there, done that," said Scott, pairing his cliché with an orthodontically-perfect smile.

A Brief, Mostly Happy Reunion

"And you?" said Julia, turning to me. "Are you ok with Zoe climbing Kanch again this spring?"

"Whether I get to spend six more days with Zoe or sixty years, this year has taught me that I must enjoy every moment with her as if it is our last," I said. "Wanda Rutkiewicz is also planning to climb Kanchenjunga this spring. She may be the best female mountaineer in the world but there is only one spot for a woman on top of that mountain and Zoe thinks it has her name on it."

During our ceremony the soothing voice of a priestess from the Zen Center in San Francisco guided our exchange of vows and rings.

In the far horizon, a tired truck dragged its way up the sloped highway. And beyond the highway, the Pacific surf roared, muted like a distant dragon.

Zoe looked dazzling in a lavender dress that highlighted her eyes. But I felt out-of-place in my rented tuxedo.

After dinner, everyone moved to the dance floor.

Zoe had chosen a local band whose lead singer tried hard to sound like Kurt Cobain.

With all eyes on us I felt awkward, but as soon as we danced to the band's rendition of 'About A Girl' by Nirvana, I felt great because I knew the words to that song.

When the last guest had left, Dave welcomed me into his family with the following wonderful (and politically-incorrect) words: "The first time Zoe told me you were from India, I thought she had said you were from Indiana. I would have never guessed you were not from around here. Don't take it the wrong way but you feel so American, son."

Later that night Zoe handed me a letter and said: "My wedding present for you. Here, open it."

The letter was printed on a California College of the Arts letterhead. It stated that I'd received admission into their MFA program in Drawing-Painting.

"Oh my God," I said, hugging her tightly. "How in the world did you pull this off?"

"I sent them a portfolio of slides developed from your watercolor series on Kanchenjunga. And I wrote a couple of essays on your behalf. Trust me, it wasn't that difficult, pretending to be you. Over the last year, I feel like I've really gotten to know you," she said.

"Wow, thanks!" I said. "How can I ever repay you, Zoe-rani?"

"Hearing you call me Zoe-rani again is reward enough, Mowgli," she said, echoing my sentiments from a few months earlier.

A solitary sandpiper scuttled along the grey-brown shoreline of Ocean Beach. As surfers rode the choppy Pacific, a foghorn served a cautionary reminder to not take the fragile promise of permanent sunshine for granted.

We sat on a large, wooden crate placed on top of a sand dune. Zoe took a bottle of beer out of her backpack and handed it to me. We shared sips of beer as we watched the sun wrestle a loose-hanging layer of fog.

A dog appeared out of the fog and stood next to us.

Zoe poured beer into her cupped hand and offered it to the dog, saying: "Why is the world so sad today?"

He drank it thirstily.

"The world is weeping because Zoe is leaving for Kanchenjunga again," I said, running my fingers through the flaxen fur on the dog's back.

A Brief, Mostly Happy Reunion

With pleading eyes, the dog looked up from her empty cupped hand. Zoe poured more beer into her palm and offered it to the dog.

Then, turning towards me, she said: "Don't be sad. I know it is time to say goodbye but a part of me will find a way to be with you, always."

The loud wet laps of the dog's tongue shattered the silence and created waves of foam on her palm.

After getting back on our feet, we carried the crate towards the incoming waves.

I took the Stars-n-Stripes and the Indian Tricolor out from inside my backpack. The great flags entwined, as I tied them together. The morning breeze made them flap around, like a pair of fabric seagulls. I laid the flags onto the bottom of the crate, which was now resting on water.

Zoe took out a photo out from inside her jacket pocket and showed it to me. It was photo of us feeding each other cake at our wedding reception, held 99 days earlier.

On the back side of the photo she scribbled with a permanent marker the words: "May Zoe-rani's and Mowgli's life adventure be extraordinary and sail smoothly with the waves, like this bottle."

She rolled-up the photo and put it inside an empty beer bottle. Placing the bottle on top of the flags, she secured it in place with a piece of chewing gum, extracted from her mouth.

The immortal flags sat united inside the crate. And on top of them sat the bottle, with our message inside. The painted surface of the bottle glistened, as the sun finally broke through the haze.

We set the crate afloat upon the waves. It wobbled its way out into the ocean but before it could make significant progress, an incoming wave pushed it back towards the shore.

Just as I was about to step-in and give the crate a heave, the tide pushed it seawards again.

Fistful of Fog

The dog came and stood next to us. We watched the crate splash the foaming sea canvas with pearly dots as it rode out into the endless ocean.

Part Five:
A Day I'd Like To Forget
(May 16, 1992)

Chapter 12: Don't Forget Me (Revisited)

Until the mid-nineteenth century, Kanchenjunga was assumed to be the highest mountain in the world. Even after Everest claimed the top spot, no mountain was considered more sacred by its residents than Kanchenjunga. This sacredness made the first known summiteers (George Band and Joe Brown) stop a few meters short of the summit, ensuring the peak remained untrodden by mortals.

Many climbers who dream of summiting Kanchenjunga don't see anything sacred about climbing an icy tall piece of rock. Most also fail to see any demonic forces residing on its slopes. Locals often refer to this demonic force as the *Yeti*. They believe once you cross the hallowed peak, you enter the land of the immortals; a land so unpolluted and lofty that it belongs as much to the snow as it does to the cloud. But to get there you have to first appease the demon.

During the month of May 1992, two women vanished into the ethereal clouds floating on the summit of Kanchenjunga. The first was world-famous Polish mountaineer, 49-year old Wanda Rutkiewicz. And the second was 25-year old Zoe Anne Kirchner: my first love, my recurring All-American dream.

Wanda was attempting to summit the mountain from the Nepal side. She was last seen alive on May 12th.

Four days later, Zoe was seen trudging her way up from Camp VI (situated at 27,003 feet). She was following the North-East Spur to North Ridge route on the Sikkim side of the mountain. Tenzing had asked Zoe to wait with him at camp and allow the heavy snowfall to subside. But she had insisted on going up, saying she had heard her mother's voice asking to meet her up top. Her body was never found but the following year a banner would be discovered near the top of Kanchenjunga by a mountaineer from Ukraine. Inscribed on the banner were the words: "Anne Kirchner: She danced on top of the mountain and drank from the fountain of dreams".

Fistful of Fog

We will be together forever but if I die young, don't forget me, Zoe had said once.

On a stormy day in the Himalayas, the fragile mandala of our life together was shattered by the painful hammer of a young death. I wish our time together would have lasted forever. But after an extended period of grief, I began to accept that our love, like most first loves, was no more permanent than a caterpillar hanging on to a leaf blowing in the middle of a wind-storm.

When I look back at my time with her, it feels like a permanent daydream, a magical memory which refuses to fade. We had triumphed and we had failed and it was this joy and this suffering which activated my delayed adulthood as I slowly transformed, less like a flashy butterfly and more like an injured moth, hesitatingly making its way out of the cocoon and into the world, flying high at times but stumbling at other times.

Acknowledgement

This novel would not have been completed without the motivation and inspiration provided by my beloved wife, Lynn Susan Sondag. Her luminous painting graces the cover of this book, for which I'm deeply grateful. The next one is for you, Lynn.

I remain eternally indebted for the love and support provided by my dear mother, Shila Ghosh. Thank you, Ma.

About The Author

Rinkesh Ghosh is a writer, entrepreneur and traveler from San Francisco. He is passionate about life sciences, the arts, and the environment. His fiction explores the fragility of love, the fragmentation of identity, and the fear of taking risks.

FIC GHOSH
Ghosh, Rinkesh
Fistful of fog

03/27/19

Made in the USA
Middletown, DE
12 February 2019